"Run . . ."

Artek tried to shout the word, but it escaped his lips only as a strangled whisper. Fear radiated from the far end of the tomb in thick, choking waves. He tried to back away from the dais, but his legs betrayed him. Against his will, he fell to his knees, bowing to the dread majesty rising before him. Behind him, Beckla and Corin did the same.

Icy wind shrieked through the ancient chamber. Crimson mist poured down the steps of the dark dais, filling the air with a bloody miasma. Trailing tattered funereal garb and yellowed wisps of dried flesh, the long-dead wizards climbed from their sarcophagi. They stood before the stone coffins, orbless eyes blazing, pointing accusing fingers at the humans. Two keening voices rose in shrill chorus.

Defilers! Trespassers! Foolishly have ye dared to transgress upon our domain!

So this is how it ends, Artek thought. Dying at the hands of the dead. He might have laughed at the irony of it, but when he opened his mouth, he could only scream.

THE NOBLES

King Pinch
David Cook

War in Tethyr
Victor Milán

Escape from Undermountain
Mark Anthony

The Mage in the Iron Mask
Brian Thomsen
August 1996

Council of Blades
Paul Kidd
December 1996

Escape from Undermountain

The Nobles
Volume 3

Mark Anthony

For Gussie

Escape from Undermountain

The Nobles
Volume Three

Random House and its affiliate companies have worldwide distribution rights in the book trade for English language products of TSR, Inc.

Distributed to the book and hobby trade in the United Kingdom by TSR Ltd.

Distributed to the toy and hobby trade by regional distributors.

Cover art by Walter Velez. Interior art by Dawn Murin.

First Printing: February 1996
Printed in the United States of America.
Library of Congress Catalog Card Number: 95-62071

9 8 7 6 5 4 3 2 1

8562XXX1501

ISBN: 0-7869-0477-1

TSR, Inc.   TSR Ltd.
201 Sheridan Springs Rd.   120 Church End, Cherry Hinton
Lake Geneva WI 53147   Cambridge CB1 3LB
U.S.A.   United Kingdom

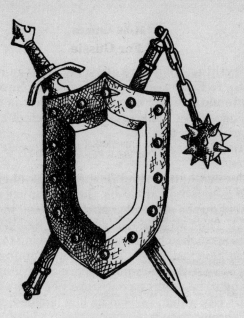

Prologue
Well of Entry

Jardis began to think that the three of them might actually make it.

"Watch yourself up there, Trisa!" he called out. His booming voice echoed around the subterranean temple.

As it had for five hundred years, the giant, sacred idol of Savras the All-Seeing sat upon its onyx dais in meditative repose. White stone hands rested calmly upon white stone knees, palms upward in a gesture of supplication. Blank stone eyes gazed from a placid stone face, while a single crystal shone like a star in the center of the idol's smooth stone brow.

Everything about the enormous statue bespoke peace, reflection, and ancient wisdom. Never in its existence had the sacred idol of Savras the All-Seeing known the blasphemous touch of a defiler. Never, that is, until now.

"Don't tell me my job, Jardis, and I won't tell you yours!"

The red-haired thief flashed a look of emerald-eyed indignation at Jardis, then continued to climb nimbly up the stone idol. Mirth rumbled in Jardis's chest. That was the exact look she had given him years ago, when he had caught her trying to pick his purse. She had frowned at him in utter annoyance, as if *he* were the one who had done something wrong. In anger, he might have turned her over to Waterdeep's city watch. Instead he had laughed, and they had become friends.

"I'm almost there!" Trisa called out as she scrambled onto the slope of the idol's shoulder.

"Talk less and climb more, Trisa," Sulbrin said through clenched teeth. Rivulets of sweat poured down the wizard's gaunt face as he knelt before the statue. Green sparks of magic flew from his hands where he gripped the polished dais. "I cannot stave off the enchantment of the idol much longer."

Oh, yes you can! Jardis countered silently. He knew Sulbrin better than Sulbrin knew himself. The wizard uttered doom far more readily than hope. Yet they could always count on him in a scrape—ever since he had helped them, two perfect strangers, in a bar fight. He'd given that nasty hobgoblin captain a magical hotfoot, and gave Jardis and Trisa the chance to escape.

Long gone now were the days when Sulbrin was a scrawny mage's apprentice who couldn't cast two simple cantrips in a row. So were the days when Trisa was a freckled street urchin picking pockets for a living. Though Sulbrin was more spare than ever inside his drab gray robe, he radiated an aura of power. And there was Trisa, lithe as a cat in her supple leathers, her beauty as dangerous as it was bewitching. Just look at them now.

Jardis grinned, shaking his head. Look at *them?* By Torm! Look at *him!*

Back when the three had met, he had been nothing more than a stripling farmboy who had run away with his father's sword. And now? Face of a lad still, yes, but he could swing a two-handed glaive with one hand, hold steady a shield in the other, and not even breathe hard. He never bothered with armor anymore, except for the studded bracers on his wrists. Just his leather breeches, and two straps around his broad, bare chest so he could sling his sword on his back. That was all he needed to make his way.

None of them were youths anymore. They were the Company of the Red Wolf. And damn them to the Abyss if they weren't going to be heroes.

"All right, I'm there!"

The thief perched atop the idol's left ear, bathed in a pearl-white glow. From a hole in the ceiling, filtering down from far above by device unknown, a single beam of moonlight pierced the dusky air. The beam fell directly upon the crystal in the center of the idol's forehead: Savras's Third All-Seeing Eye. Shards of light radiated outward, basking the column-lined temple in diamondfire.

"Remember my warning!" Sulbrin hissed. Concentration twisted his visage. Green magic still crackled around his clenched hands. "The beam must not be broken, or the doom of Savras will be upon us!"

Trisa stretched her lean form. She reached for the glimmering crystal with one hand, while in the other she gripped a circular mirror fashioned of polished silver. Jardis watched, breath suspended. Sweat trickled down the naked muscles of his chest. It was unusually hot for so far below ground.

Trisa's hands hovered above the crystal, just beyond the pearly beam of light. She shut her eyes in a brief prayer—no doubt to Tymora, Mistress of Fortune. Then, in one deft motion, she plucked the crystal from its socket and placed the mirror in its stead. For a frozen moment all three stared at the statue, waiting for the curse of Savras to strike them down.

The beam of light did not so much as waver. The idol gazed forward in beatific serenity.

Trisa thrust the crystal into the air. "I've got it!" she crowed exuberantly.

"You're going to get it, all right, if you don't quit your gloating and climb down!" Sulbrin gasped hoarsely. "My magic is failing."

"Hey, Jardis!" Trisa shouted. "Think fast!"

She tossed the crystal in a glittering arc, then sprang lithely down from her perch. Jardis raised a big hand. His fingers closed around the jewel just as Trisa landed in a catlike crouch. Groaning in relief, Sulbrin withdrew his arms. The wizard's counterspell shattered. Like a blazing serpent, white-hot fire shot upward from the dais, coiling around the idol in a coruscating spiral of crystalline death.

Jardis gazed at the stone in his fist. It winked brightly, as if it were indeed a mysterious eye.

Everyone had said they were fools to venture into Undermountain. It was said that only the mad and the desperate gambled their lives in the ancient maze beneath Mount Waterdeep in search of wealth and fame. Instead, the sane gambled on the fates of those who dared to go below. Every night the spectators gathered inside the Inn of the Yawning Portal. They crowded around the Well of Entry that led down into the uppermost halls of Undermountain, wagering on which bold adventurers would survive the journey into the labyrinth—and which would never be seen again.

Fools they called us, Jardis thought with a snort. Yet here was the Third Eye of Savras in his hand. And who were the fools now? The Company of the Red Wolf would go down in the annals of Waterdeep. And perhaps, after this, they could even stop for a while. After all, they had been traveling for years now, finding adventure and a spot of coin where the road and chance took them. But the crystal was worth an entire chest of gold—more than enough for them to take it easier for a time. They could even open that shop they always talked about when they had drunk too much ale. Trisa could be the jewelsmith she had always wanted to be, and Sulbrin could sell powders and potions to his wizard friends. And himself? Well, life as an armorer did not sound so very terrible. He could get up late, work when he wanted, and not worry about what sort of foul creature he would have to kill next. No, it did not sound terrible at all.

All they had to do now was get out.

"We did it, Jardis!" Trisa said triumphantly. She helped Sulbrin, weary but beaming, to his feet.

"We did indeed," Jardis said brightly, tucking the crystal into the leather purse at his belt. "Now, let's get out of this pit." Together, the three moved swiftly between the two long rows of columns, toward the circular portal through which they had entered the temple.

They were halfway to the door when the thunder struck.

Eyes wide, they whirled around. The beam of light falling upon Savras's brow had transformed from cool white to angry crimson. So too had the swirling tendrils of warding magic surrounding the idol. Now, a bloody miasma pulsated in the dusky air of the temple. Again came the sound of thunder. A webwork of dark cracks snaked across the surface of the statue. The silver mirror shattered. Stone crumbled from the idol's serene visage, revealing a new face below—a grotesque mask twisted in supreme fury. At the same moment, the two stone columns nearest the idol tottered wildly and toppled inward, striking each other with crushing force. A heartbeat later, the next two columns in line fell inward, then the next, each striking the floor with a deafening crash. One after another, like a child's game of Tip the Tiles, the columns fell, approaching the Company of the Red Wolf with perilous speed.

"The wrath of Savras is upon us!" Sulbrin cried.

"Not as long as we can run!" Jardis shouted back.

Pulling his companions by the arms, he lunged in a mad dash for the portal. As the three fled, columns crashed to the floor on their heels. Hearts pounding, they ran faster yet. Gradually, they began to outpace the toppling line of columns. Jardis grinned fiercely. They were going to—

Trisa let out a choking cry of fear.

"The door!"

Jardis jerked his head up. His blood froze. Like the stone iris of a gigantic eye, the temple's circular door was shrinking.

With a great roar, Jardis pressed forward, outpacing his companions, heavy boots pounding on hard stone. The portal continued to constrict with terrifying speed. Now it was ten feet across. Now eight. Now six. Jardis was out of breath and out of time. He launched himself into the shrinking door. Bracing his broad back against the rim, he pushed with both arms and legs. Knotted muscles stood out in strain. The rate of closure slowed but did not cease. In seconds the door would shear his body in two.

"Run, Red Wolves!"

Gasping, Trisa reached the door. She scrambled nimbly over Jardis. Sulbrin followed her a heartbeat after. Jardis glanced up, face pale, to see the last two columns toppling directly toward him. With a cry, he heaved himself over the edge of the door and through. The portal shut with a sharp *snick!* A second later came a great crash, as the columns shattered against the inside of the portal. But the door held. The noise faded into an echo.

Pale green light flared to life, revealing their three faces. A cool wisp of magelight danced on the palm of Sulbrin's hand. They stared at each other, panting. Then, as one, they grinned. They had made it.

"Shall we?" the wizard asked wryly.

"Let's," Trisa said merrily, dusting herself off. "I think I've had my fill of Undermountain for a long time to come."

Jardis laughed in agreement.

Together, they sped swiftly through the gloomy maze of halls and corridors, retracing the steps that had brought them to the shrine of Savras. They passed through a crypt lined with dusty stone sarcophagi. Next was the chamber filled with candles, all mysteriously ever-burning. And here was the Hall of Many Pillars. They were close now. A few more twists and turns and they would be at the Well of Entry. There waited the rope to take them back up to the Inn of the Yawning Portal, and to fame everlasting.

Nothing could stop them now.

"We're the Company of the Red Wolf!" Jardis shouted in jubilation.

"Our names will never be forgotten!" Sulbrin rasped exultantly.

Trisa howled with glee. "We're the greatest heroes that ever—"

A shaggy gray form leapt squealing from the shadows, knocking the thief to the ground. Long yellow teeth flashed in the gloom.

Jardis drew his glaive and skewered the thing. It let out a shrill shriek, then died. With a boot, he shoved the creature aside, gagging in disgust. It was an enormous rat, the size of a small pig. Yet a rat was still a rat—nothing to fret about. He reached down to help Trisa up. Suddenly he froze. The thief stared upward with blank green eyes. Blood spattered her face and clothes. Her throat had been torn out.

"Trisa?" Jardis whispered in puzzlement. She

couldn't be dead. How could she be dead? What about their shop? He knelt and roughly shook her shoulder. *"Trisa!"*

Dim shapes scuttled just beyond the circle of Sulbrin's magelight. A hungry chittering rose on the dank air, along with a foul stench. Countless pairs of blood-red eyes winked in the dark.

"We have to go, Jardis," the wizard said, in a choking voice. "It's too late for Trisa."

Dazed, Jardis lurched to his feet. Then hunger won out over fear of light, and the rats attacked.

With a shout of rage, Jardis swung his massive glaive, cleaving several of the rabid creatures in twain. Sulbrin spoke a guttural word of magic, and the wisp of magelight in his hand flared into a ball of green fire. He heaved it at the undulating gray mass. In seconds a half-dozen rats squealed as emerald flames licked at their mangy pelts. They scurried frantically around the hall, setting others ablaze. In moments the entire chamber was lit by flickering green light. Jardis stared in horror. Every inch of the vast hall was seething with gigantic rats.

Fear redoubled, Jardis swung his sword in whistling arcs, barely beating back the ravenous creatures. Sulbrin raised his hand, readying another spell. He never had the chance to cast it. A rat leapt on him from behind, and the wizard cried out in terror as he pitched forward. In moments, his body was lost amid the gnashing throng of rats, his cry cut short.

Tears streaming down his face, Jardis hewed at the rats, shouting in wordless rage. Blood oozed from a dozen small, stinging wounds. Yet somehow he kept the vermin at bay as he backed toward the archway that led out of the hall. He was nearly there. Only a few paces more.

His glaive lodged in the body of one of the rats. The blade was torn from his hand and swept away by the surging mass. Weaponless, Jardis sprang back, scrambling over the living carpet of rats. Somehow he gained the archway, stumbling into the corridor beyond, but the rats followed. Jardis ran as blood poured into his eyes, blinding him. A rat leapt forward, gnawing the back of his knee, severing the tendons. Jardis cried out in agony, nearly fell, and lurched on. Another rat lunged for his back but missed, striking the leather purse at his belt instead. The purse tore open, spilling a spray of gold coins, as well as something bright and sparkling.

The Third Eye of Savras.

For a second Jardis hesitated. Without the crystal, all of this was utterly meaningless. But the horde of rats was mere paces behind. To reach for the crystal was to die. Clenching his jaw, he limped on.

Then he saw the rope dangling ahead. Twenty feet above was a large hole in the ceiling, and beyond that, golden firelight. The Well of Entry. Two dozen faces peered down at him from above, cheering— some for Jardis, some for the rats.

With a bellow of rage and pain, Jardis threw himself forward, latching on to the rope just as rats flooded the chamber's floor. Arms bulging, he pulled his body upward. A moment later, he blinked the blood from his eyes—he had reached the top. Gripping the rope with one hand, he stretched the other toward the rim of the well.

"Wait just a minute, friend," said a grizzled man

who leaned over the edge of the well, blocking him. "You know Durnan's toll. One gold piece to go down, and one to come up. That's the rule."

With his free hand, Jardis clutched at the purse at his belt. His fingers found torn, empty leather. He looked up in terror. "I've lost it all. But I can get more! Please, I—"

The grizzled man stared down at him with cold eyes. "Cut the rope," he ordered.

"No!" Jardis cried in horror.

A knife flashed. The rope parted. A scream ripped itself from Jardis's throat as he plummeted downward.

But we were supposed to be heroes!

His scream ended as he plunged into the roiling sea of slavering rats.

* * * * *

So this is how the rabble lives, Lord Darien Thal thought in vaguely fascinated disgust.

From his table in the shadowed corner of the Yawning Portal, he gazed with heavy-lidded green eyes at the crowd that filled the smoky tavern. A great shout went up from the throng gathered around the stone-ringed well in the center of the common room. Gold changed hands, and the gamblers grumbled or gloated as best suited their luck.

Apparently some poor idiot had just met his demise in the dungeon below. No doubt the fool had been ill-equipped and ill-prepared to meet the perils that lurked in the labyrinth beneath Mount Waterdeep. Why couldn't these commoners understand that venturing into Undermountain was a sport best left to the nobility? But no, it was ever the compulsion of the poor to ape the wealthy. And if they had to throw away their lives in the process—well, they were meager enough, so what did it matter?

With his left hand, Darien raised the dented pewter goblet that a serving maid had plunked down before him. His nose wrinkled in distaste. This swill passed for wine? He thrust the goblet back down, then noticed a ruffle of purple velvet peeking out from beneath the heavy black cloak in which he had wrapped himself. Hastily, he tucked the bit of velvet back beneath the cloak, then adjusted the deep hood that concealed his visage. It would not do to be revealed as a member of one of Waterdeep's noble families. Commoners would be too wary to speak to a lord. And speaking with the inn's coarse clientele was exactly what Darien needed to do this night. A curious excitement coursed through him. There was always a certain lurid thrill to slumming.

A black beetle scuttled before him across the knife-scarred wooden table. Darien withdrew his right arm from beneath his cloak. The arm ended, not in a hand, but in a cap of polished steel that fit over the stump of his wrist. It was cylindrical in shape, without mark or adornment, save for a single slit on the end.

Darien called it the Device.

He considered his choices for a brief moment, then nodded to himself. The stiletto would do. With a *click*, a wickedly thin blade sprang from the slit in the Device. In one swift motion, Darien lashed out and skewered the beetle. He raised the blade, staring in fascination at the insect wriggling on the point. Its vain struggle made him think of the hapless commoners who sought glory in the depths below—fighting on when they were already dead.

With a sigh, Darien flung the beetle into a corner. Retracting the stiletto, he concealed the Device beneath his cloak once more. He supposed he was being too hard on these poor people. They had little enough to brighten their drab lives. Why begrudge them what small entertainments they could find? Certainly Undermountain was more than vast enough for nobles and commoners alike.

It was only in recent years that venturing into the depths beneath Mount Waterdeep had become a fashionable—if perilous—sport. Yet it was well-known that the maze was far older than Waterdeep itself. Over the centuries, countless tales had been spun about the city beneath the city, though most were half-truths liberally sprinkled with falsehoods: outlandish tales of imprisoned dragons, monsters of metal, and subterranean forests impossibly bathed in bright sunlight. Still, nearly all the stories agreed on one point, and Darien supposed there must be some degree of truth to it—that the labyrinth now known as Undermountain was created by the mad wizard Halaster over a thousand years ago.

No one knew from whence had come the one called Halaster. A few tales whispered in passing the name Netheril, the dread empire of sorcerers that legends told lay buried beneath the shifting sands of the Great Desert Anauroch. When Halaster had first come here, he found Waterdeep no more than a rude fishing village huddled by a natural harbor. Ignoring the villagers, the wizard ascended the slopes of Mount Waterdeep, and on a rocky shoulder he built a tower for himself, that he might continue his arcane studies away from all distraction. Yet—and here the tales agreed once more—the solitude of the tower was not enough.

Whether compelled by magic, madness, or some burning secrecy, in time Halaster began to delve into the mountain beneath his tower. As the years passed, he dug ever downward, excavating vast chambers in which to work his magical experiments. Some say that as he went he struck delvings deeper and more ancient yet—the tunnels of dark elves and dwarves. From these he drove the drow and duergar, and claimed the tunnels for his own. Eventually, Halaster abandoned his tower, and the uppermost levels of his labyrinth as well. Deeper and deeper he went, driven by his secret needs, until he passed from all knowledge. Soon, hordes of dire, nameless creatures crawled out of the cold and lightless Underdark to haunt the empty corridors and chambers that the mad wizard had left behind.

In later centuries, as Waterdeep grew from lowly village to teeming City of Splendors, it pressed against the rocky shoulders of Mount Waterdeep. Eventually, those who haunted the sewers beneath the city found places where the maze of foul waterways came in contact with Halaster's delvings. Knowledge of this fact soon spread among elements of the city's underworld. Thus the upper halls of Undermountain became a refuge for bands of criminals and cults dedicated to evil and forbidden gods. When the hidden Lords of Waterdeep finally assumed control of the city a century ago, most of these sinister organizations were rooted out and destroyed. After that, Undermountain was left to brood in its own silent darkness.

That is, until Durnan the Wanderer ventured below.

Durnan was the first to descend into Undermountain in recent times and return bearing tales of wonder and the riches to prove them. Seven times Durnan journeyed beneath Mount Waterdeep, and seven times he returned triumphant. At last he retired from the adventuring life and built his inn, the Yawning Portal, right over the entrance into Undermountain he had discovered. Some whispered that it was upon this very spot that the tower of Halaster once stood.

All that was nearly twenty years ago. Now Durnan was a gruff innkeeper, not a hero. Yet he kept the Well of Entry ever open. Would-be heroes came from all over Faerûn to pay one gold coin and take their chances in the maze below. A few of them found wealth and fame. Most of them found death. Either way, lucre changed hands in the tavern above as bets concerning the adventurers' fates were settled.

Nor were common freebooters the only ones drawn by the sport of Undermountain. Of course, not the least member of the nobility would be so gauche as to pay to use Durnan's public entryway. Many nobles had constructed their own private entrances into the labyrinth, and the rest curried their favor. To the nobility of Waterdeep, venturing into Undermountain to hunt trophies of kobold or goblin was no different than the manner in which country lords rode into their greenwoods in search of hart or stag. Always the nobles went in large, well-armed parties and ventured down only well-known passageways. There was little true danger in these excursions. It was an expensive and stylish game, and that was all.

In contempt, Darien eyed a scruffy band of adventurers sitting at a nearby table, making drunken plans for their own descent down the Well of Entry. It was a game to them, too—though one with far greater rewards if they succeeded, and far deadlier consequences if they failed. Yet Darien needed to find one to whom Undermountain was not merely a game. He had to find one who could brave the deadly depths like no other had before.

It was time to start asking questions.

Rising, he moved slowly through the firelit common room, making certain he stayed fully concealed within his cloak and hood. Few gave him a second look. Travelers in disguise were hardly an unusual sight at the Inn of the Yawning Portal. Sitting alone in a corner was a bent-nosed man in a travel-stained leather jerkin. He looked like a suitable candidate. Darien hesitated only a moment, then swiftly sat down opposite him.

Bent-Nose looked up, his beady eyes hazy with drink. "What in the Abyss do you want?"

"Your advice," Darien replied smoothly from the shadows of his hood.

The other man grunted in surprise. Clearly this was not a request he received often.

"You see, I have lost something," Darien continued in a low voice. "Something of great value to me."

At this, interest flickered across Bent-Nose's

weathered face. "How valuable?"

"Very."

Bent-Nose scratched his scraggly beard. "And I suppose you're looking for someone who can find it for you."

From the purse beneath his cloak, Darien withdrew a gleaming gold coin and placed it on the table. The man eyed the coin greedily.

"Actually," Darien replied affably, "I already know where this thing of import happens to be. So the task is all the simpler. I only need someone who can venture there and retrieve it."

The other man's hand inched across the table toward the gold coin. "And just where might that be?"

Darien spoke a single, quiet word.

"Undermountain."

Bent-Nose's hand began to tremble. Hastily he snatched it back.

"I can be of no help to you, stranger," he gasped hoarsely. "I'll not go back down there." His eyes went distant with remembered fear. "Do you hear me? I'll not go down there again!"

Darien watched the trembling man with a mixture of pity and curiosity. He had seen something below, something to break a man's will and send him seeking forgetfulness in drink. Something horrible. The pathetic wretch.

"Fear not, friend," Darien said in disdainful mirth. "I would hardly ask you to undertake this task for me." He tapped the gold piece with a finger. "But tell me—who shall I send on this crucial errand? Are any of these worth the price?" He gestured subtly toward the various roadworn freebooters and adventurers who filled the inn.

A strangled laugh escaped the other man's throat. "Those fools? Bah! None of them are worth the coin Durnan charges them to go down below. They'll come back mad and penniless. If they come back at all." His voice dropped to a mysterious whisper. "No, there's only one who might help you, stranger. Only one who could go down into a place like that, find what he's looking for, and come out . . . whole. But you'll not get *him*."

Darien pushed the coin across the table. His voice resonated with intensity.

"Tell me."

For a long moment Bent-Nose eyed the gold piece and his empty ale pot in turn. At last he reached out his still-shaking hand and closed it around the coin. Within the shadows of his hood, Darien smiled. He leaned forward to hear the other man's whispered words.

* * * * *

As the hours wore toward midnight, Darien moved through the inn, swathed in his disguise, approaching others who he thought might be compelled, with a gold coin or a pot of ale, to speak. They were more than plentiful. He asked each the same question. Who, better than any other, might go deep into Undermountain and find what he was charged to seek? Many names were given in answer. Some were heroes who had never existed other than in legends. Others were sots who at present snored drunkenly in a corner of the inn. Neither were of any use to Darien. However, there was one name that was repeated again and again in awed voices.

Artek the Knife.

Darien had heard of the scoundrel before. Artek Ar'talen, known also as the Knife, had once been Waterdeep's most famous and elusive criminal. He had preyed most often upon the nobility, which made him all the more abhorrent in Darien's eyes, if not those of the common folk. It was said that there was no tower so high, no vault so secure, and no crypt so deep that Artek the Knife could not penetrate it and rob it clean. That made him the perfect candidate for Darien's task. There was only one complication. Artek the Knife had mysteriously vanished over a year ago.

At last Darien found one who knew why.

"The city watch finally caught him," the woman said, quaffing the ale Darien had bought her. By her leather garb and the myriad knives at her hip, she styled herself some sort of rogue. "I guess Artek wasn't as slippery as the stories claimed. The Magisters have him locked up in their prison." She clenched a hand into a fist. "And he can rot in there forever!"

"Let me guess," Darien replied musingly. "Ar'talen enlisted your help in a robbery, promising to cut you in on the take, only to disappear with all the loot."

Anger twisted her face, and by this he knew he had hit close to the mark.

"He won't do *you* any good either," she spat. "The Magisters will never let you near him."

"I wouldn't be so certain," Darien purred. "I am rather accustomed to getting what I want."

Just then a burly freebooter careened drunkenly into Darien. The noble swore hotly, but the man only lurched onward to join several compatriots at a nearby table. Darien turned back to the woman to see that her eyes had narrowed in sudden suspicion. Too late he noticed the silken ruffle now revealed where his cloak had been knocked aside.

She grabbed the cloak, ripping it away. Even to one who did not know his identity, his high forehead and striking features clearly marked him a noble, as did his long coat of rich purple velvet and his ruffled shirt of silvery silk. The rogue hissed the words like venom.

"A *nobleman*."

Instantly, a deathly silence settled over the common room. All eyes turned toward Darien. Inwardly he cursed the insolent woman.

"I have no quarrel with you," he said coolly. Yet, he added to himself.

She drew dangerously close to him. "No? Well, I have one with you—you and all your kind. I was only a child at the time, but I will never forget the day a nobleman cast my family into the street. He took everything we owned. Then he had my parents hauled away by the city watch. They were thrown into prison, and they *died* there. I remember standing in the gutter, crying. I didn't understand what was happening. And do you know what the nobleman said? *'Do forgive me.'* " She shook with seething fury. "As if that could bring my parents back!"

Darien stared at her flatly. "You must understand, my dear," he said in a bored voice. "A lord can hardly be expected to indulge a tenant who fails to pay his rent. You see, if one allows but a single maggot into his meat, he will soon find it putrid with flies."

For a frozen moment, the woman stared at him in pale-faced rage. Then she reached for one of the curved knives at her belt. But Darien was faster and raised his right arm. Three barbed steel prongs sprang from the end of the Device. They spun rapidly, emitting a high-pitched whine. With a fluid, casual motion, Darien stepped forward and thrust the whirling prongs deep into the rogue's gut. He let them spin there a moment, then withdrew his arm. With a *click*, the blood-smeared barbs slid back into the Device.

Her eyes wide with shock, the rogue sank to the floor. There she writhed in soundless agony as she slowly died. Just as the insect had on the end of the Device. With a fey smile, Darien whispered, "Do forgive me."

He spun on a boot heel and strode through the silent common room toward the tavern's door. The rabble made no move to stop him. They didn't dare. And it did not matter that his disguise had been revealed. He had already gotten everything he needed.

"So you have managed to land yourself in prison, Artek Ar'talen," he murmured to himself. "Well, that is a small enough problem. For me, if not for you."

Laughing softly, Lord Darien Thal stepped out into the balmy spring night.

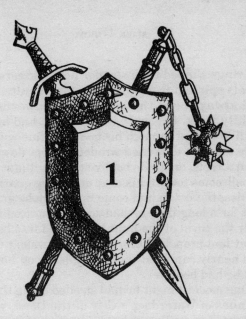

Heir to Darkness

What a fool he had been to think that he could truly change.

With your fingers, trace every crack and crevice in the walls of your prison cell. A dampness may signify weakened mortar, a puff of air an opening beyond. Notice how insects and other vermin come and go. Their paths may lead you to freedom, my son.

He had thought it would be such an easy thing, like shedding an old cloak to don one of new cloth. After all, he didn't choose this course for his life. Since childhood, he had simply known nothing else. For a time it had *seemed* enough, though not because of the gold coins pilfered from velvet-lined purses, or

the rings slipped from slender noble fingers, or the
jewels spirited from guarded stone vaults. Money
had always been the least of the rewards of his
nightly work. Far more intoxicating had been the
thrill. It flowed through his body like fine wine as he
stole through darkened windows, crept down shadowed streets, or strode boldly across brilliant candle-
lit ballrooms toward his next unwitting quarry.

Dissatisfaction had come upon him so gradually
that for a long time he had scarcely noticed it. Even
after the thrill of the hunt had dulled into boredom,
habit had propelled him onward. It wasn't until he
was nearly captured that he understood how reck-
less he had become.

One moonlit night he had strolled along the silent
avenues of Waterdeep's City of the Dead, wearing
the expensive silken robes he had just lifted from a
recently deceased nobleman. Only when the hue and
cry sounded on the air did he realize that he had not
even bothered to conceal himself as he walked.
Struck by sudden terror, he had cowered in the embrace of a decomposing corpse in a half-filled grave
as the City Watch ran past. He had escaped them,
for the moment. Yet he knew it was only a matter of
time before he grew so careless that even he could
not elude the Watch when the alarm sounded.

The truth was, part of him wanted to get caught. He
was weary—weary of scheming, of running, of watching dread flare in the eyes of others when they recognized who it was that stood before them. That night, in
the bottom of the muddy grave, wrapped in the rain-
soaked garb of a dead man, he finally made a choice.
From that moment on, he was a thief no longer.

Now to the floor. Press your ear right against the stones. Then rap sharply with some hard object—a spoon, a pebble, even your bare knuckles if you have nothing left. Move a half-pace to one side, then rap again. Listen well as you do. A change in sound may indicate a space below. And a way out.

He had not considered that nobody would believe him. But it made perfect sense, naturally. He had robbed the citizens of Waterdeep for years. What cause did they have to trust him? When the rumor spread across the city that he had given up his thieving ways, another rumor raced hot on its heels: it was all an elaborate ruse to lure the nobility into a false sense of security. They would leave their wealth unguarded, and Artek could thereby relieve them of it all the easier. Finally, he had realized there was only one way to make the people of Waterdeep understand that he had truly changed. He had to *show* them.

His chance arrived unexpectedly. He was gloomily pacing the night-darkened streets of the North Ward, pondering his dilemma, when he turned the corner of a narrow lane and saw a gilded carriage standing at a halt beneath a stone archway. Instinct pricked the back of his neck, and he melted soundlessly into a pool of shadow. Then he saw them: two masked figures in black. One gripped the harness of the horses as the animals stamped nervous hooves against cobblestone. The other reached through the open window of the carriage, roughly jerking glittering rings from the hands of a middle-aged countess, while her heavily painted face cracked in terror.

Artek knew this was his chance. Surely saving a countess would win him a pardon for his past crimes, and prove himself reformed. He moved swiftly through the shadows, drawing a dagger from each of his boots. The man who held the horses was dead before he even felt the knife slip between his ribs, piercing his heart. The second looked up and managed to let out a cry of surprise before he was silenced by a knife in his throat.

Kneeling, Artek retrieved the jewels from the dead thief's grip, then stood to hand them back to the countess. Then matters took an unexpected turn. The countess screamed. Artek tried to explain that he was returning her jewels, but she just continued to cry for help. Growing angry, he thrust the rings toward her, but she beat them away with wildly flapping hands, her shrieks rising shrilly on the night air. Too late, he realized his own peril.

Whirling around, he saw torchlight approaching rapidly from either direction, and heard the sound of booted feet. Before he could act, a patrol of the City Watch appeared in the archway, while another rounded the corner. In seconds a dozen watchmen surrounded him, swords drawn. A cold knot of fear tied itself in his stomach as he became aware of the jewels he still gripped in his sweating hands.

"It wasn't me," he said hoarsely.

The watchmen only grinned fiercely as they closed in.

Remember that every prison is merely a puzzle, and each has its own solution. To escape, all you must do is discover the answer that is already there. And while your face may be that of a man, never forget that the blood of the Garug-Mal *runs in your veins. Ever have the orc-kindred of the Graypeak*

*Mountains dwelled deep in lightless places. You have
nothing to fear from the dark, Artek. For the dark is
in you, my son . . .*

With a clinking of heavy chains, Artek Ar'talen
shifted his body on the cold stone floor, trying to ease
the chafing of the iron shackles where they dug painfully into his ankles and wrists. As always, the effort
was futile. He stared into the impenetrable dark
that filled the tiny cell. *Once a thief, always a thief.*
That was what the Magisters had said just before
they sentenced him to spend the rest of his life in
prison. On that day, Artek had finally realized that it
was impossible to change. He would be whatever
others thought him to be.

Artek was not certain how long he had been in this
place. Clay cups of foul water and bowls of maggoty
gruel came rarely and at uneven intervals through a
slit in the opposite wall, and could not be used to
mark time reliably. Certainly it had been months, perhaps as many as six. In that time, he had explored the
cell as far as his chains allowed, recalling everything
about prisons his father had taught him as a child,
but he found no hope. The walls and floors were made
of flawless stone without crack or crevice, as if forged
by sorcery rather than hewn by hand. Nor had his father's tricks worked upon the shackles, or the bolts
that bound the chains to the wall.

"I remember your words, Father," he whispered
through cracked lips. "And damn your wretched half-
orc soul to the Abyss, for they have failed me now."

With a groan, he slumped back against the wall.
His father had been right about one thing—the dark
was in him. And in the dark he would die.

It might have been minutes later—or perhaps hours, or even days—when a metallic noise ground on the dank air of the cell. Artek cracked his eyes. Chains jingling, he stiffly sat up. Had the guards finally brought him some water? He ran a parched tongue across his blistered lips. It had been a long time. He eyed the place in the dark where the slit of faint light always appeared, and through which food and drink were pushed with a stick. Puzzled, he saw only unblemished darkness. Then the grinding sound ended with a sharp *clang!*

All at once the perfect blackness of the cell was torn asunder. A tall rectangle of blazing fire appeared before Artek. With a low cry of pain, he shrank against the wall, shielding his face with his hands.

"Looks like our little friend here is afraid of the light," said a coarse voice.

"Isn't that just like a rat?" a second, wheedling voice laughed.

At last Artek's brain grasped what had happened. For the first time since he had been locked in this cell, someone had opened the door. Blinking away stinging tears, he slowly lowered his hands, trying to force his eyes to adjust. Two hazy forms stood in the open portal. Guards, one with a smoking torch. Artek supposed the light it cast was in truth dim and murky, but to his eyes, so long in the dark, it seemed like a brilliant sun.

Why . . . ? His lips formed the word soundlessly. Deliberately he swallowed, then tried again, straining to voice the sounds. This time the words came out as a croaking whisper. "Why have you come for me?"

"Somebody wants to see you," growled the first guard, a tall man with a dog's drooping face.

"What . . . what for?"

"Rats don't ask questions," snapped the second guard, a corpulent man with beady eyes. "They just do what their betters tell them if they don't want new smiles cut around their necks."

With a large iron key, Dog-Face unlocked Artek's chains from the ring in the wall. He jerked on them, pulling the prisoner roughly to his feet. Artek cried out as blood rushed painfully into his cramped limbs. He staggered, but another harsh jerk on the chains kept him from falling. Gradually the fire in his legs dulled to pins and needles. After a moment he could stand on his own, though only in a hunched position. Before his imprisonment, thick muscles had knotted his short, compact frame. Now, beneath his filthy rags, bones stuck out plainly beneath sallow skin.

"Looks like prison food hasn't agreed with you, rat," Beady-Eyes chuckled.

Artek eyed the gut straining against the guard's food-stained jerkin. "You might want to give it a try yourself," he said hoarsely.

Beady-Eyes glowered darkly, sucking in his stomach. "Bring him out!"

Dog-Face pulled hard on the chain, and Artek stumbled forward, barely managing to keep his balance.

"I can't walk with my feet shackled," he gasped.

"He's right," Dog-Face said. "And I'm not going to carry him."

Beady-Eyes scratched his stubbled jowl. "All right. Unlock his feet. But don't get any ideas about going anywhere, rat." He took the center of the chain

that bound Artek's shackled wrists and locked it to
an iron band he wore around his own thick wrist. A
yellow-toothed grin split his face. "You'll be staying
close by me."

In the corridor outside the cell, four more armed
guards waited. They all looked to Beady-Eyes. It was
clear he was their captain. He gave the order, and
they began marching down a long corridor. Two
guards led the way. Next came Beady-Eyes, who
jerked cruelly at the chain binding Artek's wrists,
followed by the remaining guards. Artek trudged
silently, head bowed, shoulders slumped.

"It seems there's little spark left in you, Artek the
Knife," Beady-Eyes chortled in a bubbling voice. "No
one would mistake the wretch you are now for
Waterdeep's most infamous rogue. It seems a year
alone in the dark is enough to break even the greatest of scoundrels."

Artek staggered dizzily. A year? A few months, he
thought, perhaps even six. But an entire year of his
life lost in that black pit? Deep inside, amid the
hopelessness that had filled him during his confine-
ment, there now ignited a single bright spark of
rage. Remembered words—spoken by father to son—
echoed in his mind.

*A good thief finds strength in weakness. Chains
can be a weapon. And sometimes a prisoner's bonds
may be turned upon unwitting captors.*

The party rounded a corner. To the left the wall fell
away, and in its place was an iron rail. Beyond this
was a vast chamber, its floor fifty feet below—the center of the prison of the Magisters, a place named the
Pit by the city's criminals. Below Artek, five levels of

cells lined the perimeter of the Pit, each bordered by a narrow catwalk. In the far wall was a massive stone slab of a door. At present, the door was raised, held up by a chain that passed through a ring in the ceiling and hooked to a large counterweight. A dozen armed guards stood before the open portal.

Beady-Eyes tugged Artek's chains, leading him toward an opening to the right, away from the Pit. The spark blazed more hotly inside the prisoner, burning away months of apathy and despair. This, he realized, would be his only chance.

He took it.

Lunging to the left, Artek jerked sharply on the chain that connected his shackled hands to the guard's wrist. With a cry of alarm, Beady-Eyes stumbled toward him, giving Artek the slack in the chain he needed. The guards drew their swords, reaching for Artek, but they were too slow.

With a shout, he threw himself past the iron railing and over the edge of the Pit. For a second he plunged downward, then abruptly stopped short. Above, Beady-Eyes shrieked in pain as he struck the iron railing. Arms above his head, Artek dangled in midair, suspended by the chain attached to the corpulent captain's wrist.

"My arm!" Beady-Eyes squealed, his pudgy face bright red. With his free hand he clutched the iron rail to keep from being dragged over the edge. "He's going to pull my arm out of its socket! Break the chain!"

The other guards stared at him.

"Break it!" Beady-Eyes wailed.

Dog-Face hurried forward, raising his sword. The

blade flashed downward in a whistling arc. At the
same moment, Artek swung his body toward the
wall. Another shrill scream sounded above just as
the chain gave way. Artek's momentum carried him
forward, and he landed in a crouch on the catwalk
bordering the highest row of cells. Glancing at the
chain around his wrists, he saw that Dog-Face's blow
had missed. The chain was unbroken, but at its center, still in the iron wristlet, was a severed hand. No
wonder Beady-Eyes had screamed, Artek thought
with grim mirth. He plucked the hand from the iron
ring and tossed it aside.

Shouts of alarm rang out across the Pit. Jerking
his head up, Artek saw guards racing along the catwalk from either direction. There was no way past
them without a fight, which left only one way to go.
Gripping the edge of the catwalk, he lowered himself
down, grunting with effort. His body was no longer
accustomed to such rigors. Drumming footfalls approached. Gritting his teeth, he swung himself forward and dropped to the catwalk bordering the
fourth level. At least his body had not forgotten
everything.

Angry curses drifted downward. A moment later, a
pair of black boots dangled over the edge of the catwalk above. A guard was climbing down after him.
Artek grabbed the man's boots and pulled. With a
scream, the guard lost his grip and plunged downward. A second later, he struck the hard stone floor
forty feet below, and blood sprayed outward in a crimson starburst. The remaining guards above swore
again but did not attempt to follow their companion.

Artek looked up. Across the Pit, guards on each of

the five cell levels raced in his direction. He leaned against the railing of the catwalk, his breath rattling in his gaunt chest.

You may not have changed, Artek, he thought. But you're certainly not the man you used to be.

Exhausted though he was, this was not the time to rest. He lowered himself over the edge of the catwalk and swung onto the third level. Emaciated arms reached out from iron-barred cells, but he ignored them. They would have to find their own way out. Arms aching, he lowered himself to the second level, then finally dropped to the main floor of the Pit.

He staggered, then gained his feet. A few feet away, a grimy old man pushing a wheelbarrow looked up in surprise. The cart was filled with gray, lumpy slop, and the old fellow gripped a dripping wooden ladle in his hand. He had been making the rounds, flinging a ladleful of the fetid slop into every cell for the prisoners to eat off the floor.

"That looks appetizing," Artek said wryly.

The old man only gaped at him.

A dozen guards poured out of a nearby stairwell and rushed toward Artek. He glanced at the door of the Pit. Another dozen guards stood before it. Now where?

A good thief is imaginative, my son. If something seems impossible, consider it. The unexpected action is the hardest of all to counter.

His black eyes drifted upward. A thrill coursed through him as he spied a way out. There was no time to consider it; the guards were almost upon him.

"Excuse me," Artek said, pushing the stunned old

man aside. He gripped the handles of the cart and, with a grunt, heaved it over. Putrid, gray gruel spilled across the stone floor, and the guards were running too fast to avoid it. Their boots skidded on the slimy swill, and they went down in a swearing tangle of arms, legs, and swords.

Artek did not hesitate. He took the sword from the body of the guard who had fallen to his death, then raced to a corner of the Pit. A massive iron ball was tied with a rope to a ring in the wall. The ball was, in turn, attached to a long chain dangling from above—the counterweight to the door.

Artek snaked his arm around the chain, then swung the sword, severing the rope from the ring. Instantly the counterweight rose into the air, taking Artek with it. Across the Pit, the guards before the door dove forward to avoid being crushed by the ponderous slab of stone as it descended. The counterweight came to an abrupt halt as the door crashed to the ground.

Artek kicked his legs, swinging at the end of the chain in wider and wider arcs. At the end of the widest arc, he let go, tucking himself into a ball. He sailed through the air, landing inside the open mouth of the ventilation shaft he had glimpsed from below.

Leaving behind the angry shouts echoing in the Pit, Artek crawled as quickly as he could through the narrow shaft. Though he couldn't be certain, he felt that it was gradually heading upward. The shaft had to lead to the surface at some point. He crawled on.

Just when he thought his cramped limbs could go no farther, he glimpsed a square of golden light ahead—an opening. His heart pounded rapidly. Was that sunlight pouring through the hole? Artek couldn't remember what the rays of the sun looked like, and now freedom was mere yards away. In excitement, he pulled himself through the golden opening, and suddenly felt himself tumble end over end through cold mists, no longer sure of where he was. After a moment of dizzying disorientation, Artek landed with a thud on a softly cushioned surface.

"I see that you're right on time, Artek Ar'talen."

Artek blinked away the fog in his head and saw that he was lying on a thick, expensive-looking rug. A sharp stench of lightning hung in the air.

Artek jumped up, but the action was never completed. Brilliant energy crackled through the air, and a blood-red aura sprang up around him, pinning his limbs to his sides and rooting his feet to the floor. He was not outside at all, but in a small chamber filled with rich tapestries, gilded wood, and many other ostentatious displays of wealth and taste. Artek choked for air, feeling as if the breath were being squeezed out of him. Struggling, he lifted his head to gaze upon the faces of his new captors.

They were a curious duo: a nobleman and a wizard. Effort racked the wizard's face as he concentrated on the spell of binding. Between his dark robe, hooked nose, and bald head, he looked like a great vulture. In contrast, the nobleman was strikingly handsome, with sharp green eyes and dark hair tied back from his high brow with a black ribbon. He was clad all in purple velvet and silver silk and, in a sophisticated affectation, had tucked his right hand beneath the breast of his long coat. He regarded Artek with calm but keen interest.

"Allow me to introduce myself," the nobleman said in a smooth voice. "I am Lord Darien, scion of House Thal, high advisor to the Circle of Nobles." He inclined his head ever so slightly.

Artek stared at the man as his thief's intuition made a sudden leap. "You," he spat between clenched teeth. "You're the one they were taking me to see."

Darien nodded, drawing a step closer. "That is correct. You see, I have a bargain to offer you, Ar'talen. It would be a simple transaction—freedom from this prison in exchange for your services. Are you interested to hear more? If not, don't hesitate to say so, and I will be happy to deliver you back into the hands of the guards . . ."

Artek swore inwardly. Why did nobles always enjoy playing such games, manipulating common people as if they were merely pieces on a lanceboard?

"Calling the guards won't be necessary," he said. "And you can tell your hired vulture to call off his spell. I won't be going anywhere. You have my word."

Darien turned to the wizard. "You heard him, Melthis. Remove the spell of binding."

The wizard gaped at him. "But my lord, surely it is unwise to trust this scoundrel."

Sparks of ire flashed in Darien's eyes. "Do you question my orders, Melthis?"

The wizard's face blanched. "Of course not, my lord," he said fawningly.

Hastily, Melthis weaved his thin hands in an intricate gesture, and the shimmering aura surrounding Artek vanished. He staggered, then caught his balance, drawing in a deep breath of relief.

Darien led the way to a table in the center of the

small chamber. He sat in a cushioned chair and motioned for Artek to take the chair opposite him. Melthis hovered two paces behind his master, hands tucked into the sleeves of his robe.

"I imagine you are wondering how I brought you here," Darien began.

Artek only gazed at him silently. That was exactly what he was wondering, but he did not want to give the lord the satisfaction of hearing it.

"You see, I have made a study of your colorful career, Ar'talen," Darien went on. He pressed his shapely hands into a steeple before him. "I learned all I could of your daring exploits, and by so doing I have come to know you. I was certain that, once you were outside your magically warded cell, you would attempt an escape. By plotting the course on which the guards would lead you, and by studying parallels in your past work, I predicted the route that you would take. From there, it was a simple matter to have Melthis bring you here." A smile coiled about his lips. "I must say, I am gratified to see my prediction proved so accurate."

This caught Artek entirely off guard. Was he really so simple that his actions could be guessed by one who had merely examined his past work?

"I don't know what you want of me, Darien," he growled angrily. If the nobleman noticed the omission of the honorific *lord*, he showed no sign of it. "But you should know that I'm not the thief I used to be. I'm not sure if I'm even a thief at all anymore." He plucked at the dirty rags that covered his emaciated frame. "Either way, I'm certainly damaged goods."

Darien shook his head, laughing softly. "No,

Ar'talen, you are not damaged. If anything, you are greater than you ever were before. For in being captured you have finally known humility. You have learned that you have limits. And that knowledge will drive you to reach beyond those limits all the harder."

Artek did not answer. Darien had been right about him so far; perhaps he was correct in this as well. It was a disturbing thought, but one he could not quite dismiss.

"So what do you want me to steal?" he asked darkly.

"Nothing," Darien replied. "Rather, there is something I want you to find. Something of great value to me—and to all of Waterdeep as well."

Darien motioned to Melthis, and the wizard filled two silver cups with crimson wine from a crystal decanter. Artek downed his in one gulp, then reached for the decanter to refill his goblet. It was expensive stuff, much better than prison swill. Darien sipped his own wine slowly as he spoke.

"Three days ago, in search of sport, a hunting party consisting of several nobles and their attendants ventured into the upper levels of Undermountain. By accident, one of the nobles, Lord Corin Silvertor, was separated from the rest of the party. Before the others could search for him, they were set upon by a vicious band of kobolds and forced to retreat to the private entrance through which they had entered the maze. Subsequent forays into the same areas of Undermountain have revealed no trace of Lord Silvertor, and it is feared that he is lost."

Artek shrugged his shoulders. He had no sympathy for nobles whose stupidity put them in danger. "And why isn't it feared that he found his way into the kobolds' stew pot?"

"This is why." Darien set a small blue crystal on the table. A faint light flickered inside the gem. "This is a heart jewel," the lord explained. "They are magical stones, each linked to the one it is created for. This one belongs to Lord Silvertor. The light within pulses in time to his heart, and by that we know he yet lives. The nearer the jewel is to its master, the brighter the light. By the faintness of the light in this jewel, we know that Lord Silvertor is lost deep in Undermountain—deeper than any hunting party has ever ventured."

Artek gazed thoughtfully at the pulsing jewel. "And I suppose you want me to go down and find your missing little lord."

Darien nodded gravely. "It is imperative that we find him, Ar'talen." His voice dropped to a dire whisper. "You see, in two days' time, there is to be a vote among all the nobility of Waterdeep. The vote will determine who is to take the seventh seat in the Circle of Nobles, left vacant after the untimely death of Lord Rithilor Koll. Lord Corin Silvertor is the leading candidate for the seat—which is well, for among his rivals are those with dark ambitions. They see the Circle as a means to rule over all the city's nobility, and as a position from which to launch an all-out assault against the hidden Lords of Waterdeep." Darien's expression was grim. "Such strife would certainly tear this city asunder. But Silvertor is loyal to the Lords of Waterdeep. That is why it is crucial that he be found in time for the election. The fate of all Waterdeep depends on it."

Artek considered these words. "So if I go down into Undermountain and find this precious lord of yours, you'll give me my freedom. Is that the deal?"

"No, it is more than that," Darien countered. "I am authorized by the Magisters to grant you a full pardon for all your past crimes. It would be as if you were never a thief, Ar'talen." Darien's sharp green eyes bore into Artek's own. "All you must do is say yes."

Artek glared at the lord. Damn the smug bastard to the Abyss. What choice did he really have? It was exactly what he wanted—to have his dark past forgotten. There was only one thing he could say. He clenched his hands into fists and spat the word like a curse.

"Yes."

Darien leaned back, smiling toothily. "Excellent." He eyed Artek's gaunt frame critically. "But we must prepare you for your task. Imprisonment has left you ill fit for the rigors of this mission." He glanced at the red-robed wizard. "You may cast the spell now, Melthis."

Artek started to spring from his chair, but he was too slow. Melthis raised his hands and uttered a string of words in the weird tongue of magic. Searing pain arced through Artek's body, and he fell to the floor, writhing. His flesh felt on fire, as if his bones and muscles were being molded like hot wax. Then, as quickly as it had begun, the pain ended. Gasping, he climbed to his feet. Something about the motion felt . . . strange.

Artek gazed down at himself, and his coal-black eyes went wide with shock. His ragged clothing had been reduced to a fine dusting of ash, but this paled in comparison to the change in his body. It was as if he had never spent those long months chained to the wall, wasting away in the dark. His skin was not pale and jaundiced, but a deep olive. No longer was he a half-starved skeleton. Now, thick muscles knotted his compact frame. He flexed his hands, staring at the fingers. Moments ago they had been calloused stumps, covered with sores from worrying his chains, but now they were smooth and strong and whole. He looked at Melthis in amazement.

Darien rose to his feet and slowly approached Artek. "Yes, I can see it," he murmured in fascination. "Though I would hardly notice it if I didn't know what to look for. You are handsome enough in a swarthy way. But the signs are there: brow ridges slightly too thick, jaw a little too protruding, shoulders a bit too heavy. And those eyes—the jet-black eyes give it away." The nobleman's lip curled up in disgust. "Orc blood indeed runs in your veins, doesn't it, Ar'talen?"

Artek glowered but said nothing. He felt suddenly naked and exposed, and not because of his lack of clothes.

Darien opened a trunk next to the table and pulled out a bundle of dark leather. He heaved it toward Artek. "Here. Put these on. I believe black is your favorite color."

Artek put on the clothes: jerkin, breeches, and boots. The supple black leathers fit his body tightly but comfortably, as if made just for him.

"Take this," Melthis said, pressing the heart jewel into Artek's hand. "It will guide you to Lord Silvertor. I have two other objects for you as well." He

handed Artek a curved saber in a leather sheath.
"This sword is enchanted, and will lend you strength
against any enemy you may encounter." Finally he
held out a small golden box. "And this is a transportation device. If you open it, a magical gate will
appear. All you have to do is step through and you
will be instantly transported out of Undermountain."

Artek belted the sword around his waist, then
tucked the heart jewel and the golden box into his
pocket. It was good to know that he had a way out of
Undermountain if things looked bad.

Darien nodded in approval. "There's only one more
thing we need to do, Ar'talen. Hold out your arm."

Artek eyed the noble warily, but did as he was
told. Melthis rolled up the sleeve of Artek's jerkin.
Then, using a quill pen and a jar of black ink, the
wizard drew an intricate tattoo on his arm: a wheel
depicting a stylized sun and moon, with an arrow
next to it. In the center of the wheel was a grinning
skull. Artek wondered what it could possibly mean.

Setting down the pen and ink, Melthis held his
hand over the tattoo and whispered a dissonant incantation. The lines of ink glowed with scarlet light,
then went dark again. Artek felt no pain, only a cool
tingling against his skin.

"What was that all about?" he asked with a frown
as Melthis moved away.

A mysterious smile played around the corners of
Darien's mouth. "Take a closer look at the tattoo,
Ar'talen."

Feeling a sudden chill at the nobleman's words,
Artek looked. At first he noticed nothing unusual.
Then he blinked in surprise. Slowly but perceptibly,

the circle drawn upon his arm was moving, the sun and moon spinning around the grinning skull.

"The tattoo is linked to the movements of the sun and moon in the sky above," Darien explained in cool tones. "No matter how deep in the ground you go, the wheel will move as they move. As you can see, the sun is just passing the arrow, for it is sunrise outside. If the sun passes the arrow twice more—that is, in exactly two days—the tattoo will send out a small but precisely calibrated jolt of magical energy. At that moment your heart will stop beating. Forever."

For a moment Artek could only gape at Darien in openmouthed shock. Then rage ignited in his chest.

Artek lunged at the nobleman. At the same time, Darien pulled his right hand from beneath his coat. Artek froze. It wasn't a hand on the end of Darien's arm, but some sort of metallic device. Three viciously barbed prongs sprang from the end of the metal cylinder, whirling rapidly.

"Killing me will get you nowhere, Ar'talen." The nobleman's voice was not angry, merely matter-of-fact. "I will have Melthis remove the tattoo only when you return from Undermountain—with Lord Corin Silvertor. Return without Silvertor, and I will do nothing." The whirling prongs drew closer to Artek's face. "Now, what do you say?"

Hatred boiled in Artek's blood. The orc in him would not rest until he had exacted his revenge upon Lord Darien Thal. But that would have to wait; right now, there was only one thing he could do. Artek hissed the words through bared teeth.

"Show me how I get into Undermountain."

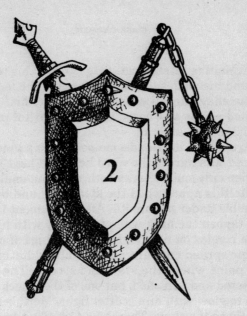

Descent Into Danger

The steep alley ended in a blank stone wall.

"No offense, but this doesn't exactly look like an entrance into Undermountain," Artek noted dryly.

He turned to watch as Lord Darien Thal and Melthis picked their way down the slimy cobblestones toward him. Dawn was breaking over the rest of Waterdeep, but in this deep alley in the Dock Ward, the shadowed gloom of night still held sway. Artek wished he could climb out of this hole and walk the city's open avenues, to feel the light of the sun upon his face. However, it was down into the dark that he was to go.

"That is why I am a wizard and you are a dungeon

rat!" Melthis hissed acidly. He clutched his robes up around his ankles to keep them out of the foul muck of the alley. "Recall your manners, Melthis," Darien chided as the two came to a halt. "Ar'talen is our friend in this, after all."

Artek shot the handsome nobleman a black look. *Friend* was hardly the word he would have chosen. Darien only smiled his smooth, arrogant smile.

Melthis approached the stone wall and began to mumble under his breath. After a moment the wizard tapped the back wall of the alley with his staff. Like ripples on a pond, concentric rings of crimson magic spread outward on the wall, radiating from the point where the staff had struck. The circles flickered and vanished, but one of the stones continued to glow with dim scarlet light. Melthis pushed lightly on the stone. There was a grinding sound, followed by a hiss of fetid air. A low opening appeared in the wall. The wizard shot Artek a smug look.

"You'll forgive me if I hold my applause," Artek said in annoyance.

Darien gestured to the dark opening. "All you need do is follow the passageway beyond, Ar'talen. It leads to one place only: the upper halls of Undermountain."

"The transport device I gave you will return you to this place," Melthis added. "We will be waiting for you."

Darien smoothed his elegant velvet coat. "Remember, Ar'talen, you have only two days to return with Lord Corin Silvertor. And if you fail to find him," he said, green eyes flashing sharply, "don't bother to return at all."

Artek tried to swallow the bitter taste of rage in his mouth. "How do I know that when I do return you'll really have Melthis remove the tattoo?" he demanded.

"You don't," Darien replied flatly. "Yet what choice do you have but to trust me?"

Clenching his hands into fists, Artek resisted the orcish urge to tear the nobleman to shreds. He glanced down at the tattoo on his arm. Slowly, inexorably, the wheel continued to spin around the grinning skull. The sun had completely passed the arrow now. Less than two days to find the missing noble. Less than two days to live.

"Be here," was all he said.

Crouching, he passed through the opening in the wall into a cramped tunnel beyond. Behind him, Melthis uttered a word of magic. The secret doorway shut with a foreboding *boom*, sealing Artek in tomblike blackness.

For a long moment he stared into the thick darkness. Gradually his eyes began to adjust. Rough walls, loose stones, and scurrying insects appeared before him in subtle shades of red. He sighed in the dank air. During those long months locked in his cell, he had thought his ability to see in the dark lost forever, for his eyes had glimpsed nothing but impenetrable blackness. Now he knew that this had indeed been due to some enchantment bound in the stones of that cell. Like his thieving skills, his darkvision was a gift from his half-orc father. And one for which he was now grateful.

In a hunched position, he began moving down the low tunnel. Countless times it bent and twisted, until he lost almost all sense of direction. Yet some deep instinct told him that he was steadily heading westward—in the direction of Mount Waterdeep. At several points he was forced to crawl on his belly over heaps of rubble where the tunnel had caved in. The foul air was oppressive, and he breathed it in shallow gasps through his open mouth.

Abruptly he came to a halt. The passageway, which had been level up to this point, suddenly plunged down before him at a steep angle. He eyed the slope critically. It would require some caution, but he could do it. Keeping his center of balance low to the floor, he inched his way over the edge of the incline.

His boot skidded on a layer of slime.

Artek's hands shot out, but it was no use. The walls and floor of the tunnel were both dripping with slick slime. The ichor was the same temperature as the cool stones, and so his heat-sensitive eyes had failed to detect it. His boots and fingers scrabbled furiously against the slimy surface. He nearly made it back up to the edge of the incline, but then he lost his grip and careened headlong down the steep slope.

His curses rang off the walls of the tunnel as he slid rapidly downward. In vain he fought to slow his descent, wondering if at any moment he would strike a blank wall or some other obstacle with bone-crushing force. Out of control, he slid faster and faster.

As suddenly as it had begun, the slope ended, leveling into a flat passageway once more. With a surge of dread, he saw that his fear of a trap was all too prophetic. Just ahead, the tunnel dead-ended in a wall bristling with pointed iron spikes. Despite the level floor, he was so covered with slime that he continued to skid, hurtling with fatal speed face first toward the spikes.

With a yell, he reached back and fumbled for the saber belted at his hip. At the last moment he drew the blade and thrust his arms out before him, clenching his eyes against the coming impact. There was a deafening *clang* of metal on metal, accompanied by a spray of hot sparks. A brutal shock raced up his arms, jarring his shoulders painfully, as he came to a sudden halt. After a moment he opened his eyes. He looked up to see the tip of a spike a hairsbreadth from his hands. The sword was longer than the spikes, its tip striking the wall just before he struck the points.

Pulling his aching arms back, he slowly sat up and slipped the saber back into its scabbard.

"I guess that was the quick way down," he said weakly. He let out a nervous laugh of relief. Stiffly, he started to climb to his feet.

That was when the floor dropped out from beneath him.

Artek swore as he plunged downward. He had become stupid as well as rusty during his long imprisonment. Of course the spikes hadn't been the real trap. They were far too obvious. Their only purpose had been to distract him from the true trick—a weight-sensitive trapdoor. And it had worked perfectly. He flailed as he plummeted through cold air, wondering how many heartbeats he had until he struck bottom.

Out of the corner of his eye, a large shape loomed beneath him. Instinct took command. Like a cat in midfall, he snapped his body around and reached out. His fingers brushed across hard stone, slipped— then caught in a sharp crevice. His descent abruptly halted. Once again pain flared in his shoulders, but somehow he managed to keep his grip on the crack. Searching blindly with his boots, he found a toehold and took the pressure off his throbbing arms. He leaned his cheek against the cool stone, breathing hard. That had been close. Too close.

"How in the Abyss did I do this blasted thieving stuff for so long?" he groaned to himself.

He didn't know. But he only had to do this one last job, and then he could give it up forever.

Shaking the vertigo from his head, he gazed around, his darkvision piercing the gloom. He was in the center of a large circular chamber, clinging to the side of some sort of irregular stone pillar. Had he not managed to catch himself, he would now be lying on the floor over forty feet below, gruesomely wounded or—more likely—dead. Craning his neck, he gazed upward. He could just make out the trapdoor through which he had fallen, perhaps twenty feet above. It was still open, but utterly out of reach. Not that it mattered. His goal lay in the opposite direction—deeper into Undermountain.

A peculiar odor hung in the air, sharp and metallic, like the scent of the air before a storm. The smell troubled him, though he was not certain why. The hair on the back of his neck prickled uncomfortably. However, there was nothing to do but start climbing. He glimpsed two stone doors on opposite sides of the chamber, both closed. Hoping that one of them might lead to his quarry, he felt for crevices and protrusions and started inching his way down the pillar.

He had gone no more than five feet when the lightning struck. Two blue-white bolts of brilliant energy rent the darkness asunder. Each sizzled hotly as it struck one of the shut doorways, then crackled around the chamber, ricocheting wildly off the stone walls. A searing bolt passed inches from Artek's face. He cringed against the scant protection of the pillar.

Only it wasn't a pillar at all, he saw now in the blazing illumination. It was a gigantic statue hewn of seamless, dark red stone. At the moment, Artek clung to the shallow ridge just above its right shoulder blade. The statue's neck ended in a jagged stump, for the head had been knocked off long ago. But the torso and legs were muscled and powerful, like those of a god. The figure's hands—from which several of the fingers had been snapped off—were outstretched in a commanding gesture. It was from these that the two bolts of energy had emanated.

After a few terrifying seconds, the lightning bolts burned themselves out in hisses of sulfur. Artek blinked, but all he could see were purple afterimages. The lightning had temporarily blinded his darkvision. At last the dull red shapes of the statue and walls came back into focus. With a sigh, he started down once more.

Two more lightning bolts arced from the statue's hands to strike the doors and careen around the chamber.

Clinging to the statue's back, Artek narrowly ducked one of the jagged arcs of energy as it crackled past. This time when the lightning dissipated he remained still, staring into the darkness while he counted his heartbeats. He made it to a hundred before the blue-white bolts struck again.

Artek swallowed hard. This did not look good.

Even assuming he could make it to the statue's feet without being struck by the magical lightning, the interval between strikes gave him just over a minute to dash to one of the chamber's doors. This would be more than enough—provided the door was not locked. However, if it was, and he could not pick the lock in time, he would be standing directly in the path of the lightning when it leapt from the statue's outstretched hands again.

As if on cue, once more searing bolts of magic bounced around the chamber before vanishing. Artek racked his brain, but he could not see a sure-fire way around this trap. Had he been thwarted in his mission already? If so, he was rustier than he had feared. *Think, Artek*, he told himself urgently. *You've got to think!* It was no use. His mind was a blank. With a groan of frustration, he smacked his forehead against the hard stone of the statue.

He noticed two things. First, this idiotic action *hurt*. Second, it resulted in a hollow echo deep inside the statue.

Artek jerked his head back, staring at the statue in astonishment. Quickly, he began running his hands across its smooth stone surface. It had to be here somewhere. Then his fingers brushed a small, slightly raised circle in the center of the statue's back. That was it. He mashed the circle with his thumb. There was a grating noise, and he was nearly thrown off the statue as a small, circular door opened between its shoulder blades.

"Now this adds new meaning to the term *back door*," Artek quipped with a satisfied grin.

He scrambled through just as lightning sizzled

around the chamber again. Pulling the door shut, he
sealed himself safely inside the statue. After a long
moment his eyes adjusted. He stood at the top of a
narrow spiral staircase. Descending the steps, he
coiled deeper and deeper, soon certain that he must
be far below the statue. Still the stairs plunged
downward. At last they ended in an iron door. It was
not locked. Tensing himself in readiness, Artek
pushed open the portal.

An empty corridor stretched beyond.

Glancing around, he saw no sign of sharp iron
spikes, trapdoors, or lightning-shooting statues. He
drew in a deep breath. Maybe he could actually relax
for a second.

From a pocket in his black leather breeches, he
pulled out the crystalline heart jewel. The sapphire
light that pulsed in its center, though still dim, was
brighter than it had been before. So Lord Corin Silvertor was still alive, and closer now, if some distance away. Holding the heart jewel out before him,
Artek started cautiously down the corridor.

Soon he found himself amid a maze of dank passageways and shadow-filled halls. High archways
opened to the right and left. Corridors doubled back
on themselves or ended abruptly in blank walls.
Some stairwells led to nowhere, while others delved
deeper into the oppressive dark. It was not at all difficult to believe that this place had been constructed
by a mad wizard. There seemed no reason or plan to
the vast labyrinth, unless it was to lead those who
wandered its ways inexorably downward.

As he went, Artek kept his eye on the heart jewel.
A dozen times the light flickered and dimmed, and

he retraced his steps until the blue gem began to glow more strongly once again. Then he would try his luck down another passageway or tunnel. It was hardly an elegant method, but it worked. Gradually the glimmer in the center of the heart jewel grew brighter. Slowly but steadily, he worked his way closer to the missing nobleman.

He wasn't certain exactly when he first noticed the sounds drifting in the musty air. At first they hovered on the edge of consciousness, filling him with a vague and nameless unease. Finally they resolved themselves into distant yet distinct noises: an echoing *boom* like that of a slamming door, the grinding of unknown machinery, and high, wordless cries that were either screams of agony or inhuman howls of bloodlust. Though the sounds were faint and far off, they were not enough so for Artek's comfort. One thing was certain—he was not alone in the maze.

Half-remembered stories drifted to mind, tales told to him as a child by his father, of the lightless warrens of the *Garug-Mal*. In turn, Artek's father, Arturg, had learned the stories from his own father. His name had been Arthaug, and he had been a high chief among the orcs who lived beneath the Graypeak Mountains. From time to time, the orcs had raided human settlements at the foot of the mountains, capturing men and women and bringing them back to the orc warrens to work as slaves, digging and tunneling. It was upon one of these human women that Arthaug had sired Arturg.

Not long after this, Arthaug was deposed in an overthrow engineered by a rival orcish chief. Arthaug was forced to flee the warrens of the *Garug-*

Mal, and he took young Arturg with him. Arthaug plotted for the day he would return to the Graypeak Mountains and become high chief of the *Garug-Mal* again. However, he died in exile—slain in a duel with highwaymen—without ever again laying eyes on the tunnels of his homeland. After his death, his half-orc son was left to fend for himself.

Fully grown at the age of ten, Arturg was brutish in appearance. However, he could pass for a human man, at least in dim light. Remembering the power of the brigands who had killed his father, he made his way in the overworld as a rogue, though he never managed to rise far above petty theft. His companion was a human witch named Siraia, who died giving birth to Artek.

Arturg raised Artek alone, teaching his son all that he knew of stealth and stealing. When Artek was seven, Arturg was caught robbing a rich merchant in Elturel. There he was beheaded, and with him died the dream of Arthaug. For Artek considered himself human, and he had no desire to return to the Graypeak mountains to claim rulership of the *Garug-Mal*.

Yet it was not so easy for Artek to escape his inhuman legacy. Darkly handsome as he was, others still sometimes glimpsed the orcish blood that ran in his veins. And though, in time, he far surpassed Arturg in skill and success, he was still a thief, just like his father. In the end, his attempt to escape his heritage had been an utter failure, landing him in the prison of the Magisters. He had been stupid to think that he could ever change. He would not make that mistake again.

"This is what I am," he growled under his breath.

Gripping the hilt of his saber, he prowled down the dusky corridors of Undermountain, forcing the old stories from his head. He had a nobleman to find.

Following the gleaming heart jewel, he passed through an open archway into a long, high-ceilinged room. Immediately his nose wrinkled in disgust. A vile odor hung thickly on the air. Something crunched beneath his boot. Kneeling, he peered at the object. It was a thin, papery tube, almost like a sheath of some sort. Examining it more closely, he saw dull green scales embedded in its surface. Alarm stirred in his chest. He had a bad feeling about this place. Hastily he tossed down the sheath.

It came from behind, a rhythmic whirring sound, along with a rasping hiss.

Artek spun on a heel. In the air before him hovered a brilliant green snake, leathery wings sprouting from its back flapping rapidly to keep the creature aloft. Crimson light gleamed in its dull reptilian eyes, and the thing opened its mouth, baring long fangs.

He dodged barely in time to avoid the stream of vitriol that sprayed from the snake's mouth. The black liquid struck the wall behind him, smoking and sizzling as it burned deep pits into the hard rock. Artek stared at the melting stone in shock.

There was another whirring noise to his left. He jerked his head around to see a second winged snake dart toward him through the air. The flapping sound grew louder, and dry hisses echoed all around. A dozen sinuous shapes drifted out of the shadows. Artek could only watch in horror as he was surrounded by flying snakes.

His hand crept toward the hilt of his saber, though he knew it would do him no good. The creatures closed in, their bodies coiling and uncoiling menacingly. The snake's venom had burned easily through solid stone. Artek could only imagine what it would do to living flesh. Even as he watched, the flying snakes opened gaping mouths, baring their hollow fangs, ready to spray.

"Duck!" a voice shouted.

Such was his terror that Artek did not even question the command. He dropped to the floor, curling into a tight ball. A fraction of a second later, a ball of blazing fire struck the flock of snakes just above his head. A blast of furnacelike air hit him. The creatures hissed and writhed as they were burnt to crisps, and the fireball dissipated as quickly as it had appeared. The blackened husks of the flying snakes dropped to the floor and did not move.

Artek uncoiled himself cautiously. Ashes drifted from the backs of his hands where the hair had been singed away, but he was otherwise unhurt. He clambered to his feet, then looked up to see a woman walking toward him.

Even if she had not just conjured a fireball, he would have mistaken her for nothing other than a wizard. A ball of blue light glowed on the end of the intricately carved staff she gripped, and myriad pouches, feathers, and bones hung from the leather belt around her hips. She was tall—a good head taller than Artek was—and sleek, with close-cropped brown hair. Her too-square jaw and crooked nose precluded prettiness, but there was something warmly compelling about her deep brown eyes. Her clothes were better suited to a young prince out hunting than a wizard or a woman—worn leather breeches, a full white shirt, and a gray vest. However, the garb was dirt-smudged and threadbare, as if she had been wearing it for a long time.

Artek gazed curiously at his mysterious rescuer as she halted a few paces away.

"I suppose that I should thank you for your help," he said cautiously.

"I suppose that you should," she said with a slightly smug expression.

"But in a place such as this," he went on pointedly, "it might be better to first ask how it was that you came upon me at just the right moment."

She shrugged her broad shoulders. "That was easy enough. I was following you, of course. I have been for nearly an hour now."

Artek frowned dubiously at this. "Call me a skeptic, but I'm not exactly a beginner in matters of stealth. And my ears are really rather good. I think I would have heard if you were following me."

"Not if I had cast a spell of silence around myself," she countered with a crooked smirk.

Despite himself, Artek laughed. He doffed an imaginary hat and bowed low, conceding his defeat.

Her brown eyes flashed with mirth. "The truth is, I don't run into many other people down here," she went on. "And monsters make for dreadfully dull conversation partners before you have to kill them. It gets a little lonely. So when I saw you from a distance, I decided to cloak myself in silence and follow." She eyed the burnt remains of the flying snakes. "And it's a good thing I did. Fine company you would be if you had been melted into a puddle of black slime."

With a shudder, Artek agreed.

"By the way," the wizard added, "my name is Beckla Shadesar."

Artek held his breath a moment. "I'm Artek Ar'talen," he said finally.

She gaped at him in open surprise. "You're Artek the Knife?" Hastily she checked the pouches hanging at her belt, counting to make certain they were all still there, and regarded him suspiciously. "You know, I think you once swindled my old employer out of a casket full of emeralds."

"It wouldn't surprise me," Artek replied dryly.

"So have you come down here to steal things?"

He shook his head slowly. "No."

To his surprise she nodded, as if she actually believed him.

"So why are *you* down here in Undermountain?" he asked carefully.

Her lips parted in a wry smile. "I think both of our tales might wait until we've had a bit of refreshment," she said in lieu of an answer. "I have a bottle of something I've been saving just for a special occasion like this."

Artek hesitated, glancing at the tattoo on his forearm. By the position of the sun in relation to the arrow, several hours had passed. However, he supposed a few moments of rest would do more good than harm. Besides, he was curious to hear the wizard's story.

"Lead the way, Beckla Shadesar," he said with a gracious gesture.

Artek followed the wizard through a door in the far end of the hall into a dusty corridor beyond. As they turned a corner, Beckla suddenly cried out in alarm.

"Artek, look out! It's on you!"

The wizard reached out her hands and shouted a word of magic. Blue energy crackled from her fingertips, striking Artek's side. He let out a howl of pain, dancing around in a circle, swatting at his hindquarters.

"That's not a snake," he gritted through clenched teeth. "That's the scabbard for my sword!"

The wizard affected a sheepish look. "Oops."

Artek glared at her. "You nearly set my rump on fire, and all you can say is *oops*?"

She crossed her arms. "Well, I'm sorry," she countered petulantly. "Sometimes I make mistakes. I'm only human, you know. I suppose you're not?"

Artek grunted. She couldn't know how close to the mark her question had hit. "I think I definitely need that drink now," he muttered.

It wasn't far. At the end of a dim corridor was an iron door. Beckla waved her staff, and the door glowed briefly, then swung open of its own volition.

"It's not much," Beckla said cheerfully, "but I call it home."

She wasn't joking. Beyond the door was a cramped and dingy stone chamber. It was decorated with flotsam and jetsam scavenged from the ancient tunnels and halls: worm-eaten furniture, threadbare tapestries, and dusty shelves overflowing with moldering books and scrolls. Beckla motioned for Artek to enter and then followed, closing the door behind them. She waved her staff, and the portal locked with an audible *click*.

"It keeps the wandering creatures out," she explained. "Otherwise, I'd never get a wink of sleep."

They sat on a pile of musty cushions, and Beckla rummaged in a nearby chest. "I have some food, if you want it," she said. "It isn't great stuff, but considering that it's conjured out of thin air with a spell, I really can't complain." Then she held aloft a purple glass bottle. "Now *this* is the real thing. Dwarven firebrandy. I found it on some dead adventurers a while back. I think we'll get more use out of it than they did."

Beckla grabbed two clay cups, blew the dust and spiders out, and filled them with the clear firebrandy. She handed one to Artek. They clanked the cups together, and the wizard downed her drink in one gulp. With a bemused smile, Artek followed suit. Instantly a delicious warmth spread outward from his stomach. Until now, his magically restored body had still felt slightly strange and alien, as if it weren't really his own. But the firebrandy melted his tense muscles, leaving him feeling extremely comfortable. Beckla refilled their cups.

"So are you ever going to tell me what you're doing down here?" he asked amiably. He sipped his firebrandy. Suddenly, his mission did not seem quite so urgent.

Beckla giggled, slurping from her own cup. "Actually, there isn't that much to tell. It isn't all that easy to make a living as a wizard these days. And I've taken some jobs I'm not proud of to make ends meet." She sighed deeply, leaning back on the grubby cushions. "I have dreams, of course. Someday I want to have my own tower, and a personal laboratory so I can perform experiments, and devise amazing new spells that no one has ever seen before. I'd be one of the most famous wizards in all of Faerûn." She shook her head ruefully. "But a tower and a laboratory cost gold—lots of it. And, unfortunately, that's one thing I haven't figured out how to conjure yet."

The wizard sloshed more firebrandy into their cups as she went on. "A year ago, I took a job working for a moneylender in the South Ward of Waterdeep. His name was Vermik. He was vile-tongued and foul-tempered, but he paid well, so I put up with him. Vermik came up with a clever scheme. He had me ensorcell all the coins that passed through his shop to seem slightly heavier than they really were. That way he could shave gold dust from them, and no scale would reveal the trick. Though he took only a little from each coin, a great many went through his business every day, and he was making a killing. Until . . ." Her words trailed off.

"Until what?" Artek asked.

Beckla swallowed hard. "Until I transmogrified him into a green slime."

Artek choked on his firebrandy. "You what?"

"It was an accident," the wizard huffed defensively. "I didn't mean for the spell to go awry. He had a bad headache, and I was trying to help."

"Like you were trying to help me when you thought my sword was a snake?" Artek replied smartly.

She shot him an annoyed look but otherwise ignored the offending comment. "Anyway, I couldn't figure out how to change Vermik back. Personally, I think it simply brought his physical appearance in accord with the nature of his soul. Needless to say, his henchmen didn't appreciate the finer points of irony. In revenge, they came after my head. Because I'm rather partial to it myself, I decided it would be a good idea to look for a hiding place. I planned to lurk for a while in the sewers beneath Waterdeep. Then I stumbled on a way into Undermountain, and I figured there couldn't be a better hiding place." She held her arms out in a final gesture. "And here I am. I can't say that I like living in this pit. But at least I *am* living."

"A year is a long time," Artek noted. "I imagine Vermik has given up the chase by now. You could probably return to the surface."

"I would if I could," the wizard replied mournfully. "What I wouldn't give to breathe real air again—not this wet, moldy stuff that passes for air down here. I've heard there's a well a few levels up that leads to a tavern, but I've never been able to find the way there. Of course, the nobles have their own entrances into this hole, but they're well hidden. Besides, they only open if your blood is bluer than sapphires. Then there are the sewers. According to the rumors, the city's sewers lead all the way down here. Maybe they do, but once I spent five days slogging through sludge, only to end up right back where I started."

She let out a forlorn sigh. "But that's the problem with Undermountain. It's a whole lot easier to get in than it is to get out, as you're bound to discover yourself."

Artek reached into his pocket, fidgeting with the small gold box Melthis had given him.

"I suppose now it's my turn to tell you what I'm doing here," he said jovially.

Dimly, he noticed that his words were rather slurred.

His tongue seemed oddly thick. He took a deep swig of his firebrandy, hoping that would improve things, then began his story. By the time he finished, Beckla gripped her cup, staring at him in astonishment.

"You were locked in the Pit?" she said incredulously. After a second she burst into a fit of wild laughter. "That must have been terrible!"

"It was absolutely awful," Artek agreed, snorting with mirth. He tried to bring his cup to his lips, but his hand wouldn't seem to behave properly. "They served us gruel with live maggots. And that was on good days!"

Beckla let out a howl of glee. She tried to refill Artek's cup from the purple bottle but missed altogether, spilling dwarven firebrandy on the floor. The volatile liquid quickly evaporated.

"So how are you supposed to find this missing nobleman anyway?" Beckla managed to gasp.

"With this." Artek pulled out the heart jewel and tossed it to the wizard. She fumbled with the glowing stone and finally managed to clutch it. "But he could be almost anywhere in this labyrinth. Even with the jewel, it could take weeks to find him." He thrust out his arm, pointing to the magical tattoo, grinning broadly. "And if I don't get back out in two days, this thing will kill me!"

This statement sent them both into breathless paroxysms of laughter.

"At least I have this," Artek choked through his mirth. He showed her the golden box. "When I find the nobleman, all I have to do is open this and a magical gate will appear, leading back to the surface."

Beckla gazed at the box with wide eyes. "Oooh.

That's very nice!" She looked from side to side, then giggled mischievously. "Listen, I have a secret to tell you."

Artek leaned dizzily closer. "What is it?"

She bit her lip, then smiled crookedly, speaking in an exaggerated whisper. "I know where he is. Your lost lord. He's not far. I could take you right to him."

Artek sat up straight. Instantly the giddiness drained from him. That was the advantage of dwarven firebrandy, and the reason it was such a rare and expensive commodity. Its highly intoxicating effects ceased the moment one wished them to. He stared at her, his black eyes deadly serious.

"You know where Lord Corin Silvertor is?"

The wizard's face quickly grew solemn as she too willed away the effects of the firebrandy.

"I do."

Artek bore into her with his black eyes. He could see her pulse fluttering in the hollow of her throat, but she did not look away. Thief's instinct warned him that she was not telling him everything. But she was not lying. Of that he was certain. She did indeed know where to find the lost lord.

"Take me to him," he said intently.

"Take me with you," she replied in an even voice.

For a silent moment the two gazed at each other. Then a reluctant smile spread across Artek's face; this time, it was not from the firebrandy.

"It looks like we have a deal, wizard."

Beckla beamed brightly in reply. She stood, gripping her wizard's staff. "All right, thief," she said crisply. "Let's go rescue us a nobleman."

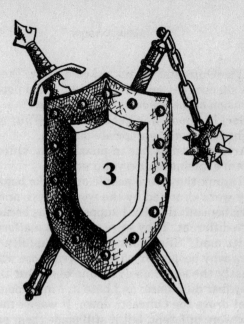

3

Outcasts

Artek and Beckla came to a halt before a high basalt archway shaped like a gaping mouth. Whether the maw was open in laughter or a scream was impossible to tell. Green mold clung to the stony lips, and black water dripped from jagged teeth. Distant sounds drifted through the archway: grunts, snarls, and high-pitched howls. They were almost like the noises of animals. Almost, but not quite. Beyond the mouth lay darkness.

"This archway marks the border of the territory of the Outcasts," Beckla whispered. A faint blue radiance bathed her face, emanating from the wisp of magelight hovering on the end of her staff.

"The Outcasts?" Artek asked quietly. The oppressive silence seemed a living thing. It did not like the intrusion of their words. "Who are they?"

Beckla shook her head grimly. "*What* are they might be a more appropriate question."

Artek gazed at her in puzzlement. Quietly, the wizard explained her cryptic words.

"I think they were people once," she began. "But they were shunned by the world above and driven down beneath the city. I suppose it was because they were different. They were the city's malformed, its ill, its mad." She shook her head ruefully. "I don't know why people are so terrified of those who aren't exactly the same as everyone else. But they are. They fear difference, and hate it. I imagine that was what drove the Outcasts down. It wasn't their fault they were different, but it still made them pariahs. I think that over the years, one by one, the unwanted of Waterdeep retreated down into the sewers beneath the city, and many eventually found their way into the halls of Undermountain."

Beckla gazed thoughtfully into the darkness with her deep brown eyes. "There's a whole world down here beneath the city," she murmured. "One that those who walk the daylit streets above have no idea even exists."

Artek let out a grunt. He knew well what it was like to be despised simply because he was not like others. Would the Magisters have been so deaf to his claims of innocence had orcish blood not run in his veins? He could feel sympathy for the Outcasts, for those who had chosen to live in the dark below rather than be feared in the light above.

"So it's these Outcasts who have Lord Corin Silvertor?" he asked finally.

Beckla nodded, confirming his guess. "They're holding him prisoner deep in their territory."

"Well, I don't suppose a ragtag band of misfits will give us much trouble," Artek said gruffly.

At this, Beckla shook her head fiercely. "You don't understand, Artek. The Outcasts are not what they used to be. Anyone scorned by the world above is welcomed among them. But they hate those who are whole—those like us. And over the years that hatred has . . . *changed* them."

A chill snaked down Artek's back. "Changed them?" he asked slowly. "How?"

She gripped her staff with white-knuckled hands. "I think their hatred melded with some dark magic that lingers in these corridors even now, so long after Halaster created them. The very stones exude an evil enchantment like a foul odor. The Outcasts fled the world above because they were perceived as monsters. And over time, down here in the darkness, they have become just that. The atmosphere of Undermountain has twisted them. I've never laid eyes on any of the Outcasts myself—few who do so survive. But according to the stories, they're not *human* anymore." Beckla could not suppress a shiver.

Artek stared at her in grisly astonishment. "So why wouldn't they just kill Lord Silvertor?" he asked. "From the description I got, Silvertor is young and handsome. If what you've said about the Outcasts is true, they would loathe him."

"Yes, they would," the wizard agreed solemnly. "But you don't know the whole story. The Outcasts don't kill those who intrude upon their territory." Revulsion choked her voice. "Instead they twist their bodies and minds, turning the intruders into Outcasts like themselves."

This time it was Artek who shivered. It was a horrible image. "How do you know all this, Beckla?"

The wizard flashed a wan smile in his direction. "I have my ways."

He frowned at this enigmatic answer, and she let out a soft laugh.

"Actually, it's no mystery," she explained. "I'm not the only one hiding out down here. And rumors tend to travel pretty swiftly through these dreary tunnels."

Artek nodded, temporarily satisfied with her answer. An uneasy feeling gathered in his stomach. He glanced down at the dark ink tattoo on his arm; the arrow was now halfway between sun and moon. Already six hours had passed. He didn't like the idea of meeting up with the Outcasts, but he had little choice. If he wanted to live, he had to venture into their territory.

He shot the wizard a questioning look. "Are you certain you still want to come with me, Beckla?"

"That little golden box of yours might be the only way I'm ever going to get out of here." She crossed her arms, fixing him with an even gaze.

"You could just kill me and take it, you know."

Her lips parted in a crooked grin. "If I was going to do *that*, wouldn't I have done it by now?"

Despite his fear, he let out a laugh. "I suppose so."

Together, they stepped through the archway's gaping mouth.

While elsewhere the dank air of Undermountain had been oppressive, here it was downright menacing. As they went, the darkness parted sluggishly before Beckla's flickering ball of magelight and closed turgidly behind them, like oily water in the wake of a ship. Artek found himself taking shallow breaths; he was reluctant to draw the noxious atmosphere into his lungs, as if once inside his body it might fester, filling him with its dark disease. He knew that they were not welcome here.

The two walked down a twisting tunnel; its walls were strangely curved and ridged. A dark, glistening mucus covered them, dripping onto the floor, which was nauseatingly soft and spongy under their feet. In all, the tunnel seemed as if it had not been hewn of stone, but was alive. Artek felt as if they had been swallowed by a gigantic creature, and were now moving down its long, sinuous esophagus. Hot bile rose in his own throat. He tried to force the queasy image from his mind, but had little success.

They had gone only a short way when the moist tunnel divided. They paused, and Artek pulled the heart jewel out of his pocket. The blue light glimmering in the center was stronger now. He moved a few paces down the right-hand passageway. The gem flickered. He retraced his steps, then padded down the left-hand tunnel. The glow inside the heart jewel steadied and strengthened.

"This way," Artek whispered.

Beckla followed after him, and the two moved down the slime-covered passage. Before long the tunnel forked again, and again. Each time Artek used the glowing heart jewel to determine which

way they should take. Soon they found themselves in
a labyrinth of networking tunnels, branching and re-
joining countless times in a chaotically braided pattern. Artek began to wonder if they could ever find
their way back out if they needed to. He did not voice
his fear.

A distant thrum vibrated in the air. It was so low
that they felt it more than they heard it, reverberating beneath their feet, almost like the sound of a
beating heart. Otherwise, the winding tunnels were
utterly silent. The grunts and howls that had drifted
out of the mouth-arch had ceased. The quiet was
even more disturbing.

"Where are the Outcasts?" Artek hissed when the
silence became almost unbearable.

Beckla bit her lip nervously. "I don't know. But I
almost wish they would just show themselves. I don't
think facing them could be any more horrible than
wondering and waiting."

There was nothing to do but keep moving. The
tunnel opened up before them, and they found themselves in a smooth-walled chamber. Glossy shapes
were embedded in the wall, livid and throbbing, like
huge organs. Sickened, they hurried across the
squelching floor and moved through a circular opening in the far wall.

Artek glanced at the heart jewel in his hand. The
light in the center was so bright they hardly needed
Beckla's magelight. The glow pulsed steadily, echoing the lost lord's heart. Silvertor was still alive. And
by the rapid rate of his pulse, Artek guessed he was
terribly afraid—as well he should be in this place.
But the nobleman was close now, Artek was sure.

They rounded a sharp bend, then skidded to an abrupt halt. Something was embedded in the tunnel wall, something alive. It writhed beneath a translucent sheath of tough mucus, like an insect inside a chrysalis. In dread fascination, Artek and Beckla approached.

It was a person. For a moment, Artek thought it might be Lord Silvertor, but as they drew near, he saw that this was not so. It was a woman, some other prisoner of the Outcasts. She struggled vainly against the viscous bonds that held her within the wall. Her eyes bulged when she saw them, and she pressed her face against the clear sheath that covered her, stretching it. She opened her mouth, screaming. No sound came out, but Artek could understand her words by the movements of her lips. *Help me*, she was screaming. *Please, by all the gods, help me.*

"We've got to cut her free!" Beckla cried.

Artek reached for the saber at his hip. In horror, he froze. It was too late.

Slick tendrils snaked out of the wall and plunged into the woman's body. They pulsed like veins, pumping her full of dark fluids. She screamed, convulsing violently. All at once she fell still. As Artek and Beckla watched in revulsion, her body began to change. Her skin dissolved, revealing glistening muscles and organs beneath. As if of their own volition, her body parts began to undulate, rearranging themselves into hideous and alien new shapes. The woman twitched and shuddered. She was still alive, but she was transforming into something else.

"There's nothing we can do," Artek gasped, feeling

sick. He grabbed Beckla's arm. "We have to go!"

The wizard nodded jerkily and stumbled after him. They careened down the tunnel, passing more prisoners embedded in the moist, fleshy walls. All were in the process of being transformed; all were beyond hope.

The tunnel opened into another chamber, one with pink walls and a ribbed ceiling. Thick green liquid bubbled in a pool in the center of the room. A caustic stench hung in the air, burning their eyes and noses. The jewel in Artek's hand flared brilliantly.

"He's got to be here!" he gasped, gagging on the stinging air. He spun around, searching the slime-covered walls.

"There!" Beckla choked, pointing.

They rushed to the far side of the chamber. A body was embedded in the wall, struggling beneath a taut, fibrous sheath. Artek peered through the covering, dreading what he would see. He glimpsed a young man with a pale face, golden hair, and terrified blue eyes. It was the lost lord—Corin Silvertor.

"I think he's all right," Artek uttered in relief. "It looks like the transformation hasn't begun."

"Then we've got to get him out," Beckla replied urgently. "And fast!"

Artek drew his saber and slashed at the glistening sheath. It was tougher than he would have guessed. He pushed harder, until at last the tip of the blade penetrated the membrane. Clear yellow fluid oozed out. Clenching his jaw to keep from gagging, Artek slid the saber down, cutting open a large slit, and more ichor spilled out.

"Give me a hand!" he cried.

Together, he and the wizard reached into the slit, grabbing hold of Silvertor. They strained backward. At first there was resistance, but then, with a sucking sound, the young man slid through the opening in a gush of thick fluid. At the same moment, livid tendrils sprang out of the wall, searching blindly for living flesh into which they could pump their vile secretions. Clutching the lord, Artek and Beckla fell to the floor, hastily rolling out of reach of the waving tentacles.

Breathing hard, they climbed to their feet, pulling Silvertor up with them. The young man wobbled precariously, then managed to stand with their assistance. Foul-smelling ichor dripped from his once-fine clothes of blue velvet and ruffled white silk. With trembling hands, he wiped the slime from his face. Even as Artek's swarthy looks denoted his orcish blood, so too the young man's fine, elegant features indicated his noble heritage.

Lord Corin Silvertor smiled weakly as he gazed at Artek and Beckla. "I must say, your timing is impeccable," he said in a haggard but cultured voice. "I know not who you may be, but I must thank you for rescuing me. I am forever in your debt. Know that I and my family will lavish great rewards upon you for this deed. Anything you wish of me, you have only to ask it."

"Anything?" Artek growled.

"Anything!" Corin agreed enthusiastically.

"Then shut up," Artek snapped. "We're not out of here yet."

"What's wrong?" the lord gasped, his blue eyes going wide.

Artek did not answer the question, but gazed around the chamber. "Can you hear them, Beckla?" he whispered.

She nodded slowly. "They're coming."

The word escaped Artek's mouth like a hiss. "Outcasts."

All around the room, large bubbles appeared in the soft floor and walls. They swelled rapidly like blisters, their outer skins shining glossily.

"I don't like the looks of this," the wizard said in a low voice. Artek only nodded.

"What's happening?" Corin cried anxiously, wringing his hands.

The other two ignored him. Reaching into a pocket, Artek pulled out the small golden box that Melthis had given him. He fumbled with the tiny latch, then swore as the box slipped from his sweaty hands. It fell to the slimy floor, slid, then came to a halt on the very edge of the pit of roiling green liquid.

Beckla shot him a scathing look. "And here I thought thieves were supposed to be dexterous and graceful."

"Everyone has their off days," Artek snapped.

With a wet, sickening sound, a blister in the opposite wall burst open. A twisted form climbed out, trailing sticky strings of ichor—an Outcast. It was a thing of grotesque distortion, all bubbling flesh, rubbery limbs, and glistening organs fused together in the vaguest mockery of a human form. Bulging eyes sprouting from a half-exposed brain focused malevolently on the three humans. The misshapen creature began dragging itself toward them.

Another straining blister exploded, then another, and another. All around the chamber, Outcasts pulled their slimy bodies out of the walls and floor. Each lurched, jumped, or slithered forward as best suited its own contorted shape. A score of lopsided mouths grinned evilly, revealing countless teeth as sharp as glass shards.

The Outcasts advanced, and Artek and Beckla retreated toward the boiling pit. Corin cringed behind them, whimpering softly. At least the twit was no longer blathering, Artek thought darkly. It was small consolation.

Artek came to a halt, his boot heel on the very edge of the pit. He bent down cautiously and snatched up the golden box before it could topple over the rim. Eyeing the bubbling vat warily, Beckla lowered the end of her staff into the green liquid. There was a hiss and a puff of acrid smoke. Hastily she pulled out the staff, and her eyes went wide. The end had completely dissolved away.

"I think we're in trouble, Artek," she gulped.

"You don't say?" he said caustically.

The Outcasts closed in.

"Quick, Artek!" Beckla shouted. "You've got to open the gate!" She thrust her staff forward. A bolt of blue energy shot out, striking an Outcast only a few paces away. The thing let out an inhuman shriek, its flesh smoking, but it continued to lurch toward them.

"I hope I don't have to know any magic words to use this thing," Artek muttered. This time he wrenched the lid open by force, breaking the finely wrought gold latch.

Instantly a small silvery disk rose out of the box. The disk grew swiftly, floating in midair, until it was as wide as Artek's arms. Through its shimmering surface he could just make out an image: the stone walls of the alley where he had parted ways with Melthis and Darien Thal.

There was no time for hesitation.

"Jump!" Artek shouted.

He grabbed Beckla's and Corin's hands and threw himself toward the disk. At the same moment the Outcasts lunged for them, and a rubbery hand brushed Artek's arm. Then he broke the surface of the shimmering disk and fell through the gate, dragging the others with him. It felt exactly as if they had plunged into icy water. The dim scene of the alley wavered before them, drawing nearer, as if they were slowly surfacing from the bottom of a cold, deep pool.

Then, with a terrible wrenching sensation, the vision of the alley was torn away. The three spun wildly, as if caught in a fierce riptide. Artek cried out, feeling Corin's hand separate from his own, but his voice made no sound in the frigid void. The cold sliced his flesh and splintered his bones. Then all sensation vanished as the three plunged downward into endless darkness.

* * * * *

For countless centuries, the subterranean chamber had dwelled in dark and perfect silence. In all that time, no living thing had ever breathed the room's dank air, or disturbed the silken carpet of dust that covered the stone floor. Few creatures dared to live this far below the surface of the world. Here, within this forgotten chamber, shadows had always reigned.

Until now.

A throbbing hum resonated in the air, shattering the ancient silence. A brilliant silver line appeared in the dusky air, causing shadows to flee to the corners of the room and cower. Crackling, the silver line widened into a jagged rift. Three large shapes tumbled out of the gap. Then, as suddenly as it had appeared, the blazing gate folded inward upon itself and vanished. The sharp smell of lightning lingered in the stale air.

With a groan, Artek pulled himself to his feet and shook his head dizzily. Only once before had he ever felt this groggy, and that had involved a jug of blood-wine, a half-orc barmaid, and a dance called The Dead Goblin. After a moment, his darkvision adjusted, and he saw Beckla sprawled on the stones some distance away. Hastily he moved to the wizard, fearing that the fall had injured her, but his sharp ears caught a muttered string of strikingly graphic curses and oaths. He grinned, his slightly pointed teeth glowing in the darkness. Beckla was just fine.

Gripping the wizard's hand, he hauled her to her feet. Wavering blue light flared to life on the end of her staff, illuminating the chamber. Nightmarish friezes covered the walls, and grotesque statues lurked in the corners. Artek shuddered. Whatever this place was, it had been created by a mad and evil genius.

Beckla spoke with a frown. "Granted, it's been a

while since I've been to the surface, but this doesn't exactly look like the streets of Waterdeep to me."

"I don't understand," Artek replied in confusion. "When I opened the gate, I saw the alley where I left Darien Thal. We were heading right toward it. And then . . ." He shook his head, trying to remember the disorienting seconds after they had jumped through the gate.

Beckla gazed at one of the friezes. The stone relief depicted a tangled mass of writhing bodies tumbling into a jagged pit. Nervously, she looked away. "I have a very bad feeling about this," she said grimly.

"You're not the only one," Artek gulped.

Beckla looked around in the dim light. "So what happened to the lump? I mean, the *lord*?"

Artek glanced about. "Silvertor let go of my hand as we passed through the gate," he said. "The fool could have landed anywhere nearby."

Suddenly, a cry of fear emanated from one of the shadowed corners of the chamber.

"Help! Help!" a voice wailed piteously. "I've been caught by a terrible monster! It's going to eat me! Please, somebody—help!"

Artek and Beckla exchanged looks of alarm, then dashed toward the corner. Artek's hand dropped to the hilt of his saber, while Beckla gripped her staff tightly. Artek swore inwardly. That foppish young lord was his one ticket to freedom—and to continued life. If the fool had managed to get into trouble already, Artek was going to . . . well, he wasn't going to *kill* Silvertor—he needed the lord alive—but he would come up with something *extremely* unpleasant.

Artek and Beckla reached the opposite corner of

the chamber. The wizard's magelight pierced the gloom to reveal Lord Corin Silvertor, flailing wildly in midair, hanging by his coat from the jaws of a huge beast. His pale face was agape with terror. In the shadows behind him loomed a terrifying, evil shape that looked like a cross between a lizard and a wolf. For a frozen second, Artek stared in horror. Then laughter rumbled in his chest. Next to him, Beckla burst into peals of mirth.

"What's wrong with you two?" Corin cried fearfully. "Can't you see that the dastardly monster has got me! So far I've been able to hold the foul beast at bay with my bare hands, but I don't think that I can stave it off much longer! You've got to help me. Please!"

This was too much for Artek and Beckla. They leaned against each other, shoulders shaking, howling with laughter. Corin gaped at them in terror and confusion. Then, aided by Beckla's glowing blue magelight, realization gradually dawned on him.

The monster was made of stone. In the soft light emanating from Beckla's staff, the thing was clearly revealed to be a statue. Cracks covered its dusty shape, and one of its gnarled legs had been snapped off and lay nearby. The collar of Corin's velvet coat had snagged on a sharp tooth in the statue's gaping lower jaw, suspending the nobleman in midair. Apparently it had caught him when he tumbled out of the gate.

"Well, isn't this awkward," Corin said sheepishly.

"For you, at least," Beckla snorted.

The nobleman gave her a wounded look but said nothing.

Artek scrambled up the basalt statue and perched on its flat skull. He drew a dagger from his boot and cut the fold of blue velvet that had snagged the stone tooth. With a yelp, Corin fell to the floor, and Beckla helped the stunned lord to his feet. The nobleman did his best to arrange his expensive clothes, but they were torn and smeared with dark slime. He brushed his long, pale hair away from his high forehead.

"You could have warned me before you cut my coat, you know," he said indignantly as Artek lightly hopped down from the statue.

"I know," Artek said amiably, slipping the dagger back into his boot.

Corin's blue eyes grew large at this impertinence. He stared at Artek and Beckla, then swallowed hard. "You two aren't dangerous, are you?"

Beckla smiled nastily. "As a matter of fact, we are."

Fear blanched Corin's boyishly handsome face.

Artek shot Beckla an annoyed look, then turned back toward the nobleman. "Don't worry, Silvertor. We may be dangerous, but we came here to rescue you. This is Beckla Shadesar. You can tell she's a wizard by her peculiar notion of humor. She's on the run from her old master, who she turned into a green slime. And I'm—" He licked his lips nervously. Why didn't this ever get any easier? "I'm Artek Ar'talen."

A strangled sound of fear and surprise escaped Corin's throat, and he hastily backed away. "You're Artek the Knife?"

"Oh, get over it," Artek growled.

Apparently this was easier said than done. Corin shrank against a wall, hand to his mouth, staring at his rescuers in turn, as if trying to decide of which he should be the more afraid. Artek turned his back on the nobleman; they had other matters to worry about.

"So where do you think we are?" he asked Beckla. "The gate could have transported us anywhere on the continent of Faerûn."

She shook her head. "I'm not certain. But I have an idea. And I don't much care for it."

"What is it?"

"I'll show you."

The wizard bent down and picked up a loose pebble from the crumbling floor. Laying it on her outstretched palm, she murmured an incantation. A pale white aura flickered around the pebble. Beckla drew in a deep breath, then blew on the stone. The aura vanished. The pebble was dark and ordinary once again.

"I was afraid of that," Beckla sighed.

"Am I supposed to be impressed?" Artek asked dubiously.

She scowled at him. "As a matter of fact, you are. I just cast a spell of teleportation on the pebble."

"But it's still here."

"Exactly. That's because the walls of this place are imbued with an enchantment to prevent anything from magically transporting in or out."

"Wait a minute," Artek protested in confusion. "The walls of *what* place?"

Beckla spoke a single grim word.

"Undermountain."

Artek swore an oath. Instinctively, he knew the wizard was right. This place had the same oppressive feel as the rest of Undermountain. No, it was even stronger.

"The enchantment is Halaster's doing," Beckla went on. "The mad wizard wanted to make certain no one found an easy way out of his maze."

"So how deep are we?" Artek asked hoarsely.

"Let's find out," Beckla replied without relish.

She whispered another incantation over the pebble, and it began to glow again. With a final word of magic, she cast the pebble into the air. It did not fall, but floated high above them.

"The ceiling represents the surface world, and the floor the very bottom of Undermountain," Beckla explained. "The pebble will tell us where we are now."

The wizard made an intricate gesture with her hand. The pebble began to descend. It continued to sink slowly as they watched in growing alarm. At last it came to a halt halfway between floor and ceiling.

"Is that very deep?" Artek asked nervously.

Beckla nodded. "If we were still in the halls where we met, the pebble would be no more than a foot below the ceiling." A haunted look crept into her brown eyes. "I don't think anyone has ever been this deep in Undermountain before. At least, not any who lived to tell about it."

Cold dread filled Artek's stomach. "But that's impossible," he said emphatically. "You said that we couldn't teleport out of the maze. You didn't say that a gate would fail as well!"

"A gate is different from a teleport spell, Artek." Beckla fixed him with a piercing look. "It should have worked. What did you do?"

"It wasn't me!" he said defensively.

"Well, *somebody* did something."

At this Artek nodded, scratching his chin. "You're right. And there's only one person who might be able to help us understand exactly what happened."

As one, Artek and Beckla turned to glare at Corin.

"What?" the lord gasped in shock, clutching a hand to his chest. "You can't possibly believe that I had anything to do with this."

"No, I don't," Artek replied gruffly. "But I think it's time we heard your story all the same."

Corin mopped his face with the ruffled cuff of his coat. The effort did little besides smear around the grime, but the nobleman was oblivious to this fact.

"Let's see," Corin began. "It all started when Lord Darien Thal invited me on a hunt into Undermountain. I had never ventured into Halaster's halls before, and I was thrilled at the prospect. It's all the rage these days, you know."

Artek and Beckla rolled their eyes but kept listening.

"The hunting party set out from Lord Thal's private entrance into Undermountain," Corin went on, his enthusiasm growing. "We were a grand sight. A dozen strong, and all bearing bright swords. Of course, I had my trusty rapier here." He patted the slender blade at his hip.

Artek barely managed to stifle a snort. A real monster wouldn't even feel the bite of that rat-sticker. Nobles, he thought derisively—they were all fools of fashion, and nothing more.

"I was having an absolutely marvelous time." Corin's bright expression darkened. "That is, until I got lost. It was my own fault. I lingered behind to examine a fascinating stone vase—I think it was Third Dynasty Calishite—while the others continued on ahead. When I tried to catch up, the rest of the party was nowhere to be seen. We had been making for a place called the Emerald Fountain. I tried to find the fountain, hoping to meet the others there, but it was no use. And then," said Corin, shuddering, "the Outcasts captured me."

"Wait a minute," Beckla interrupted. "Why were you going to the Emerald Fountain?"

"It was Darien's idea," Corin answered. "He said it was a magical font, and that if I drank from its waters, I would gain wisdom beyond my years. I could do with a little extra wisdom, as I am to take the seventh seat on the Circle of Nobles in two days' time."

"It's not wisdom you would have gained from drinking from the Emerald Fountain," Beckla said darkly. "Death is all you would have found in its green waters."

"But Darien's my dearest friend!" Corin protested. "Why would he tell me to drink from the fountain if it wasn't safe?"

Artek bit his lower lip. That was a good question. "Tell me something, Silvertor," he said. "If you were not present when the vote was held, who would ascend to the Circle of Nobles in your stead?"

Corin shrugged. "Why, I imagine Lord Thal is the next in line. But what does that—oh!" The young lord's eyes went wide with sudden realization.

Artek nodded. This was all starting to make sense. He plied Corin with more questions about Darien Thal and the hunting trip and soon pieced together a story. While he wasn't certain if it was exactly right, he knew it couldn't be far from the truth.

Without doubt, Lord Darien Thal wanted the vacant seat on the Circle of Nobles for himself. He had invited Corin on a hunt into Undermountain, secretly planning for the young lord to meet with an unfortunate "accident," after which nothing would stand between Darien and the seat on the Circle. Yet Darien had not counted on Corin getting lost before the foolish young lord could be disposed of.

That's where I came in, Artek thought angrily. Darien did not want to take the chance that Corin would somehow manage to stumble on a way out of Undermountain in time for the vote. He needed someone to go below and finish the job. All along it had been Artek's task not to rescue Corin, but to make certain that he never returned from Undermountain. The golden box from Melthis had not malfunctioned at all. The gate had taken them exactly where Darien had intended—deeper into Undermountain.

"*Guhr og noth!*" Artek swore. It was an orcish oath, learned from his father. Rage boiled in his blood at the one possible conclusion.

Lord Darien Thal had betrayed him.

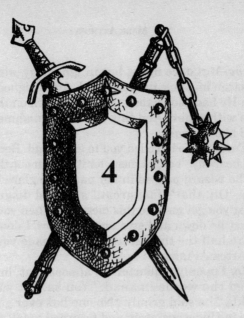

4

Webs of Deceit

Arms crossed over her chest, Beckla paced in agitation before a leering statue of some nameless beast. Corin watched, apprehension written plainly across his boyish face.

"This is just wonderful," the wizard said acidly. "I thought you were going to get me out of this dump, Ar'talen, and now I'm deeper than ever." She let out a sharp sigh of exasperation. "I suppose that will teach me to trust a thief."

Artek slumped against a wall. He stared blankly at the bas-relief carving of lost souls falling into the dark void of the Abyss. So this is how the line of Arthaug ends, he thought bitterly. Not in glory, ruling over the

Garug-Mal once more, but in ignominy, alone and forgotten in a hole in the ground. Artek sighed dejectedly. He had been wrong to turn his back on the darkness within him. And this was the punishment that deed had wrought.

"I'm sorry to have led you to a bad end, Beckla," he said hoarsely. "I didn't mean for it to turn out this way."

The wizard paused in her pacing to glare hotly at him. "Oh, that's just great," she said disgustedly. "First you get me into this mess, and then you decide to just lie down and give up. You know, I don't think you're half the thief all the stories made you out to be, Artek Ar'talen."

No, I'm only a quarter, he almost spat, but swallowed the words instead. "You said it yourself, Beckla," he said grimly. "No one has ever gone this deep in Undermountain and returned to tell about it. In an entire year, you couldn't find a way out of this maze's uppermost halls. So what chance do we have this deep down?"

Beckla clenched her too-square jaw angrily but said nothing.

After an uncomfortable silence, Corin cleared his throat. "Excuse me," he said in a meek voice. "I know I'm hardly the most qualified person to offer an opinion on this matter, seeing as I'm the one who's theoretically being rescued here." He made a vaguely hopeful gesture with his hands. "But couldn't we at least *try* to find a way out of this dreadful place? It certainly seems like the reasonable thing to do."

Artek let out a derisive snort. "You see this?" He thrust out his arm, pulling up the sleeve of his jerkin to reveal the magical tattoo. "In less than two days, this thing is going to kill me. And in less than two days, the nobility of Waterdeep is going to hold its vote, and Lord Darien Thal will ascend to the seventh seat on the Circle of Nobles."

He jerked the sleeve back down, covering the tattoo. "Don't you understand? There's no point in trying to escape. Even if we *could* find a way out of this hole, it would certainly take us more than two days, and by that time I'd be dead. And if you managed to get out, Corin, I'm sure the first thing Darien would do in his new position of power would be to find a way to dispose of you."

Chagrined, Corin fell silent and hung his head.

"Well, that still leaves *me*," Beckla snapped. "Or had you forgotten? I certainly still want to try to find a way out of this pit."

"Then be my guest," Artek grumbled. He turned his back on the wizard.

Anger burned in her brown eyes. She ran a frustrated hand through her close-cropped brown hair. For a moment she bit her lip, considering something. Then, abruptly, she spoke several harsh, guttural words.

"Morth al haugh nothok, Artek Ar'talen! Bettah al nothokari!"

The words sliced at Artek like knives. It had been years since he last heard them. Drawing in a hissing breath, he spun around, advancing on the wizard. "Where did you learn to speak that?" he demanded fiercely.

Beckla stepped backward, momentarily startled by the fury blazing in his black eyes. Corin stared at the two in open alarm. Then, visibly, the wizard steeled herself. "I once traded spells with an orcish sorcerer," she said evenly, a sly smile on her lips. "Of course, I learned a few things other than spells from him. And I heard him use that oath once or twice."

Artek shook with rage. Old memories surfaced in his mind, of a father berating his child for being too afraid to pick a rich merchant's purse. "Do you know what those words mean?" he choked.

Beckla nodded solemnly. " 'Your heart is not that of an orc. It is that of a goblin.' I think that's an accurate translation, don't you?" She clucked her tongue at his shocked expression. "Come now, Ar'talen. Don't be so surprised. All the stories say that orcish blood runs in your veins."

Artek opened his mouth, but he could find no reply. Only once had Arturg used those words with him, but once had been enough. There was no greater insult among orc kindred than to have one's heart compared to a goblin's. It was an accusation of cowardice, a brand of worthlessness. As a child, Artek had done everything he could to please his father in order to make certain that he never heard those hateful words again. Now this arrogant wizard had dared to speak them herself.

"You have no *right*," he began, clenching his hands into fists.

"And why not?" she snapped harshly. "It's all true, isn't it? You're the one who's giving up." She shook her head. "Maybe the stories are wrong. Maybe it isn't fell orcish blood that runs in your veins, Ar'talen. Maybe it's the blood of lowly goblin worms after all."

The wizard had gone too far. Artek felt a fierce, primal fury stirring deep inside. As always, he fought to contain it, but this time it was no use. The rage welled up hotly in his stomach, burning as it coursed through his veins. A red veil descended over his eyes, and a rushing sound filled his ears. The dark, animal part of himself that he always kept carefully locked away now rose to the fore. It terrified him, but it was intoxicating as well. Raw power trembled in his limbs. His orcish side was free.

Artek snarled, baring his pointed teeth, his handsome face twisted into a sinister mask. Corin let out a cry of fear, leaping backward. Beckla paled, shocked by the fury her words had unleashed.

"Damn you!" Artek hissed, advancing on the startled wizard. Words sprang from his mouth as if someone else spoke through him. "You have no right. I am *Garug-Mal!* I will rend your flesh for this insult. I will splinter your bones!"

Artek grabbed Beckla and shoved her roughly against a stone wall. His hands encircled her throat. The desire to kill seared his mind. The wizard's body shook, but she clenched her jaw and gazed unflinchingly into his eyes, refusing to show fear. This only enraged his orcish side further; his fingers contracted tightly. Beckla gasped for breath as her airway inexorably closed.

No, Artek! Don't do it!

The voice was faint and distant, barely piercing the roaring in his brain. He ignored it, gritting his teeth as he tightened his grip.

Don't kill her!

This time the voice was stronger. Uncertainty tinged his rage. He hesitated.

This doesn't have to be you!

At last he recognized the voice. It was his own—at

least, that of his human side. For a second, dark and
light halves warred within. Then, with a strangled cry,
he tore his hands away from the wizard's throat and
lurched back. Beckla stumbled forward, clutching her
throat, gulping in ragged breaths. Artek shuddered,
staring at his clenched hands, sickened at how close to
killing they had come. He looked up. Though her lips
were tinged with blue, the wizard was grinning.

"That was dangerous, Beckla," he said, his voice
low and grim. "I could have killed you. I almost did.
You took a foolish gamble."

"But it worked, didn't it?" she rasped smugly.
"Corin and I need you, Ar'talen. We have to stick together if we're to have any hope of getting out of
here. I guessed that only a little orcish anger would
burn through your stupid self-pity, and I was right."

Artek scowled at her. "Well, you don't have to act
so pleased about it."

"Oh? And why not?"

He had no answer to that, and settled for a sullen
grunt instead. Risky as it had been, the wizard's
plan had worked as intended. Despair and hopelessness had been burned away by his rage. Artek
wanted nothing more now than to have his revenge
on Lord Darien Thal, and the only way he could
achieve that was to escape from Undermountain. He
found himself returning Beckla's grin. As violent as
his orcish side was, it had its uses.

Corin gasped as he realized what the wizard had
done. "Oh, bravo, Beckla!" he exclaimed, clapping his
hands together, tattered lace cuffs fluttering. "That
was simply brilliant. A virtuoso performance." He
snapped his fingers as an idea occurred to him.

"Why, perhaps it would hearten Artek further if I uttered the same epitaph. Now, what were the words?" He braced his shoulders and lowered his voice, speaking the words with exaggerated bravado. *"Malth al nothilk, Artek Ar'talen!"*

For a moment Artek and Beckla stared at the puffed-up lord. Then both burst into laughter. Corin frowned in confusion.

"I don't understand," he sputtered. "Why are you laughing? Aren't you supposed to be absolutely furious with me? I just said your heart was a goblin's!"

"No, you didn't," Artek replied.

"Well, what did I say?" the nobleman asked indignantly.

Beckla let out a snort. "You said, 'Your ears are made of cheese, Artek Ar'talen.' "

The two broke into renewed peals of mirth. Corin stared at them with a hurt expression until Artek took pity on the lord.

"Don't worry, Corin," he said. "We'll make an orc of you yet." He gave the young man a friendly slap on the back, and Corin stumbled forward, eyes bulging at the force of the blow.

"Er, thank you," he murmured. "I think."

His black leather creaking, Artek prowled back and forth. He knew what they needed to do—get out of Undermountain. Now, how by the Shadows of Shar were they going to do it? The obvious thing was to attempt to work their way upward through Halaster's mad labyrinth. However, according to Beckla's spell, they were terribly deep—deeper than anyone had gone and managed to return in nearly a thousand years. Artek didn't like those odds, and instinct told him that there was little hope in heading upward. But what other alternative was there?

His black eyes glittered sharply. The inkling of an idea crept into his cunning mind. He turned toward the wizard. "Beckla, you said that Halaster enchanted the walls of Undermountain so that no one could magically teleport in or out."

"That's right."

"So how was it that the gate Melthis gave me was able to transport us so much deeper? Doesn't that mean that it *is* possible to teleport here?"

The wizard shook her head. "No, it doesn't. Like I said earlier, gates are different. A spell of teleportation instantly moves a person or object from one place to another. And Halaster's magic blocks such spells. But when you pass through a gate, you don't really move at all. Instead, the gate magically brings two different places close together. It's space that moves, not you."

Artek frowned at this explanation. "I don't exactly follow you."

"I suppose that's why I'm the wizard," she replied dryly. "Here, I'll show you." She reached out and grabbed the pebble that still hovered in midair from her earlier spell. She held her hands flat and apart, the pebble resting on her left palm. "Say I'm the pebble, and I want to get from my left hand to my right. If I cast a teleport spell, it's like jumping from hand to hand instantly." With a deft flick of her wrist, she tossed the pebble and caught it in her right hand. "But a gate works more like a window opening between two places. Effectively, it brings the two locations next to each other." She moved her hands until they were touching. "Then it's only a short step sideways from one place to the next." She tilted her right hand, and the pebble rolled onto the left. She tossed the pebble toward Artek. "Got it?"

He snatched the pebble out of the air, then held it between his fingers, studying it thoughtfully. "Got it." He digested this new information, and gradually his plan grew clearer. "So instead of trying to find our way up through an endless maze, all we need to do is find another one of these gates."

"If there *are* any others," Beckla amended cautiously.

"There have to be others," Artek replied. "All the stories tell how Halaster abducted living things—people and monsters alike—for use in his magical experiments. He had to have some way to bring them down here. And from what you've said, a gate is the only way."

Beckla crossed her arms over her white shirt, her expression skeptical. "I still say our surest bet is to head upward. But I suppose it wouldn't hurt to look for any gates on the way."

That was close enough for Artek. "Then it's settled," he said firmly. "Darien hasn't beaten us yet. And neither has Undermountain. One way or another, we're going to get out of here."

Corin jumped excitedly. The lord had become quite caught up in Artek's stirring speech. "Oh, this is going to be positively fun!" he exclaimed enthusiastically. "I had no idea that getting lost could lead to such a marvelous adventure."

Artek bit his tongue. Corin would find out soon enough for himself that this was going to be anything but *fun*.

Artek had noticed earlier that there were no doors

in the room—at least, none readily apparent to the casual eye. All four walls of the chamber were of solid stone, each covered with a grotesque frieze of tortured souls. But Artek was not going to believe their quest was over before it had even begun. He doubted that even a mad wizard would build a room without a door—what would be the use? Thief's instinct told him that there had to be a way out of the chamber. All they had to do was find it.

"All right, let's search the walls and floor," Artek told the others. "There has to be a hidden door in this room somewhere. Look for anything at all that stands out or seems unusual in some way."

He moved to one of the walls and began running his hand over the bas-relief carvings that covered it, searching for any seams or inconsistencies in the stone. Corin and Beckla exchanged unsure looks, then followed suit. Each pored over his or her respective wall, attempting to find any sign of a secret portal. Before long, Artek's head throbbed with concentration. The friezes made it difficult. The intricate relief carvings of writhing bodies could be obscuring something—a crack, a hole, a gap—he might otherwise see. However, there was nothing to do but keep searching.

Just when he was beginning to lose hope, Beckla let out an excited whoop. "I think I've found something, Artek! There's a thin seam around the neck of one of these carvings. I think the head is some sort of knob. It looks like it could turn."

That sounded promising. Artek hurried toward the wizard. "That's good, Beckla. But don't touch it yet. If the knob is a trigger for a secret door, it could be trapped. We need to check it out before we turn it."

"Oh," Beckla replied as she snatched her hand away from the carving. "Oops."

Artek halted in alarm. The last time Beckla had uttered that word, she had nearly set his hindquarters on fire. He shook his head slowly, staring at her. "Please tell me you didn't . . ."

Beckla grinned at him weakly. "I did."

The wizard gestured to the twisted stone figure on the wall. Its screaming head now pointed backward. Artek lunged forward, reaching out to turn the figure's head back around, but it was too late.

There was a hiss of stale air, followed by a low grating sound. The floor vibrated beneath their feet, and the three stared around the room in surprise. At first it was not apparent what was happening—until Corin voiced the truth.

"Look at the walls!" the nobleman cried. "They're closing in!"

Artek swore in alarm. The young lord was right. The chamber's two long walls were slowly but inexorably moving inward. Artek gripped the figurine, turning the head back around. It was no use. The trap had been sprung, and the walls continued to close in. Artek guessed they had no more than a few minutes before the slabs met and crushed their bodies to a pulp. The open stone mouths of the writhing damned no longer seemed to be screaming, but laughing.

"Quick!" Artek shouted over the rumbling. "There's got to be another trigger, one that will stop the trap!"

Hastily, he began searching one of the walls as it pressed forward. Needing no other inducement besides fear, Corin and Beckla leapt toward the other wall and did the same. As they searched, they were forced to keep stepping backward as the walls closed in. There were fifteen paces between them, then ten, then five. Frantically, Artek kept searching. He felt something brush his back. Glancing over his shoulder, he saw Beckla staring at him with wide eyes. The walls were no more than two arm lengths apart.

"That's odd," Corin announced. "The arm on this figurine looks almost like a lever."

"Well, then pull it!" Beckla cried urgently.

Corin put his hands behind his back. "Oh, no. Not before Artek checks it. You heard what he said before."

Artek craned his neck, gazing with wild eyes at the nobleman. "Pull it, Corin!" he shouted.

The lord shook his head. "If I pull that lever, we may find ourselves in worse trouble yet. You told Beckla not to . . ."

"Never mind!" Artek barked. His back was against one wall, the other just four feet away. Three feet. Two. "Just pull the lever!"

Corin sighed in exasperation. "Well, this is all very contradictory. But here goes . . ." He gripped the stone arm and pulled the lever. The floor dropped out from beneath their feet, and the three plunged downward, screaming. The two walls met with a clap of thunder above their heads, grinding together with bone-crushing force. For a moment more they continued to fall through darkness. Then, with three grunts, they struck a hard stone floor.

Artek groaned as he sat up. Magically restored though it was, his body still wasn't used to all this falling and landing, if it ever had been. He probed gently with his fingers, wincing as he found numerous tender spots. However, nothing seemed to be broken.

Pale blue magelight flared into being. Beckla slumped against a wall, gripping her staff, grimacing but whole. With painful effort, Artek turned around, wondering how Corin had fared. He stared in amazement as the nobleman leapt easily to his feet, briskly dusting off his tattered finery.

"That was positively thrilling," Corin said exuberantly. "The danger! The excitement! The narrow escape!" His blue eyes shone brightly. "I don't suppose we could do it again?"

"Are you sure we can't kill him, Ar'talen?" Beckla grumbled, slowly pulling herself to her feet with the help of her staff.

"Don't tempt me." Joints and muscles protesting, Artek stood.

Corin eyed the others speculatively. "You know, I'm beginning to get the distinct impression that neither of you likes me very much."

"Wherever would you get such an idea?" Artek replied facetiously.

"Oh, I don't know," Corin mused. "I suppose it's all this talk about wanting to kill me. One might construe that as an indication of dislike."

"Really? What a fascinating interpretation."

The nobleman beamed. "Why, thank you, Ar'talen!"

Artek and Beckla exchanged meaningful glances. There was no need for words.

By the glow of the magelight, the three stood at the beginning of a corridor. Smooth stone walls rose to a flat ceiling high over their heads. Artek could see the trapdoor through which they had fallen. It was now blocked by the bases of the thick stone walls that had nearly crushed them in the room above. The darkness was dense and stifling here, retreating sullenly before the magical light of Beckla's staff, and only a few paces at that. A rank odor like the putrid reek of decay hung in the air, so thick that it almost seemed to leave on oily residue on their skin and inside their lungs. It was a stench of evil.

With no other options evident, the three started down the corridor. The tunnel plunged straight through the darkness, without openings or side passages. The sickening odor grew more intense as they walked, but there was nothing to do but swallow their bile and press on. Soft, ropy strands dangled from the ceiling. Artek guessed they were moss or fungal growth, for they glowed with a faint and noxious green light. They ducked to avoid the strands and kept moving.

Though he couldn't be sure, Artek had the sense that the passageway was leading gradually downward. He swore inwardly. They needed to go up, but it seemed everything they did only took them farther down. It was as if Undermountain itself were somehow conspiring to pull them deeper.

After a time, the inky mouth of a smaller tunnel opened up to the left. The fetid stench was stronger here, pouring like black water out of the side opening. Yet it wasn't just the smell that spilled from the tunnel—there was a malice as well, distant and faint, but chilling all the same.

"There's something down there," Beckla whispered nervously.

Corin nodded, his smudged face pale. "And what-

ever it is, I don't think it's terribly friendly," he added
in a squeaky voice.

"Just keep moving," Artek countered. He felt the
malevolent presence as well. He wiped his sweaty
palms on his leather jerkin and kept his sensitive
eyes peeled.

They continued down the murky passageway. The
mouths of more tunnels opened to their left and
right. Some were blocked by fallen rubble, and
others were dry and dusty. But the same pungent
reek wafted outward from several tunnels, as did the
aura of evil. Without deciding aloud to do so, the
three picked up their pace. Then Artek detected it—
a subtle shift in the movements of the air.

"There's a space ahead," he whispered excitedly.
"And a faint breeze. I think there's a way out. Come
on, it's not far."

The others needed little urging. They started into
a jog, hurrying down the passageway. At the same
moment, the aura of malice swelled behind them.
They reeled, nearly overwhelmed by the vile emana-
tions of hatred. Something was following them, and
it was gaining.

"Run!" Artek yelled.

Gasping, they hurled themselves down the tunnel, the darkness following thickly on their heels. An
eerie whispering sound echoed all around. Lungs
burning, the three kept running. All at once the
walls of the tunnel fell away, and they found themselves dashing across a cavernous chamber. Strange
white shapes littered the floor, crunching brittlely
underfoot. Dense clumps of the same strands that
had filled the tunnel hung from the high ceiling like

a weird inverted forest, filling the room with a ghastly green glow. Artek caught another wisp of fresh air, stronger now. Then he saw it on the far side of the hall—a faint rectangle glowing amid the gloom. A doorway.

"Hurry!" he shouted, heedless of what might hear his voice.

The eerie whispering grew louder, filling the chamber. Thick blackness poured out of the opening behind them like a putrid flood. Legs pounding, Artek outpaced the others. As he neared the doorway, he saw that it was covered with more of the same green, glowing strands. With a cry, he hurled himself at the portal. Instantly his cry became one of pain as bitterly cold threads burned the skin on his hands and face. The silken material stretched under the force of his impact, then abruptly snapped back, throwing him roughly to the ground.

He stared up at the door in surprise, rubbing his throbbing hands. Then he leapt to his feet, drew a knife from his boot, and slashed at the chaotic weave that covered the door. The blade bounced back, jarring his wrist painfully. He had not so much as damaged one of the cords.

"What *is* this stuff?" he said in hoarse amazement as the others came to a halt behind him.

Beckla drew in a sharp breath, staring upward. "I think I know."

The strange whispering grew to a maddening din. The threads hanging from the ceiling stirred. Ghostly shapes scuttled down the glowing strands.

"Webs," Corin gasped. "They're spiderwebs!"

As they watched in horror, half a dozen bloated

forms dropped down from the tangle of webs above, while several more scurried from the opening through which they had entered the chamber. They were spiders, but like none Artek had ever seen. They were huge, each the size of a dog. Their bulging bodies, as pale and waxy as corpses, were eerily translucent, and their long gray legs trailed off into dim tendrils of gray mist. Dark saliva bubbled from their vague pincer mouths, and their multifaceted eyes shone malevolently, like flame reflected off black jewels. Whatever these things were, it was clear they were not truly alive, but wraiths, in hideous spider form. As they drew near, Artek realized the nature of the white shapes littering the chamber's floor. They were bones.

Together, the three backed toward the web-covered doorway.

"So, are you having fun yet, Silvertor?" Artek said darkly.

"Actually, this is a little more fun than I had anticipated," the lord answered with a gulp.

"Mystra save us," Beckla breathed.

The spiders advanced on their misty legs.

Artek drew the curved saber Melthis had given him. The hilt tingled in his hand—it was the first time he had drawn it in combat. Warm energy flowed up his arms as red fire glimmered along the edge of the blade. A wraith spider lunged forward, and Artek swung the saber. The creature let out a mind-piercing shriek as two of its legs fell to the floor. For a moment, they twitched of their own volition, then evaporated into wisps of fog. The spider lurched backward.

Beckla uttered an arcane incantation. Blue energy crackled from her fingertips. It struck two of the wraith spiders, but passed through their ghostly bodies. They continued to scurry forward.

"My magic has no effect on them!" the wizard shouted in terror.

"Nor does my rapier!" Corin cried as he thrust without result at one of the creatures. He retreated hastily.

"Then work on freeing the door!" Artek gritted through clenched teeth. "I'll try to hold the spiders back as long as I can."

He swung the saber in whistling arcs, and a dozen more many-jointed legs fell to the floor, turning to mist. The spiders advanced more slowly now, wary of Artek's crimson sword. The plan was working for the moment, but there were too many of the wraiths. It was only a matter of time until one got through.

"I don't want to tell you your job," he growled, "but you might want to hurry, Beckla."

"Quiet!" the wizard snapped. "I'm thinking." She studied the webs that crisscrossed the door. After a moment she nodded. "All right, if my magic won't work on these things, let's see what some good, old-fashioned, mundane fire will do."

Beckla uttered a command, and the end of her wooden staff burst into scarlet flame. She thrust the blazing brand at the webs. Instantly the sticky strands ignited, engulfed by brilliant fire. In seconds they were burned to fine ashes, clearing the doorway.

"It worked!" Corin cried excitedly.

"Come on, Artek!" Beckla shouted. "Let's go!"

Artek started to back away from the spiders, toward

the now-open door. Then he suddenly froze. The saber in his hands jerked violently. As if imbued with a life of its own, the blade danced forward, pulling Artek roughly with it. He tried to release the sword, but his hands were suddenly glued to the hilt. Seemingly of its own will, the saber swung at one of the wraith spiders. Artek stumbled wildly, trying to keep his balance as he was carried along by the blade.

"What are you doing, Ar'talen?" Beckla demanded frantically. "The door's open. We've got to go!"

"I can't let go of the sword!" he gasped. "It won't let me retreat!" He lurched as the sword thrust itself at a spider, pulling him along with it. With a surge of rage, he realized the truth. "Damn Darien to the Abyss. This thing must be cursed!"

Beckla let out a fierce oath. "All right, I'll see if I can use my magic to remove the—"

The wizard's words turned into a scream as a pale form dropped down from above, landing on her back. Her cry was cut short as ghostly pincers dug into the back of her neck. Her body went limp, and she fell to the floor. The still-burning staff slipped from her fingers, rolling away.

Out of the corner of his eye, Artek saw Beckla fall. He strained against the dancing blade in his hands, face twisted in effort, then managed to turn it on the spider that clung to the wizard. The saber sliced through the thing's bloated abdomen. It waved its thin legs, then exploded into a puff of foul vapor.

Grim satisfaction turned to cold terror as Artek realized that his back was now toward the other wraith spiders. Sensing their prey's vulnerability, they chittered hatefully, closing in. Artek knew he had mere moments to live.

His eyes fell upon Beckla's burning staff, and an idea struck him. But he could not let go of the cursed saber. There was only one chance.

"Corin!" he shouted. "Grab the staff and hold it over your head!"

The lord stared at the approaching spiders, frozen in horror. He did not move.

"Now, Corin!" Artek screamed. "If there is any drop of truly noble blood in your veins, do it!"

The young lord blinked. Mechanically, he obeyed Artek's orders. He gripped the staff, then thrust the blazing end over his head just as the wraith spiders closed in. Flame licked the bottom of a clump of pale webs dangling from the ceiling. For a terrible second, Artek thought his plan had failed. Then crimson fire snaked up the hanging strands, and all at once the chamber's entire ceiling burst into roaring flame. Gobs of burning web dropped down, landing on the wraith spiders. They shrieked and writhed as they were engulfed in crackling fire.

As his enemies were consumed, Artek felt the cursed saber release his arms. He thrust the blade back into its sheath, then bent down to scoop up Beckla's motionless form. He threw the limp wizard over his shoulder.

"Run, Corin!" he shouted over the roar of the flames.

This time the lord obeyed. They dodged falling clumps of blazing spider web and dashed through the door. Leaving behind the blazing inferno of death, they ran into cool darkness.

Ancient Footsteps

When they no longer heard the roar of flames and the echoing shrieks of the wraith spiders, Artek slowed to a halt, still balancing the motionless wizard over his broad shoulders. A second later, Corin—unable to see in the thick gloom—collided with Artek's back. The nobleman stumbled, caught himself, then leaned against a slimy wall, clutching his chest and gasping for breath. Artek glanced down at Beckla's face. Her eyes were closed, her skin deathly pale. He couldn't tell if she was breathing or not. They needed to stop and rest, but not here, not in this open stone corridor. There was no telling what things might wander by and catch them unaware. They needed someplace out of the way, someplace safe.

Then something caught Artek's eye. Set as it was into a deep alcove, he almost didn't notice it, even with the aid of his darkvision. It was a small wooden door. Resting behind a portal they could barricade would certainly be preferable to sitting in the middle of a drafty passageway. Artek made for the alcove, and Corin stumbled after him, feeling his way through the murk.

The door was locked. Artek drew the dagger from his boot, slipped the tip into the iron lock, and gave it an expert twist. The door swung open with a groan. Beyond was a small chamber bathed in leprous green light that emanated from phosphorescent fungus clinging to the room's damp walls. It was not a wholesome light, but at least Corin would be able to see. They entered the room, and Artek shut and relocked the door behind them.

"I must say, I've had better accommodations," Corin noted in a quavering voice.

"But you can't beat the price," Artek replied dryly.

There was little in the room but a few heaps of rusted metal and rotted wood. Atop one of the piles of refuse was a yellowed human skull. A drooping, frayed tapestry hung on one wall, and Artek yanked it down and spread it on the cold floor. As gently as he could, he laid the limp wizard down on the worm-eaten cloth.

"How . . . how is she?" Corin asked quietly, hovering over them.

Artek shook his head. It didn't look good. He laid a hand on Beckla's throat. Her flesh was as cold as ice, and he could feel no pulse. He held his dagger before her mouth, but the cool steel did not fog. She was not breathing. Artek turned her head, and on the side of her neck were a pair of small, dark wounds.

"The wraith spider bit her," he said grimly. "I suppose the thing was poisonous." A tightness filled his chest, and his eyes stung. He had only just met the wizard, but she had helped him when he was alone, and he considered her a friend. "Beckla is dead, Corin," he said hoarsely.

"No, she isn't."

Artek glared up at the nobleman. "This really isn't the time for your boundless optimism, you know."

Corin looked at him in surprise. "But I didn't say that," he gulped.

Artek frowned. "Well, if you didn't say it, then who did?"

"Hello there!" called a cheery voice. "It was me! I said it!"

Artek leapt to his feet and Corin spun around. Both stared in confusion. There was nobody else with them in the chamber.

"Over here!" It was the voice again: odd and hollow, almost like the sound of a low flute. "On the rubbish heap. No, not that one. *This* one!"

Artek and Corin blinked in shock as their eyes finally fell upon the mysterious speaker—a yellowed skull. Lower jaw working excitedly, it hopped and spun atop the pile of refuse.

"Surprised, eh?" the fleshless skull gloated.

"You could say that," Artek said cautiously, wondering if they were again in danger.

The skull clattered its teeth happily. "Good! I like surprises! The name is Muragh, Muragh Brilstagg.

At least, that was my name when I was alive. Of course, I'm not half the man I used to be. By Lathander, I'm more like an eighth! Some fool soldier cut my body away, and then went and threw my head in the harbor. The fish had a good time with me. Do you know what it's like to have your eyeballs eaten by eels and your brain sucked out by starfish?" The skull rattled its jaw, as if shuddering. "Let me assure you, it isn't much fun."

Maybe the thing wasn't dangerous, Artek decided, but it certainly was talkative. He approached the skull. "You said that our friend isn't dead, Muragh. What makes you think so?"

"I don't *think* so," the skull replied smugly. "I *know* so."

And arrogant as well, Artek amended inwardly.

"The wraith spiders may not be alive themselves, but they don't like to feed on the dead," the skull explained in a reedy voice. "Their venom only stuns— that way they can wrap their prey in webs and snack at their leisure."

A chill ran down Artek's spine. The skull's words conjured a grisly image. He glanced back at the still form of the wizard. "So how long will it take for the effects of the venom to wear off?"

"Not long," Muragh replied. "No more than three or four—"

"Hours?" Artek interrupted hopefully.

"Days," the skull said.

Artek's heart sank. He couldn't simply leave Beckla here for three days with no one to protect her but a talking skull. It was too much of a betrayal— and that would make him no better than Darien

Thal. But in three days he would be long dead.

"Wait a minute!" Corin piped up. "I think I have something that might help." The nobleman fumbled about his grimy velvet coat, searching the pockets. "Aha!" he exclaimed, pulling out a small object. "Here it is." He held up the item—a glass vial, filled with a thick, purplish fluid.

"What is that?" Artek asked dubiously.

"A healing potion," Corin replied. "My family's healer gave it to me before I embarked on the hunt. I hadn't thought of it before—it wouldn't do much good if Beckla were dead. But if she's only *injured* . . ."

Hope surged in Artek's heart. "Give me that," he snapped, snatching the vial from Corin's hand. Kneeling beside Beckla, he unstopped the cork and carefully poured the purple potion into her mouth. For an agonizing moment nothing happened. Then the wizard swallowed and coughed, her chest heaving as she drew in a ragged breath. Her eyes flew open, and she sat bolt upright.

"The spider!" she screamed.

Artek gripped her shoulders tightly, looking her directly in the eyes. "It's all right, Beckla. It's over. We're safe now."

For a moment she continued to stare in terror, then she sighed deeply and nodded, indicating she understood. She winced abruptly and lifted a hand to her brow.

"My head hurts," she groaned.

"Spider venom hangover," Artek said with a wry grin. "It will pass."

"That's easy for you to say," she grumbled petulantly.

The complaint, more than anything, assured Artek

that the wizard was indeed well. "I think you had better meet our new friend, Beckla," he said. "Something
tells me you're going to find him very interesting."

"Hello, wizard!" Muragh exclaimed. The yellowed
skull hopped up and down while Beckla gawked in
astonishment.

Though it took far more words than Artek considered necessary, especially given their lack of time,
they finally managed to glean the whole of Muragh's
story. What was more, the skull happily provided even
more details this time, and Artek read much between
the lines. In life, Muragh had been a priest of Lathander—and at least as loquacious as he was now. He
relentlessly pestered an evil mage to give up his dark
ways, and the mage secretly cast a magical curse on
Muragh. Shortly thereafter, Muragh's loose tongue
landed him in a bar fight in which he received a knife
in the heart, and his body was tossed into a dark alley.
Though dead, Muragh found that he could still think
and talk—apparently thanks to the evil mage's curse.
However, if the mage thought that undeath would
drive Muragh mad, he had erred.

After decomposing for a week or so, Muragh was
found by a drunken soldier. Of course, soldiers are a
superstitious lot. This particular fellow—thinking
the talking corpse to be a fiend sent to torment him
for his sins—cut off Muragh's head and tossed it into
Waterdeep Harbor. There, as Muragh so graphically
described, the fish stripped the flesh from his skull.
Eventually, he was found by the mermen who dwell
in the deep waters of the harbor. Annoyed with his
constant prattling, they took the skull to Waterdeep's City Watch, where Muragh fell into the hands

of the duty-wizard.

For a time the wizard kept Muragh, using him as a watch-skull to protect his library. However, when thieves broke into the wizard's tower, they stole Muragh, thinking him to be a thing of value. That was a mistake. They soon found that no one would pay good gold for a chatterbox skull, and tossed Muragh into the sewers.

In time, the waters flowing beneath the city carried Muragh into Undermountain, and the skull had rattled around Halaster's labyrinth ever since. Occasionally, wandering creatures picked him up out of curiosity and carried him for a time, only to drop him before long in some new place. Eventually, he came into the possession of someone named Muiral. Though Muragh was extremely vague on this point, it seemed that Muiral grew weary of his incessant talking and locked him in this chamber. Here he had dwelled alone—until Artek and Corin discovered him.

"I can't tell you how wonderful it is to have company again!" Muragh exclaimed. Though his ivory cranium was nearly devoid of flesh, a few wisps of rotted hair still fluttered atop his crown. "Moldy stone walls don't make for great conversation partners, and even I get tired of hearing my own voice after a dozen years."

"There's a surprise," Artek murmured wryly.

"So now you know what I'm doing down here," the skull finished. "What about you three?"

After a moment's thought, Artek decided that it could do little harm to tell Muragh their tale. If the skull had truly dwelled for so long in Undermountain, perhaps he would know something of use. Artek quickly explained all that had happened, and ended by describing his plan to find a gate out.

"Absolutely amazing," Muragh exclaimed.

"Our story?" Artek asked.

"No. Your plan. It's the stupidest thing I've ever heard."

Artek's eyes narrowed at this insult. "And I suppose you could come up with a better idea?"

"Of course," Muragh replied smartly. "A Thayan rock slug could come up with a better plan than that."

Artek crossed his arms, fixing the skull with a dubious look. "I'm waiting."

Muragh did not need to be asked twice to talk. "Finding a gate out of here on your own is about as likely as growing wings and flying." Muragh cackled with laughter at this, teeth clacking. "Not that there aren't gates that lead out of Undermountain—there are. But you could hardly expect Halaster to simply leave them sitting around in plain sight. He was mad, not stupid. The only ones who might be able to tell you where you could find a gate out are the old wizard's apprentices. And that means you have to find one of the Seven first."

The three gathered closer, listening as Muragh told of Halaster's seven apprentices. Nearly a thousand years ago, the wizard forsook his tower on the slopes of Mount Waterdeep and descended into the vast labyrinth he had created below. When he did not return from Undermountain, the Seven—powerful mages in their own right—boldly ventured into the dark depths in search of him. There they found magical tricks and deadly obstacles, and the deeper they went, the more difficult grew the riddles, the more perilous became the traps. The Seven soon realized that this was a test set for them by their master. Believing that whoever reached Halaster first would become his most favored—and thus heir to his most powerful magic—the Seven strove against each other. Each tried to go deeper than the rest and be the first to find their mysterious master.

Whether or not the apprentices ever succeeded in finding Halaster, no one knew. Only one of the Seven ever returned from Undermountain: Jhesiyra Kestellharp, who became the Magister of Myth Drannor, an ancient kingdom whose ruins lay far to the East, near the realm of Cormyr. The other six apprentices remained in Undermountain, and whether they still searched, granted unnaturally long life by their magic, the histories did not tell.

"It sounds as if these apprentices have the power to help us, all right," Beckla said when Muragh had finished his tale.

"If any of them are still alive," Artek added.

"Muragh, old boy," Corin said, addressing the skull as one might a servant. "You seem to know a great deal about this place. Can you take us to one of the Seven?"

"As a matter of fact, I can," the skull replied glibly. "But I won't."

Only by great force of will did Artek restrain himself from grabbing the insolent skull and heaving it against one of the stone walls. "Are you playing games with us, Muragh?" he said.

"No, no!" the skull said hastily. "Believe me, you really don't want to meet Muiral."

Muiral? Wasn't that the person who had locked
Muragh in this room? Artek picked up the skull and
glared into its empty eye sockets. "Let me get this
straight," he said angrily. "You managed to annoy
this Muiral with your chattering, and now you're
afraid to take us to him because you think he will do
something to hurt you. Am I right?"

Muragh worked his mandible vigorously, but
Artek held the skull tight. "You don't understand,"
Muragh whined fearfully. "Muiral won't just hurt
me. He'll hurt *you*, too. Don't you see? He's the one
who created the wraith spiders. And I guarantee you
that there are more of them than you encountered in
that chamber. Muiral loves spiders. He's part spider
himself. I don't know how he did it, but he fused
himself onto the body of a giant spider. He won't help
you." Muragh shook pitifully in Artek's hands.
"Please don't take me to Muiral. Please!"

Beckla bit her lower lip. "I think he's telling the
truth, Artek."

"Have pity on the poor chap, Ar'talen," Corin
added worriedly. "He's been through a great deal."

Artek glowered at the skull. At last he sighed in
exasperation. "All right, I believe you, Muragh. We
won't go looking for Muiral. The truth is, I really
don't care to face any more of those wraith spiders."
He shook his head. "But if we can't go to Muiral for
help, where are we going to find another one of Halaster's apprentices?"

"Actually, I have an idea," Muragh said cheerfully.
The skull leapt from Artek's hands, fell to the floor,
and rolled toward the doorway. "Well, don't just
stand there," he said in annoyance. "Open the door.

In case you hadn't noticed, I don't have hands."

The three exchanged dubious looks. At last Artek shrugged. Following a talking skull seemed an unlikely way to escape from this maze, but he supposed they had little choice. He unlocked the door, then scooped Muragh into his arms as they headed out into the corridor.

"We need to be very careful here," Muragh said in a hollow whisper. "Right now we're on the edge of Muiral's Gauntlet."

"Muiral's Gauntlet?" Artek asked softly.

"Is there an echo in here?" Muragh replied acidly. "Yes, Muiral's Gauntlet. The room where you encountered the wraith spiders is part of it, but only a small part, and not the worst. Not by far." The skull whistled sadly through his teeth. "Muiral's quite mad, of course. Searching for his master and failing addled his brain. What little sanity he still possessed after that was destroyed when he grafted himself onto that giant spider's body. These days his only pleasure comes from toying with the victims he gates down from the surface. He sends them into his Gauntlet and watches to see how far they can get through the maze of dangers he's created."

"Let me guess," Beckla said uncomfortably. "No one ever makes it out of Muiral's Gauntlet alive."

Muragh grinned, despite his lack of flesh. "Well, Muiral certainly wouldn't think it very much fun if they did."

"So where are we going, if not into the Gauntlet?" Artek asked nervously.

"This way." The skull tugged at Artek's hands, leading him toward the mouth of a side tunnel. "Before I ended up here, I got caught inside a gelatinous cube. Not a fun experience, by the way—very cold and slimy. It was the cube that brought me into Muiral's Gauntlet. I remember the path by which it slithered here. And I recall seeing something very interesting along the way."

Artek glanced sharply at the skull. "Something interesting? What is it?"

"You'll see," Muragh replied mysteriously.

After this the skull became unusually reticent. Artek decided not to press for more answers, but rather to enjoy the quiet. His ears were ringing from Muragh's previous chatter. He walked stealthily down the narrow passageway, following the tugs and jerks of the skull in his hands, as Beckla and Corin came behind. Unfortunately, after the acid pit and the fire in the spider room, the wizard's staff was a lost cause. However, it seemed she could make do without it, for a wisp of blue magelight danced on her outstretched hand, lighting the way for the group.

Guided by Muragh's tugging, they traveled through a tortuous series of dank corridors and murky chambers. Before long Artek lost all sense of direction. At first, here and there, they encountered glowing wisps of green webs dangling from the ceiling, and from time to time they caught a whiff of the same evil scent that had permeated the wraith spider lair. However, as they progressed, they soon left all traces of the eerie webs and spiders behind. Though still dark and stifling, the air here was no longer so oppressive and menacing. The three humans found themselves breathing a little easier. It seemed Muragh knew what he was doing.

Artek glanced down at the tattoo on his arm. The moon had passed the arrow now. In the world above, night had fallen. Not that it really mattered—it was always night down here.

"How much farther, Muragh?" Artek asked quietly.

"We're close now," the skull piped up brightly. "And you can quit whispering, you know. We left Muiral's territory behind ages ago."

"Maybe I like whispering," Artek replied.

"Suit yourself," Muragh sniffed.

Artek started to clench his hands. How much force would it take to shatter an old skull, he wondered?

"Hey, stop that!" Muragh complained. "You're giving me a headache!"

By force of will, Artek managed to keep his fingers from squeezing. "Sorry," he grumbled.

"I'm touched by your sincerity," the skull quipped sarcastically. "Now turn left here."

They passed through an archway and found themselves descending a narrow spiral staircase. The steps were slick and treacherous. Several cracked beneath Artek's boots, and one gave way completely when Corin trod upon it. If not for Beckla's quick hand pulling him back, the nobleman would have crashed into Artek, and both would have gone tumbling breakneck down the steep staircase. The steps seemed without end as they delved deeper into the darkness.

Finally the staircase stopped, and they stepped through an opening into a passageway so broad that it was not so much a corridor as an avenue. A line of basalt columns ran down the center of the hall, supporting the arched ceiling high above. The columns were skillfully carved into the shapes of trees, conjuring the illusion of walking down a sylvan boulevard under the shadows of dusk.

Artek let out a low whistle, turning his head to try to take in the grandeur of the subterranean road. "I'll give Halaster one thing—he knew how to think big."

"Actually, Halaster didn't build this passage," Muragh said. "It's even older than the mad wizard. This road was built by dwarves of the clan Melairkyn. In ancient days, they constructed an entire city here, called Underhall, far beneath the surface."

"What happened to them?" Beckla murmured in awe.

"No one knows for certain," Muragh replied. "They disappeared centuries before Halaster stumbled onto their delvings in the course of his excavations. Most likely they were slain by the duergar—dark dwarves who skulked in these halls until Halaster showed up. He decided he wanted Underhall for himself. Not being keen on sharing, Halaster eradicated the duergar like so many rats. After that, Underhall became part of Undermountain proper."

Artek took a deep breath. The weight of years hung heavily on this place. He almost could hear the ghostly ring of hammers, drifting in the air like echoes from the past.

"Is this what you wanted to show us, Muragh?" he asked.

"No, over there," the skull said, clacking his jaw in the direction of one of the stone columns.

Artek and the others approached the column. Scratched into the dark stone were several lines of strange, flowing writing. Beneath the writing was an arrow that pointed down the ancient road. The words looked somehow familiar, but Artek could not make them out. Whatever it was, it wasn't written in the common tongue. He shook his head, his annoyance growing.

"Muragh," he warned, "please don't tell me that you brought us all this way just to look at thousand-year-old markings."

"What's wrong with you, Ar'talen?" Muragh complained. "Can't you read what it says?"

"No, I can't," Artek snapped. He glanced questioningly at Beckla.

"Don't look at me," the wizard told him. "I can't read it either. Though I'm willing to bet it's a naughty poem," she added with a disgusted glance at the skull.

"Excuse me," Corin said suddenly, pushing past them to get a closer look at the column. He peered at the words with his blue eyes, then clapped his hands excitedly. "Oh, this is absolutely fascinating!"

Artek and Beckla stared in shock at the nobleman.

"You can read this, Corin?" Artek asked.

"Of course," Corin replied smoothly, as if it were a silly question. "It's written in Thorass."

"Thorass?"

"That's right," the nobleman said. "Thorass, also known as Auld Common. It's the tongue our ancestors spoke long ago, and from which the current common tongue is derived. I learned to read it as a child, studying the old Silvertor family history. It goes back centuries, you know. In fact, it all started when—"

"I'm sure your family's story is enthralling, Corin," Artek interrupted. "But we're in a bit of a hurry. Do you think you could just tell us what this says?"

Corin studied the words a moment more, then nodded to himself. " 'On this, the fiftieth day of our search for our master, came we to this place,' " he translated.

"That's it?" Artek asked.

"That's it," Corin confirmed. "Oh, except for this." He pointed to the last two lines of writing. "The message is signed, *Talastria and Orannon*."

"And who are they?" Beckla wondered.

Artek made a leap of intuition. "I think I know," he said. "The message says that they came here in search of their master. Who could that be, except for Halaster himself? So Talastria and Orannon were two of his apprentices."

"Whew!" Muragh groaned. "I thought you were never going to get it!"

"You could have just told us, you know," Artek noted caustically.

"What? And spoil all your fun?"

Artek bit his tongue. It wasn't worth a reply. The important thing was that they had found the ancient trail of two of Halaster's apprentices.

"Come on," Artek said. "This arrow must indicate the direction the apprentices were traveling in. If we follow, we may find what became of them—and maybe a way out, too."

Together, they hurried down the underground avenue in the direction the arrow had indicated. Clouds of thick dust settled sluggishly in their wake. Their shadows, conjured by Beckla's pale magelight, rippled across the passage's walls like weird giants from an ancient nightmare. Artek tried not to look at them—this was an eerie place. In silence they continued on as countless tree-columns slipped by.

It was Beckla who saw the words scratched into the wall beside a keyhole-shaped archway. The stones of the arch itself were oddly scorched and cracked.

" 'It took us many days to destroy the fire elementals that barred this door,' " Corin translated slowly. "But now the way is clear, and our search continues, on this the fifty-sixth day of our quest.' "

As before, the message was signed *Talastria and Orannon*. Beneath it, an arrow pointed through the archway. They stepped through the opening and into a dim corridor. Artek shivered. It was strange to be retracing the ancient steps of the two lost apprentices. Steeling his will, he started down the corridor. The others followed. After the loftiness of the main avenue, this passage was cramped and forbidding— apparently, it had been a lesser way of Underhall. Dark water dripped down the smooth stone walls and trickled across the floor. Unconsciously, the three humans drew closer together.

When they came to a flight of stairs, an arrow scratched into the wall pointed down. Talastria and Orannon had come this way. Artek led the others down a hundred slimy steps before the corridor leveled out and continued on again through the darkness.

"What are all these strange silvery marks on the wall?" Corin wondered aloud. Though he spoke in a whisper, the sound of his voice hissed uncomfortably around the corridor. No one had an answer for him.

Four more times they came to a flight of steps, each longer than the one before. At the head of every stairway, an arrow indicated that the two apprentices had

descended it. Breathless, they reached the bottom of
the fifth flight only after Artek had counted five hundred steps. It was there that they finally learned the
answer to Corin's question. Another message was
scratched into the hard surface of the wall.

" 'We know not what day of our search this is, for
all sense of time was lost to us in the arduous battle
for the five stairs,' " Corin said, reading the ancient
inscription. " 'Upon every step of every stair waited a
fiend of the underworld, conjured by our master's
magic. To gain but a single step, we were forced to
slay a slavering fiend. We destroyed a hundred on
the first stair, two hundred on the next. Never did
we stop—save to rest briefly and restore our magic—
until we destroyed the five hundredth fiend on the
fifth and final stair. We are both gravely wounded
from the ordeal, yet surely only something of the
greatest worth could lie beyond such a terrible barrier. It is our belief that the end of our search is near
at last. And surely, once we find our master, he will
make us whole once more.' "

"A fiend on every step," Beckla echoed with a
shudder. "It must have taken the apprentices years
to get past these stairs. The silvery marks on the
walls must be scars left from the spells they cast to
destroy the creatures."

Artek nodded grimly. "Let's see what they found
at the end of their search."

It was not much farther. After a hundred paces,
the corridor ended in a pair of massive stone doors.
Emblazoned on the door were letters of gold. The letters spelled out two words that they all now easily
recognized: *Talastria* and *Orannon*. The group ex-

changed uneasy looks, and Artek pushed on the doors. They swung open easily. Beckla held out her hand, and the flickering magelight illuminated the long chamber beyond.

The sides of the chamber were littered with count-less fragments of stone. Only after a moment did Artek realize that some of the fragments were shaped like clawed hands, others like leathery wings, and still others like grotesque heads—they were parts of gar-goyles. Dozens of them had once lined the chamber, but now they were smashed to bits. At the far end of the room was a dais of dark stone, and on the dais rested two oblong boxes hewn of porphyry. No, not boxes, Artek realized. Sarcophagi.

"It's a tomb," Artek said softly as he sensed the truth. "Talastria and Orannon thought they would find their master at the end of the stairs, on the other side of the fiends. Instead, all they found was their own tomb—no doubt created for them by Ha-laster himself."

"That's a cruel joke," Corin said, aghast.

"On us as well as on them," Beckla replied glumly. "I doubt a dead apprentice is going to be able to show us a gate out of this hole."

"Don't be so hasty," Muragh replied testily. "There might be something in here that could help us."

Artek drew in a deep breath. "I suppose it's worth a try. We came all this way, so we might as well spend a few minutes poking around."

Together, they stepped into the tomb of the lost ap-prentices. It was an eerie place. Artek could almost imagine the two wizards, wounded and dying after their battle on the stairs, stumbling into this chamber

only to find the two waiting sarcophagi. Did they laugh
madly as they laid themselves within their own coffins?
Artek did his best to shake the disturbing image from
his mind. While Beckla and Corin began poking around
in the shattered remains of the stone gargoyles, he
headed for the dais at the far end of the chamber.

All at once an icy wind rushed through the tomb.
With an ominous *boom*, the stone doors swung shut.
Artek spun on a heel, staring back at Beckla and
Corin in surprise. As one, the wizard and the noble-
man gasped. A chill danced up Artek's back.

"What is it?" he whispered, clutching Muragh
tightly.

"I think you'd better turn back around, Artek,"
Beckla gulped.

Dread rising in his throat, Artek did as the wizard
suggested. His heart froze. Even as he watched, the
heavy stone lid that covered one sarcophagus slid to
the side and fell to the dais with a crash. A moment
later, the lid atop the other stone coffin followed suit.
A dry, musty odor drifted on the air: the scent of ancient decay. Then, with majestic and malevolent
slowness, a form rose out of each sarcophagus. Tattered robes of black cloth fluttered around withered
forms, parchmentlike skin peeled from gaunt faces,
and gold bracelets clinked coldly on shriveled arms.

"By all the blackest gods," Artek murmured in a
mixture of awe and terror. "They're still alive!"

"No," Muragh countered weakly. "Not *alive*."

Crimson flames flared into being in the hollow pits
of their eyes as Talastria and Orannon reached out
their undead hands toward the defilers of their tomb.

Beauty Perilous

"Run . . ."

Artek tried to shout the word, but it escaped his lips only as a strangled whisper. Fear radiated from the far end of the tomb in thick, choking waves. He tried to back away from the dais, but his legs betrayed him. Against his will, he fell to his knees, bowing to the dread majesty rising before him. Behind him, Beckla and Corin did the same.

Icy wind shrieked through the ancient chamber. Crimson mist poured down the steps of the dark dais, filling the air with a bloody miasma. Trailing tattered funereal garb and yellowed wisps of dried flesh, the long-dead wizards climbed from their sarcophagi. They stood before the stone coffins, orbless eyes blazing, pointing accusing fingers at the humans. Two keening voices rose in shrill chorus.

Defilers! Trespassers! Foolishly have ye dared to transgress upon our domain!

The words pierced Artek's skull, flaying his mind. He clutched his hands to his ears, but he could not shut out the deafening shrieks.

Accursed breathing ones! Our guardians may be no more, but still ye shall not profane our tomb. Ye shall pay for this violation with your throbbing hearts!

The undead apprentices stretched out their leathery hands, and scarlet energy crackled on the tips of their clawlike fingers. Artek grunted in fear as he felt a tugging deep in his chest. With stiff, terrible slowness, the mummified wizards took a lurching step forward. They reached their ragged arms out still further, hands blazing with fell magic.

Artek screamed in pain. He threw his head back, arching his spine. His heart leapt wildly, straining against the inside of his rib cage, as if at any moment it would burst from his chest and hurtle through the air to the waiting hand of Talastria or Orannon. A moment later, Beckla and Corin echoed his cry, writhing as their own beating hearts were called by the dread wizards.

The undead horrors continued to hobble forward, until they stood upon the very edge of the dais. The nearer they came, the more the pressure in Artek's chest increased. He gnashed his teeth in agony as a trickle of dark blood oozed from his nose. He could not breathe. So this is how it ends, he thought dimly. Dying at the hands of the dead. He might have laughed at the irony of it, but when he opened his mouth, he could only scream.

The wizards grinned evilly, empty eye sockets blazing. A little closer, and their dire magic would be strong enough to rip the beating hearts from the chests of their defilers. Together, Talastria and Orannon took one more stiff step forward.

Numb and dried as they were, their feet did not sense the stone step beneath them. The two undead wizards lurched forward at the unexpected drop. Their brittle   mbled upon striking the top step of the dais. Withered a ms shot out as the apprentices fought to preserve their precarious balance. The sudden motion caused ancient sinews to snap like old bowstrings. Talastria and Orannon let out a terrible, soul-rending shriek, and then, like grisly puppets with their strings slashed, they pitched forward. Their desiccated bodies struck the sharp stone steps and burst asunder. Disarticulated bones rolled down the steps, crumbling as they went.

By the time the remains of the two wizards reached the floor before the dais, all that was left were shards and scraps. For a moment, scarlet sparks of magic sizzled around the crumbled remnants of the gruesome mummies, but these, too, were soon extinguished. Yellow dust settled to the floor. After ten centuries, Talastria and Orannon were truly dead.

Artek slumped forward as the near-fatal magic released his heart. He clutched his chest, drawing in deep, ragged gulps of air. Gradually the wild throbbing of his heart slowed to a more steady pace. Turning his head, he saw Beckla and Corin pull themselves to their knees. The wizard wiped the blood from her lips with the back of her hand. Corin was hunched over, retching, but then he managed to straighten himself, his blue eyes wide in his pale face.

Muragh had rolled a short distance away. "Well, I guess that will teach you to respect the dead," the skull said in a slightly smug tone.

Artek did not even bother to reply, having had more than enough of dead things for the moment. Stumbling to his feet, he moved to help Beckla and Corin up. All were rattled by the experience, but no one seemed gravely injured.

"Now what?" Beckla asked hoarsely after recovering some of her composure.

Artek straightened his leather jerkin, then ran a hand through his short black hair. He gazed around the ancient tomb. "I can't say that I really care to hang around this place any longer than we have to, but I suppose we should look around. Talastria and Orannon may be dead for good, but there still could be something here that might help us."

"Very well," Corin agreed weakly. "But if any more corpses pop out of coffins, we're leaving."

For once the nobleman received no argument.

Carefully they began to search the tomb, examining the walls and poking through the broken statuary. They had been searching for only a few moments when a sound drifted on the air: a low grunting interspersed with high-pitched squeaks and damp snorts. Artek froze.

"Do you hear that?" he hissed to the others.

Beckla nodded. "It sounds like some sort of animal," she whispered back.

Corin stared at them in alarm. "I really think we

ought to be going now," he gulped.

Artek shook his head grimly. "Not without knowing what's likely to be following us when we do." He cocked his head, listening. There it was again: a grunting, shuddering sound from the far end of the tomb. Steeling his will, Artek pulled the dagger from his boot and stealthily made his way toward the stone dais. The animal sounds grew louder. Whatever the thing was, it was definitely lurking behind the dais.

Clutching his dagger, Artek soundlessly ascended the steps. He moved carefully between the two stone sarcophagi and cautiously peered over the back edge of the dais. The sniffling sound reached his ears clearly now. Something gray, scaly, and muscular crouched in the shadows behind the dais. Artek's darkvision adjusted to the murk, and his jaw dropped in surprise. He backed away, hurrying down the steps, and returned to the others.

"It's a gargoyle," he whispered.

Beckla glanced at the shattered remains of the bestial stone statues that littered the tomb. "A gargoyle?" she asked in confusion. "Like these?"

Artek nodded darkly. "Only it's alive."

Corin clutched a hand to his mouth. "Alive?" he gasped through his fingers. "But what's it doing?"

Artek frowned in puzzlement. "I'm not entirely sure. But I think that it's . . . *crying*."

Beckla and Corin traded startled looks. "Crying?" they echoed as one.

"Maybe you'd better come look for yourselves," Artek told the others. "I can't be certain, but I don't think it's too dangerous. If it was, it probably would have attacked us by now."

Beckla was game to try, but Corin had to be tugged along forcefully.

"Hey!" Muragh piped up. "Don't forget me!"

"I should be so lucky," Artek grumbled, picking up the enchanted skull.

Keeping close together, they ascended the dais and peered over the back edge. Beckla held out her hand. Blue magelight drove away the shadows, revealing the creature below.

In the light, Artek saw that it was indeed a gargoyle. The creature huddled on the floor with its back turned toward them. Its scaly hide was rough and gray as stone, and rocklike muscles knotted its powerful frame. Stubby bat wings protruded from its broad back, and onyx horns sprang from its knobby head. The gargoyle's gigantic shoulders shook as it grunted and sniffled.

"The poor thing," Beckla sighed.

Artek and Corin stared at her. "The poor thing?" Artek repeated in disbelief.

The wizard glared at him. "It's sad," she replied in annoyance.

At the sound of their voices, the gargoyle let out a snort and looked up. Both Artek and Corin jumped back, but Beckla did not so much as flinch. Somehow the creature's doglike face was more endearing than frightful. Sorrow shone in its glowing green eyes.

"What's wrong with you?" the gargoyle growled in a gravelly voice. "Why are you just standing there? Aren't you terrified of me?"

Trembling, Corin opened his mouth to speak, but Beckla elbowed him sharply in the side. The nobleman's mouth promptly snapped shut.

"No, we're not," the wizard answered seriously.

The gargoyle let out a dejected sigh, wings drooping. "I was afraid of that. Not that I'm surprised—I never was any good at guarding the tomb. Now I'm the last, and an utter failure." The gargoyle sniffed, wiping the dampness from its scaly cheeks with a clawed hand.

"Corin," Beckla asked, "do you have a handkerchief?"

"Of course," the nobleman replied in confusion. He pulled a slime-covered silk cloth from the pocket of his velvet coat. "But what do you—?"

Beckla snatched the handkerchief from his hand, then hopped down from the dais. She held the cloth out toward the gargoyle. "Here," she said gently.

The gargoyle stared at her in surprise, then hesitantly accepted the handkerchief. The creature lifted the grubby cloth to its long muzzle, then let out a trumpeting snort. When it was finished, it politely offered the dripping handkerchief back to Corin.

The nobleman accepted it reluctantly, looking vaguely queasy.

Artek watched all this with growing fascination. He crouched on the edge of the dais and eyed the gargoyle critically. "Excuse me," he said carefully, "but I was always led to believe that gargoyles were terrible and ferocious creatures—stone statues given magical life for the sole purpose of maiming and killing."

"They are," the gargoyle agreed.

Artek scratched his stubbly chin. "Well, no offense intended, but you don't exactly fit the bill."

More tears welled up in the creature's glowing green eyes. "I know," it said forlornly.

"Now look what you've done, Ar'talen," Beckla

scolded him. "You've made him cry again."

Artek shook his head in astonishment. He was having a hard time dealing with this. He gave the gargoyle a questioning look. "All right, then maybe you should tell us exactly what you *are* doing here, ah . . ."

"Terrathiguss," the creature finished. "Terrathiguss the Gargoyle."

"Well, at least your name is somewhat frightening," Artek acknowledged.

"Do you really think so?" Terrathiguss asked. "Not much else about me is." Muscled limbs flexing easily, the gargoyle climbed onto the dais and gazed around the tomb at the shattered remnants of the other stone gargoyles. "I don't know what went wrong. We were all created at the same time. Talastria and Orannon made us, you see. They used their dying energy to conjure us into being, and ordered us to keep guard over their tomb. But I was the last one they made." The gargoyle shook its head ruefully. "And somehow I was different."

"Different?" Artek asked.

The gargoyle nodded solemnly. "Do you mind if I sit?" Startled by the creature's manners, Artek could only nod. With a clawed hand, Terrathiguss fastidiously dusted off a corner of one of the sarcophagi. Then the creature perched neatly on the stone coffin.

"For a thousand years, my brethren and I stood guard over this tomb," Terrathiguss went on in his gruff yet oddly warm voice. "Oh, it wasn't as boring as you might imagine, for we spent most of that time in stone form. Time passes very quickly for us when we stand as statues. I suppose it's rather like sleeping for a living creature, though I can only guess." The gargoyle shrugged its massive shoulders. "Anyway, we became flesh only when interlopers entered the tomb. And then we promptly tore the defilers to shreds."

Terrathiguss shook his head sadly. "At least, my brethren tore the defilers to shreds. At first I joined them, but before long I realized that it wasn't the same for me as for the other gargoyles. They seemed to truly enjoy rending hapless adventurers limb from limb. They would laugh loudly, and always fought over who got to eviscerate the last screaming victim. During the first century or two, I tried killing a few adventurers myself. But I only felt sorry for them, and I dispatched them as quickly and painlessly as I could." The gargoyle rested its knobby chin on a clawed hand. "As time went on, I took to just hiding behind the dais and letting the others do all the work. My brethren never seemed to notice. They were always too busy having fun."

"But what happened to the others?" Beckla asked, glancing at the broken statues.

"I'm not sure exactly," Terrathiguss replied. "None of us were. One day we woke up from our stony sleep to find that one of our brethren had cracked and crumbled during our slumber. After that, every time we awoke, we saw that another one or two had fallen to ruin while we were sleeping. I suppose it was simply age. Even enchanted stone can crack with time, and even magical creatures can die."

"So you're the last?" Corin asked breathlessly. Caught up in the creature's tale, he had forgotten his fear.

"I'm afraid so," the gargoyle said glumly. "I woke when you first entered the tomb, and I hid behind the dais. Now I see that I was the only one to wake.

There were three others besides me when last we became stone. All must have crumbled since then." The
gargoyle's voice turned into a sob. "What a cruel joke
that I am the last! I should have attacked you when
you entered the tomb. I should have protected my
creators. Instead I hid like a coward, and now Talastria and Orannon are no more. I suppose I will crum-
ble, too, now that they are destroyed."

Beckla tapped her cheek thoughtfully. "I'm not so
certain. It seems to me that if you were still under
their power, you would have turned back to stone
with their destruction. But you're still flesh. I think
that perhaps you are free of them."

The gargoyle glanced up at Beckla in surprise.
"Free?" A look of wonder crossed his doglike face.
The green light in his eyes flashed. "Free." He mur-
mured the word again in amazement.

As the gargoyle contemplated the wizard's words,
Artek drew the others aside.

"So what are we going to do with it?" he asked
quietly.

"It's not an *it*," Beckla replied testily. "It's a *him*.
I'm going to call him Guss."

"Whatever for?" Artek asked.

"Terrathiguss is too long," Beckla explained. "And
it really doesn't suit him. He's much too nice to have
that kind of a name."

Artek shook his head, trying to follow her reasoning. "But why call it—I mean *him*—anything at all?"

"Because we're adopting him," Beckla said crisply.

"Oh, how delightful!" Corin exclaimed happily.

"Are you insane, wizard?" Artek hissed. "In case
you hadn't noticed, he's a *gargoyle*. We are *not* adopt-

ing him!"

"Quiet, Ar'talen!" Beckla said crossly. "You'll hurt his feelings."

Sputtering, Artek tried to come up with a sensible reply to this madness. Beckla breezed by him, approaching the gargoyle.

"It's decided, Terrathiguss," she said cheerfully. "We're trying to get out of Undermountain, and you're welcome to come with us. I would like to call you Guss, too—it's a much nicer name for you. But it's all up to you, of course."

The gargoyle leapt to his feet in surprise. "Well, I like Guss just fine," he gasped, "but do you really mean the rest? You want me to come with you?"

Beckla nodded solemnly. "We do."

"All of you?" Guss asked. He looked hopefully at Artek.

Artek opened his mouth, but a sharp glance from Beckla made him rethink his reply. "Yes," he grumbled darkly. "All of us."

"You might be sorry, you know," Guss said gravely. "I was created by dark wizards as a creature of destruction. I am evil by nature."

Beckla smiled. "I rather doubt that."

The gargoyle grinned back at her, displaying row upon row of sharp teeth. Somehow the expression was more charming than terrible. Artek was forced to admit to himself that Guss did seem friendly. And it couldn't hurt to have a gargoyle on their side.

"Look at this!" Corin said suddenly.

The nobleman had been rummaging inside one of the stone coffins, and his eager face was covered with dust. He gripped a tattered book in his hand.

The others gathered around Corin as he opened the
tome. The brittle yellow pages were covered with the
same spidery writing as the messages the two apprentices had scratched on the walls.

"I think it's their diary!" Corin exclaimed excitedly, thumbing through the book.

Artek peered more closely at the tome, but he
could not make out the ancient writing. "Can you
read it?"

Corin frowned, squinting at the murky text, then
shook his head. "It's written in Thorass, all right.
But I'm afraid the ink is too faded to make out more
than a word or two. Perhaps I could—wait a minute!
What's this?"

The nobleman flipped back to the page that had
caught his eye. It displayed a map showing twisting
halls joining myriad chambers. "I think this is the
great avenue of Underhall we were in before," Corin
said, pointing to a broad passage.

"What's this?" Beckla asked, pointing to a chamber with an X marked inside it and a line of text
scrawled beneath it.

Corin studied the words for a moment. "I think I
can make this out," he murmured, then nodded.
"Yes. 'To the lair of our sister Arcturia.' "

Artek looked up in interest. "Their sister? What
does that mean?"

Muragh bounced up and down in his hands. "Are you
an idiot?" the skull piped up urgently. "Who else could
be the sister of Talastria and Orannon besides—"

"Another apprentice," Artek finished in amazement. He rubbed the top of the skull with his knuckles. "Good thinking, Muragh. Especially for someone

who doesn't have a brain."

"Thanks," the skull huffed in annoyance, squirming but unable to escape Artek's grip.

"Well, what are we waiting for?" Beckla demanded, hopping off the dais. "Let's go find this Arcturia."

At first, Guss was reluctant to step outside the door of the ancient tomb, fearing he would turn to stone. But Beckla gripped his clawed hand and coaxed him through the portal. Finally he crossed the threshold, then cringed, eyes clenched shut, waiting for doom to fall upon him. Nothing happened. When he opened his glowing green eyes and looked down at his hands, they were still scaly flesh. He looked up at Beckla in wonder, then gave her a toothy grin.

Following the map, they made their way back up the five sets of stairs and down the broad, dusty boulevard hewn by the Melairkyn dwarves. Turning down a side passage, they wended their way through a maze of corridors until at last they came to the chamber marked on the map. There was nothing inside the small stone room but a round pool of dark water.

"Don't tell me this was a wild goblin chase," Artek said glumly.

Beckla cautiously approached the pool, held out her hands, and spoke several words of magic. The dark water suddenly shone with a radiant blue light. Beckla nodded in satisfaction, then withdrew her hands, and the light faded.

"The pool is enchanted," she said, turning to the others. "While I can't be entirely certain, I think it's a gate."

"Either that or it will transform us into two-headed slime worms," Artek said. "We probably ought to do a few tests before we jump in."

"For once I agree with you, Ar'talen." The wizard started back toward the others. As she did, her boot heel skidded on the damp stones beside the pool. She reached out to balance herself, but it was too late. With a cry, Beckla fell backward into the dark surface of the pool.

The others rushed to the edge of the pool. Artek peered into the murky depths. "I can't see her!" he said frantically.

"And you won't, no matter how hard you look," Muragh replied, his reedy voice grim. "Not if this really is a gate."

"But where has it taken her?" Corin asked, wringing his hands.

Artek made a decision. "There's only one way to find out."

The nobleman's eyes went wide. He started to back away from the pool. "Oh, no. You don't intend to—"

"Grab him, Guss!" Artek shouted.

The gargoyle caught the squirming lord in his stony arms. "Got him, Artek," Guss grinned. "Ready?"

Artek gave a sharp nod. "As I'll ever be." He tightened his grip on Muragh. "Let's go."

Together they leapt into the pool.

Chill water closed over their heads, and they plunged down through freezing darkness. A brilliant light appeared below and grew rapidly into a silvery rectangle. Together they fell through the glowing gate. Artek's senses were abruptly turned on their sides as he found himself not *falling* through the portal like a trapdoor, but rather *stepping* through it, as if walking past a sheer curtain of cool silk and into a shining room beyond.

"Greetings, wanderers," said a shimmering voice. "Welcome to my abode."

For a moment Artek was utterly disoriented. At last he blinked and saw that he and the others indeed stood in some sort of chamber, but he could make out few details. Everything was washed in glowing silver light. Then the light dimmed as a figure stood before them, and they all gasped.

She was beautiful. Her skin was as green and radiant as emeralds, and long hair tumbled about her shoulders in waves of polished jet. She wore a pale, diaphanous shift that seemed to accentuate the lushness of her smooth body rather than conceal it. Blue wings—as fine as those of a dragonfly—fluttered gently behind her. Eyes as bright as the sun shone from her delicate, nymphlike face.

Finally, Artek found his tongue. "Arcturia?" he murmured in wonder.

Her laughter was like clear water on crystal. "Indeed, I am Arcturia," she said in her bell-like voice. "And who else had you expected to find beyond the gate?"

Artek turned to glance at the portal behind them. It looked like a polished silver mirror hung within the carved stone archway, reflecting not this room, but rather the chamber with the dark pool. Even as Artek watched, the portal flashed, and the image changed, showing a shadowed hallway. After a few moments the silvery door flashed again. Once more the image shifted, now displaying a vast throne room.

"Many gates lead to this one," Arcturia said in answer to his look of wonder. "But that need concern you no longer, for now you have found me. Come—you must be thirsty, hungry, and tired. I will take you each to a place where you may find rest and peace."

Rest and peace. The words echoed deliciously in Artek's mind. Suddenly he could think of nothing else. It was exactly what they needed, but could they truly find it with one of Halaster's apprentices?

Arcturia reached out a slender hand toward Corin, whose eyes seemed to glaze over as he looked upon her with a rapt expression of joy. She smiled and led the nobleman away into the silvery light. He did not resist. Soon she came back to lead Beckla and Guss away in turn. They did not resist either, and Artek found he could only watch them be taken away. He could not move, and he was not sure if he even wanted to.

At last she came for Artek. She slipped her cool fingers into his. *Come*, her voice whispered gently in his mind, though her ruby lips moved only to smile.

Muragh jerked in the crook of Artek's arm. "I don't like this," the skull hissed through yellowed teeth. His few wisps of rotted hair waved in agitation. "She's a little too friendly, if you ask me. Something is wrong here."

However, the skull's urgent words were no more than a dull buzz in Artek's ears. As if in a dream, he seemed to float forward, following the green-skinned maiden.

"Artek, don't do this!" Muragh cried out. "Listen to me, I know what—"

Utterly unnoticed, the skull slipped from Artek's arm, clattering to the floor and rolling away. With an absent smile, Artek followed after Arcturia.

As they proceeded, he caught brief glimpses of the others. Corin sat in a velvet chair at the end of a long

dining table laden with pewter platters, crystal bowls,
and goblets of beaten gold. His grimy clothes had been
replaced by new finery of blue silk trimmed with silver
braid, and his golden hair was neatly drawn back from
his powdered face by a cloth ribbon. Two servants in
elegant kneecoats waited upon him, heaping his plate
with steaming delicacies and filling his cup with crimson wine. The nobleman sighed happily, then dug ravenously into the rich feast laid out before him.

Artek wondered if that was what life was like in
House Silvertor. Then the scene passed by, and
thoughts of the nobleman drifted from his mind. A
moment later he glimpsed Guss. The gargoyle sat
upon a greensward, surrounded by wildflowers.
Bathed in the warm light of an unseen sun, Guss
leaned contentedly against an oak tree. He plucked a
purple flower and held it beneath his muzzle, closing
his eyes in bliss as he breathed deeply.

Artek thought he should call out to Guss in greet-
ing, but Arcturia gently pulled him onward, and he
quickly forgot about the gargoyle. They passed an
archway through which Artek glimpsed a dim chamber. He could see Beckla standing before a wooden
workbench. Her face was intent as she ground colored powders with mortar and pestle, and combined
glittering potions in glass beakers. She held a cru-
cible over a candle's flame, and glowing blue smoke
billowed out to her evident satisfaction. It seemed
that she was researching a powerful new spell.

At last Arcturia brought him to a halt in front of a
wooden door. Again her voice whispered in his mind,
though her lips did not move. *Beyond this door you
will find all that you desire, Artek. Open it . . .*

The emerald-skinned woman seemed to fade away into the silvery light, leaving Artek alone. He gripped the brass doorknob. For a moment he hesitated, but it was as if he could not control his hand. A force was pulling him from the other side of the door. He opened it and stepped through.

"Father!" a clear voice cried. "You're home!"

A small form raced across the cozy, firelit room and flew into his arms. It all seemed so familiar. Artek found himself lifting the dark-haired boy into the air.

"You're getting big, Arneth!" he said. He was not sure how he knew the boy's name, but he was certain that the boy knew him.

"Yes, I am," the boy replied seriously. "What did you bring me?"

Artek reached into his pocket and pulled out a brown paper packet, though he could not remember putting it there. "I hope this will do."

Arneth took the packet and opened it. "Candy!" he exclaimed happily. "Thank you, Father!" The boy dashed away with his new treasure.

A pretty woman in a green dress set a steaming bowl down on a wooden table. She looked up and smiled, her sun-gold eyes glowing. "Your supper is ready, Artek."

Artek caught the woman in his arms and held her tightly. He felt lucky to have this warm home, bright son, and beautiful wife. It was all he had ever wanted in life. Why question things? He was going to enjoy it to the fullest. He glanced at the door through which Arneth had disappeared, then grinned broadly.

"It's not stew I'm hungry for," he said wickedly,

squeezing the woman tight.

She laughed, filling the air with a tinkling sound, like the ringing of a crystal bell. "Very well, husband," she said. "But there is something I must do first. Wait just a moment, and I will return."

She pushed him gently into a chair, brushed a soft finger against his lips, and disappeared through the door he had entered. Artek leaned back, sighing contentedly, dreaming of the pleasure that was to come.

"Artek!" a distant voice said. "Artek, pick me up! Please!"

The voice was so faint and hazy that he thought he had imagined it. He started to slip into his daydreams once more, but something nudged his foot. He looked down in surprise to see a skull on the floor, its jaw working frantically. For a moment he stared at the thing in amazement, but soon found himself bending down to pick it up.

"Artek!" The skull hopped madly in his hands. "It's me! Muragh! Wake up, you fool!"

Memory flooded back into Artek's mind. "Muragh," he gasped in surprise. "What are we doing here? Where are the others?"

"They're trapped in illusions, just like you are," the skull said urgently. "And let me tell you, rolling all the way here to warn you was not easy. You're all in terrible danger!"

"Danger?" Artek asked. "What do you mean? And what's all this about illusions?"

"Look through my eyes," the skull said. "Then you'll understand."

"What do you mean?"

"I'm not alive—illusions don't work on me," Muragh

explained hastily. "There's a crack in the back of my skull. If you look through it, you can see out of the holes in my eye sockets. The magic in my skull will filter out the illusions you perceive. Hurry!"

Artek still found himself unable to think clearly. He lifted the skull and, squinting, peered through the crack in the back of Muragh's cranium.

Artek stood in shock. Still gazing through the skull, he looked all around. No longer was he in a warm, firelit chamber. It was a room, all right, but the walls were covered with mold. There was no fireplace, no door in the wall through which Arneth had run. There was a table and chair, but both were rickety and worm-eaten. The chill truth crashed over him in a wave, and a pang of loss clutched his heart. It was an illusion—the house, the fire, Arneth, all of it. All of it, perhaps, except the woman.

"You said we were in danger, Muragh," he whispered intently.

"Arcturia isn't what she seems," the skull replied. "She plans to use you and the others as subjects for her experiments."

"Experiments?"

"Yes! I heard her talking to herself after she left you here. She plans to—"

The skull was interrupted by a clear voice from outside the door. "Here I come, husband," the voice purred. "I hope that you are ready."

Artek stared at Muragh in terror as the door began to open.

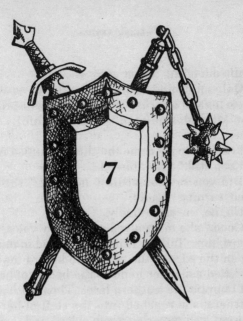

The Black Dart

The beautiful woman with sun-gold eyes stepped through the door, her green dress swishing softly. Artek smiled nervously, folding his hands behind his head and trying to lean back casually in the chair. Something sharp dug into the small of his back, and he grimaced in pain.

A faint shadow touched her smooth brow. "Is something wrong, my love?"

He forced a smile. "No, dearest. Only a passing sadness that you were away. But it has gone, now that you have returned."

Her red lips coiled into a pleased smile, and she turned to shut the door. As she did, Artek whispered quietly out of the corner of his mouth.

"Quit squirming, Muragh! You'll give us away." As Artek leaned against the skull to conceal it from view, Muragh's pointed jaw dug painfully into his spine.

"I can't help it," came the skull's muffled reply.

"Keep still!" Artek hissed.

"Did you say something, my love?" the woman asked, turning around.

"Uh, no," he said, loudly.

"Good," she murmured in a sultry voice, moving toward him. "Talking is not what I had in mind." Sitting on the edge of the table, she leaned toward him and lifted a slender hand to the bodice of her gown, as if to untie the leathern laces. Then, with startling swiftness, she reached into the cleft of her bosom, drew out a shimmering green object, and thrust it toward Artek's face. It was a tiny serpent with ruby eyes and emerald scales.

Artek grabbed her wrist and held it fast. The snake hissed, baring its fangs, mere inches from his face.

"Why do you resist me, my love?" the woman crooned, straining against his grip. Evil light flashed in her golden eyes.

"Because I do not care for poison snakes," Artek said through clenched teeth. He tightened his grip on her wrist.

"You judge me wrongly, my love," she countered. "This is a dreamserpent. Its bite will bring you only sleep, so that you will not feel pain as I transform your exquisite body."

"Transform?" Artek asked. "How?"

Strange exultation twisted her beautiful face. "You are strong, my love." She ran the fingers of her free hand down his cheek, his throat, his chest. "I could do much with you. You could bear it. I would give you the arms of an ogre, the claws of a lion, the scaled armor of a dragon, and the poison stinger of a scorpion." She trembled with excitement. "You would be utterly magnificent!"

She would make him a monster? Little did she know that he was *already* part monster. Crimson rage flared in his brain.

"I will be nothing for you, Arcturia!" he cried.

He leapt to his feet and slammed her hand—still clutching the dreamserpent—against the table. In one swift motion, he drew his dagger and plunged it downward. A shrill, inhuman scream pierced the air as Artek pinned the woman's hand to the table. Then the illusions that masked the chamber wavered and vanished, revealing the true nature of all within.

The beautiful woman was gone. Her skin was still emerald, but now it was composed of overlying scales, like those of the serpent. Wicked spurs of bone protruded from her elbows, her shoulders, and her knees. Instead of hair, a writhing mass of slimy black tentacles sprang from her head. Her wings were not a fairy's, but rather a foul insect's, and they buzzed spastically as she tugged to free her wounded hand. She shrieked again, baring long yellow fangs.

Apparently, Arcturia had made herself the subject of her own experiments.

Grabbing Muragh, Artek hurried through the door. No longer was the space beyond bathed in silvery radiance. The air was dank and murky, and fetid water streamed down the bare stone walls. The others were there, and they all looked up at Artek in shock and confusion. Beckla had not been experimenting with vials and beakers, but with broken sticks and dirty stones. Guss sat upon a heap of festering garbage, holding a clump of worms in his hand. And still in his grimy attire, Corin sat before a rickety table littered with cracked clay plates. The lord stared down at the bowl of putrid, black sludge he had been eagerly spooning up. His face went green.

"What . . . what happened?" Beckla asked, shaking her head.

"It was all an illusion," Artek explained. "Arcturia conjured visions from our fantasies in order to control us, so that she could use us for her experiments."

"Experiments?" Corin echoed in a quavering voice.

"I'll explain later," Artek said gruffly. "Right now we've got to get out of here."

He looked up at the stone archway through which they had entered the mad apprentice's lair. The gate flashed, and in it they saw the image of the chamber where they had dived into the dark pool. "Come on!" he shouted, urging the others toward the portal.

"Wait!" screamed a grating voice, bringing them to a halt. In dread they turned around. Arcturia stood before the open door of the side chamber, clutching her bleeding hand. "Stay!" she cried. "Don't you understand? I can make you beautiful. Like me!"

"We're leaving," Artek growled.

Rage and desire twisted her hideous visage. "If I cannot have you, then you will die!" she shrieked. Her golden eyes blazed malevolently as she clenched her wounded hand into a fist. Dark blood welled forth. Foul words of magic tumbled from her tongue, and the blood began to glow with scarlet force.

"The gate!" Artek shouted in alarm. "Now!"

They leapt for the portal just as Arcturia released her spell. Like a red serpent, deadly magic flashed from her wounded hand, speeding across the chamber to strike them down. Together, Artek and the others broke the gleaming surface of the gate. But just then, the image within flashed and changed. It was too late to stop. They fell through the gate as Arcturia's magic exploded behind them, shattering the archway. Screaming, they plunged down into nothingness.

* * * * *

Muragh said that six of Halaster's apprentices still lurked in Undermountain, Artek thought grimly. Just two more to go now.

He stared at the magical tattoo on his arm. Even as he watched, the wheel of dark ink moved slowly around the grinning death's head. The stylized sun had just passed the arrow. Somewhere far above— just how far he knew not—dawn was breaking over the city of Waterdeep. One whole day had passed already. He had only one more day to complete his mission. Only one more day to live.

He had found Corin Silvertor. That was something, at least. But they still had to escape from Undermountain, and it seemed they were farther from finding a way out than ever. A part of him wanted to give up, to lie down and die here in the darkness, but he was filled with rage at Darien Thal's betrayal. He could not quit, not now. The desire for revenge was too hot. Too strong. It would drive him on to the bitter end. He supposed he should be thankful for his orcish side, but it was that dark and feral part of him that had got him into this mess in the first place. He pulled down the sleeve of his jerkin, concealing the tattoo.

Artek surveyed his surroundings. Despite the murk, his darkvision let him see the rough walls of damp stone. The gate had dropped them into a natural tunnel of some sort, hewn by time and the flow of water. As quickly as it had appeared in midair, the sizzling gate had closed behind them. Neither Arcturia nor her crimson magic had followed them through the portal, but there was no telling where the gate had deposited them. For all they knew, they were deeper than ever in Undermountain.

In the darkness, he could make out the shapes of the others nearby. Corin lay curled in a ball, hands pillowing his head, snoring blissfully. Artek shook his head, wondering if the young nobleman truly understood the danger they were in. Maybe to Corin, this was all simply a grand adventure, like the fantastic tales told by a wandering minstrel. Artek almost envied the lord. Would that he himself had lived such a sheltered life, and knew the calm of such ignorance. But he had not, and he knew better.

Not far off, Guss kept watch in one direction down the tunnel, while Muragh rested on a rock facing the other direction. The gargoyle had cheerfully offered to stand sentry. "I've just woken up from a two-century long nap," he had explained.

Muragh, in contrast, had been less than cooperative. "I won't be able to talk to you if I'm that far away!" the skull had complained. That was precisely the idea. Artek had ignored Muragh's protests and set him down on a rocky perch to keep watch.

He could hear the skull faintly now, muttering to himself in wounded tones. In truth, Artek did not care for the idea of stopping to rest, but after the ordeal in Arcturia's lair, Corin had been swaying on his feet, and Beckla's face had been drawn and haggard. Much as he hated to admit it, Artek needed rest as well. Time was precious, but all the time in the world would do them no good if they dropped from exhaustion. However, he had not been able to find sleep as easily as Corin.

With a start, Artek realized that Beckla's sleeping form was no longer next to that of the nobleman. He heard a rustling sound behind him and turned to see the wizard approaching out of the shadows, a wisp of magelight bobbing above her head. She knelt beside him.

"I brought you some water," she said softly. "And something to eat."

He accepted both gratefully, only then realizing how thirsty and hungry he was. The water came from damp moss, which he squeezed over his open mouth. The moisture produced was musty and bitter, but cool against his parched tongue. Beckla broke a piece off of some sort of round loaf and handed it to Artek. The food was soft, rich, and slightly nutty. He ate it ravenously.

"Where did you find a loaf of bread?" he asked in amazement after finishing the last morsel.

"Actually, it's not bread," the wizard replied. A

weak grin touched her lips. "It's fungus."

Artek's eyes grew wide. He tried to spit out the last mouthful, but it was too late. Grimacing, he felt it slide down his throat and into his stomach. "You could have told me," he grumbled.

"Would you have enjoyed it so much if I had?" she asked.

"No," he was forced to admit.

Beckla broke off a piece of the fungus and popped it into her mouth. "It's really quite good. Besides, one can't be picky after living down here for a year. If it won't kill you, you eat it."

"Nice philosophy."

They were quiet as Beckla finished eating. Eventually Artek found himself gazing at Guss's dark form. The gargoyle stood as still as stone, gazing down the corridor.

"He can't be as good as he seems," Artek said quietly.

Beckla looked up in surprise. "You mean Guss?"

Artek nodded. "Guss said it himself—he was created to be a creature of evil. How can we be certain he won't suddenly turn on us?"

Beckla sat cross-legged, arranging her tattered shirt and smudged vest. "It's not how you're born that matters," the wizard replied firmly. "It's what you do with yourself. That's all that really counts."

Bitter laughter escaped Artek's throat. "Is that so?" he sneered. "Then why did the Magisters throw me in the Pit for a crime I didn't commit?" He did not let her answer, but went on. "I'll tell you why. It was because they knew orcish blood runs in my veins. In their eyes I was born part monster, and thus a monster I am bound to be." He shook his head ruefully. "And maybe they were right. Maybe I never will be anything else."

Beckla was silent for a long moment. Finally she gave his clothes a critical look. "Have you ever considered wearing something besides black?" she asked.

"What's the matter with black?" he asked defensively. "It's a very dignified color."

"It's a well-known fact that only evil people wear black," Beckla replied. "You might consider trying white for a change. It could do wonders for your image."

Artek let out a dubious snort. "I'll keep it in mind," he muttered. "So what about you? What's your unattainable dream? Back in Arcturia's realm, I saw you working happily with potions and powders—at least, you thought you were."

Beckla was silent for a moment. At last she held out her hand. The shimmering wisp of magelight floated down to hover above her hand. She moved her fingers, and the glowing puff danced, changing from blue to green to yellow and back to blue again. Abruptly she waved her hand, and the light vanished. She reached out, motioning as if pulling something from behind Artek, and the wisp of magelight appeared in her hand once more.

"That's a fancy trick," Artek said, impressed.

Beckla released the light, and it floated above her head once more. "But that's all it is," she said ruefully. "A trick. A ruse to entertain commoners and simpletons, and nothing more." She bit her lower lip, staring away into the darkness, then finally turned to regard Artek with her deep brown eyes. "I'm a small-time wizard, Ar'talen. I know a few real spells, and I can fake a dozen more. But I can't do anything more than a thousand other would-be wizards can. Do you know what real mages, so mighty in their high towers and mystic laboratories, call people like me?" She shook her head in disgust. "Runts. That's what they say when they see us. If they bother to look our way at all."

"You're good enough to have survived in this maze for a year," Artek offered.

But Beckla's eyes grew distant, as if she had not heard. "Just once I'd like to be the mage in the tower," she whispered. "I would learn the deepest, most powerful spells, discover the mysteries of the most ancient artifacts, and create new magic the like of which no one has ever seen." She shook her head fiercely. "But even if I dwelled in the highest tower, I would not look down on those outside. I would open my doors to all the so-called runts. I would welcome them into my study, and teach them real magic, so they would never again have to hang their heads in shame when another mage walked by!"

Only then did she realize that she had clenched her hands into fists. She fell silent, forcing her fingers to relax.

"You'd give anything for that, wouldn't you?" Artek asked softly.

She swallowed hard and suddenly looked away, as if his words had cut her somehow.

"We should be going," she said. "I'll wake Corin." She swiftly stood and walked away, leaving Artek to stare after her.

Artek told Guss that they were ready to move on, then went to retrieve Muragh. He returned to find Corin happily munching on a piece of something soft and white.

"What is this food that Beckla found?" the lord asked with his mouth full. "It's absolutely delicious!"

Artek held in a smile. "I think it's some kind of bread."

"I'll have to get the recipe," Corin said as he popped the last bite into his mouth.

They were all ready, and Artek considered which way to go. The tunnel looked the same in either direction: jagged stone walls, damp floor, and stalactites hanging like teeth from the ceiling. It was Guss who had an answer.

"Can't you hear it?" the gargoyle asked, cupping a clawed hand to his pointed ear. "There must be an underground river down there somewhere."

Artek took a few steps forward and cocked his head, listening. He could barely hear a faint rushing noise, and new hope glimmered in his heart. All rivers, even those underground, must eventually run into the sea. This just might be the way out they were looking for.

"Good work, Guss," he said, giving the gargoyle an affectionate slap on the back. Immediately he regretted the action—the creature's spiky hide *hurt*. He clutched his stinging hand.

"Sorry about that," Guss said sheepishly.

"My fault." Artek winced. "I forgot that you're made out of stone." He shook his hand, and the pain dulled to a throb. "Now let's get moving."

Artek led the way down the tunnel, holding

Muragh in the crook of his arm. Beckla followed on his heels, her magelight floating above her head. Corin came next, and Guss brought up the rear, keeping watch on the darkness behind. Before long the water on the floor became a swift-flowing rivulet. They were heading down—always down, cursed Artek inwardly.

The sound of running water grew steadily louder, until it thrummed off the stone walls. Soon a damp spray drifted in the air, cool against their cheeks. They rounded a sharp bend in the tunnel, and the voice of the river became a thundering roar. A vast space opened before them. Beneath their feet stretched a steep, rock-strewn slope, and at the bottom raced a broad expanse of dark, frothy water. Beckla's blue magelight glinted off the onyx surface of the subterranean waterway.

"This must be the River Sargauth!" Muragh exclaimed, practically leaping from Artek's hands as his jaw opened and shut in excitement.

"The Sargauth?" Artek asked.

Muragh managed to approximate a nod. "It has to be. Only the Sargauth could be this large. According to all the stories I've heard, it winds its way through the middle levels of Undermountain until it joins up with Skullport, the pirate city hidden in the sea caves that border Waterdeep Harbor. Once it passes through Skullport, the Sargauth flows out into the harbor."

A thrill raced through Artek's mind. If the skull was right, then the river could be their means of escape. "How do you know all this, Muragh?" he demanded.

"Is it the orc in you that makes you so positively dense?" the skull asked testily. "Remember, I spent a good deal of time floating in Waterdeep Harbor before the mermen found me. I know every underwater rock and cave in that big puddle."

"And I'm sure you'd tell us about every one if we give you half a chance," Artek said with a snort. Before Muragh could reply, he gripped the skull's mandible, holding it tightly shut. Ignoring Muragh's muffled grunts, he gazed at the dark river. Here was a road to freedom. All they had to do was figure out how to travel it. "We need to find a way to float on the river, to let it carry us out of this maze," he murmured, more to himself than the others.

Apparently Corin heard his words. "Er, how about if we use that?" the nobleman asked tentatively. As one, the others followed Corin's pointing hand. Beckla quickly raised her magelight higher. Artek let out an oath.

It was a ship.

The ship rested by the shore of the river nearest to them, caught on a jagged spur of rock that jutted up from the dark waters of the Sargauth. It was a two-masted schooner, small, sleek, and highly maneuverable. Such crafts were a common and much-feared sight along the Sword Coast, for they were favored by pirates for their speed and agility. By the look of it, this ship had been trapped here for many years. The remnants of the sails hung listlessly from the masts in gray shreds like cobwebs. Most of the rigging had rotted and snapped, and blotches of black mold covered the hull like some leprous disease. The ship listed precariously to the starboard side, pressed against the rocks by the swift-moving current of the river. However, there was no breach visible in the hull. If the ship could be freed from the rocks, it might yet be seaworthy.

Artek scrambled down the slick slope to the bank of the river, and the others followed quickly behind. Upon close examination he saw that the rocks had indeed punched a hole in the hull, near the prow of the ship. However, the gap was small and, at present, above the surface of the river. If its makers had known their craft, the ship would still be dry inside. True, once it was righted, the hole would be below the surface. Yet the ship likely could sail some distance before it took on enough water to founder, maybe even far enough to reach the sea. Dim but still visible, the ship's name was painted across the prow: *The Black Dart*.

Artek smacked a fist against his palm. "This is it. This is our way out, I'm sure of it. All we have to do is find a way to free the ship."

Beckla crossed her arms, surveying the vessel. "Easier said than done. I imagine her crew tried their best to free her from the rocks, and *they* couldn't manage it. A ship like this would have a score or two of sailors aboard. I don't know how the four of us could succeed where forty failed before."

"You mean the *five* of us!" Muragh corrected indignantly.

Artek squatted down, studying the ship. The wizard was right, of course. No doubt *The Black Dart*'s crew had indeed tried to free her. An image drifted to mind of the pirate schooner laden with booty, its crew rough and merry, as it evaded the tall ships of Waterdeep's Harbor Watch. It sailed into a cave, meaning to hide in the underground waterways until the coast was clear. When the captain finally ordered them to sail back down the Sargauth, they found they were caught on the dark rocks, which their lookout had missed in the gloom. Despite their struggles, the ship remained caught between river and rock, like a piece of metal between hammer and anvil.

Artek wondered what had become of the crew. Had they jumped ship, hoping the chill waters of the Sargauth would carry them back to lighted lands? Or had they remained here in the dark, dying slowly of starvation and madness? He shivered, forcing the latter thought from his mind. No crew of sailors would choose to remain here, he told himself. Not unless they were ordered to by their captain. And even then they would probably mutiny. But it hardly mattered—Artek saw no point in exploring the ship. They probably would never be able to free it.

He stood up with a sigh. "Maybe there's no use in wasting our time here," he said glumly.

"Actually, I might be able to arrange something," Guss said. The others stared at the gargoyle in surprise. "I have a way with stone," the monster explained with a toothy grin. "I was conjured from it, after all." He pointed to the boulders that trapped the ship. "I'll go have a talk with those rocks over there. The rest of you get ready, just in case it works." The others exchanged curious looks as Guss wandered over toward the rocks.

The aft section of *The Black Dart* lay only a few feet from the shore, and its deck was tilted in their direction. With a running leap, Artek launched himself

into the air and managed to grab the edge of the deck.
With a grunt, he flexed his arms, heaving himself up
and onto the deck. He searched until he found a bit of
rope that seemed only slightly rotted. Looping it
around the aft mast, he threw the end over the side to
haul Beckla and Corin up. Moments later, the two
stood beside him on the slanted deck, Muragh
clutched tight in Corin's white-knuckled hands. Neither nobleman nor skull had appreciated being
hauled up like so much cargo.

"Hold on, Guss!" Artek called out above the roar of
the river. "We should look around first before we try
anything!"

The gargoyle, squatting on the jagged spur of rock
that trapped *The Black Dart*, waved up at the others
on the deck. Figuring that Guss had heard and understood, they turned to look for an entrance into the
ship's hold.

But the din of the river had drowned out Artek's
words, and Guss mistook his call as a signal to pro-
ceed. He knelt atop the slick heap of boulders, and
stroked the rocks with a hand, almost an affectionate gesture. He seemed to whisper to the stones.

All at once, the massive boulders shifted. Leathery wings flapping, Guss rose into the air, hovering
above the outcrop. There was a low groan, and a
shudder vibrated through the schooner. Guss gestured toward the bank, and the rocks shifted again,
rolling toward the edge of the river. As they did, the
ship gave a violent jerk.

Artek, Beckla, and Corin stumbled wildly, grabbing at railing, mast, or post to keep from being
flung overboard. Timbers creaking, the ship began to

right itself. The deck rose beneath their feet, became level, and continued to roll, tilting alarmingly to the port side. They screamed as they were tossed again. Artek feared the schooner was going to capsize, throwing them into the icy waters of the river. However, a moment later the ship rebounded, rolling back in the other direction. When it became level again, the schooner wobbled, then finally stabilized on its keel.

With a grating sound, the ship slid past the rocks that had blocked its way. Dark water swirled around its hull as the schooner drifted out into the swift center current of the river. A damp breeze tugged at the tattered sails. Artek let out a cry of surprise—they were moving.

"Guss!" he called, as the gargoyle settled onto the deck, stubby wings flapping. "I told you to wait!"

The gargoyle slumped. "Oh, dear! I must have misunderstood. I'm sorry."

Beckla smiled. "Oh, it's all right—we're moving now, and that's what counts. How *did* you get those stones to shift, anyway?"

Guss shrugged his massive shoulders. "I just asked them if they would mind moving a few feet to the side, that's all. Rocks are really very cooperative, as long as you're polite."

Beckla stared with mouth agape, clearly unsure how to respond. For his part, Artek didn't really care how Guss had managed to move the rocks, or even that the gargoyle hadn't listened. Beckla was right—the ship was free, and that was all that mattered.

Beckla tossed her glowing magelight into the air. The blue wisp rose to the top of the foremast, hovering there to cast its light over the ship. Rough walls of stone slipped rapidly by as the schooner sailed down the Sargauth.

"Do you think the crew drowned?" Beckla asked. The deck was empty except for a few weathered crates and barrels, with no sign of the pirates who had once manned the schooner.

"They must have abandoned the ship once it got stuck," Artek said. "I certainly would have. Maybe their bodies are strewn about the maze. Or maybe they're at the bottom of the Sargauth."

"Now *this* is an adventure!" Corin exclaimed merrily.

Without warning, the schooner lurched roughly to one side. Artek grabbed for a worm-eaten railing, barely managing to keep his feet. He turned around, then swore hotly. Corin stood at the prow of the schooner, hands on the ship's wheel. As Artek watched, the nobleman whistled cheerfully and spun the wheel around. The ship lurched in the other direction, drifting dangerously near the cavern wall.

Artek stumbled forward. "Give me that!" he said, pushing the surprised lord away. Artek carefully turned the wheel, bringing the rudder back to center. The ship steadied, sailing down the middle of the river once more.

"Were you actively trying to dash this ship against the walls of the cavern?" Artek growled angrily.

"I was only trying to steer," Corin replied in a small voice.

"Leave the wheel alone. Go over to those old crates and sit down. And don't touch anything else!"

The nobleman nodded silently, then hung his head. He trudged toward the crates and sat with a sigh, staring at the deck. For a moment, Artek wondered if he had been too harsh with Corin. The lord was young, after all, and had only meant to help. Finally, Artek shook his head. He had other things to worry about.

Moving to the rear of the ship, he examined the aft mast. The sails were rotted and rent with holes, but they might manage to hold some air. A stiff wind blew down the cavern in the same direction as the river's current. If they could position the sails right, they might add a little of the wind's speed to the river's, making their progress swifter.

"Beckla, come help me for a moment," Artek said. As she approached, he pointed to a horizontal boom. "If we move this cross-mast, we might be able to catch some wind in the sails."

Beckla nodded and gripped the boom.

Artek turned around to untie a frayed rope. "Now push when I say—" His words turned into a cry as the boom struck the back of his head with a resounding crack.

"Oops," said Beckla.

Artek spun around to glare at the wizard, rubbing the back of his head. A painful lump was already starting to rise. "You know, I'm really starting to get tired of hearing you say that."

Before she could reply, the ship suddenly tilted to the side again, nearly sending them sprawling to the deck. Artek looked up to see a figure standing before the ship's wheel.

"Corin!" he shouted angrily, marching forward. "Didn't I tell you to keep your hands off that wheel? Now get away from the—"

His words faltered as he saw the lord look up in
pale-faced surprise from his seat on the old crates. If
Corin wasn't steering the ship, who stood at the
wheel?

As if to answer the question, the figure turned
around and grinned. Artek's blood froze. The thing
was clad in grubby breeches and a loose, tattered
shirt that once might have been white. A grimy red
scarf covered its head, and a curved cutlass hung
from its cracked leather belt. It was a pirate, clearly
long dead. Its bloated flesh was wet and rotted, and
one eyeball dangled loosely from the socket. The
sickly reek of decay drifted thickly through the air.
Even as Artek watched, a chunk of putrid flesh
dropped from the pirate's arm, falling to the deck
with a nauseating *plop*.

"Artek, I think you'd better turn around," Guss
said grimly.

Reluctantly, Artek tore his eyes from the undead
pirate. He turned to see a trapdoor opening in the
deck of the ship. More pirates climbed out, shambling as they spread across the deck. Artek counted
ten of them, then twenty, then thirty, and still they
kept coming. All wore rusted cutlasses at their hips.
And all of them were quite dead.

The crew of *The Black Dart* had not abandoned
the ship after all.

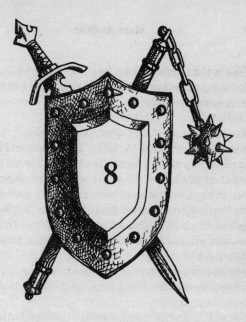

River of Death

Dropping stray gobbets of rotten flesh, the zombie pirates shuffled toward them.

Artek heard a wet, squelching sound and glanced over his shoulder. Panic clutched at his heart. More half-decomposed zombies clambered out of a trap-door near the prow of the schooner. The scent of decay wafted in the air, thick and choking. Clutching Muragh, Corin stumbled hastily toward Artek, Beckla and Guss close on his heels. Back to back, they all huddled together in a tight knot, staring in horror at the approaching zombies.

"There must be at least forty of them," Artek said.

"Sometimes I hate being right," the wizard sighed.

"Well, this time your guess was dead on."

"Must you use that word, Ar'talen?" Corin asked in a squeaking voice.

"What word?" Artek demanded.

The nobleman swallowed hard. "Dead."

There was no time to reply. The zombies closed in, trapping them in a foul circle. Beckla raised her hands, ready to cast a spell. Guss extended sharp onyx claws. Corin tossed down Muragh and drew his slim rapier in trembling hands. Artek's fingers brushed the hilt of the saber at his hip. He hated to draw the cursed weapon, knowing that once he did he would not be able to stop fighting until all the zombies were destroyed—or he joined them in death.

The pirates shuffled to a halt not a half-dozen paces away, exuding a noisome reek, and then one of their number shambled forward. By its tattered red kneecoat and the gold earring dangling from its moldy ear, Artek guessed that this zombie had been in life the captain of *The Black Dart*. A decomposed parrot missing most of its feathers still perched on the captain's shoulder, clinging with skeletal claws to the tarnished epaulets of the captain's coat.

"Aaawk!" the bird gurgled. "Stooowaways, cap-taaaain!"

"Aaaye, sooo theeey beee," the captain replied in a slurred voice. Writhing worms dropped from the zombie's festering lips. "Aaand yooou knooow whaaat weee dooo wiiith suuuch laaandlubbers."

"Aaawk!" the parrot cried again. "Waaalk the plaaank! Waaalk the plaaank! Waaalk the pl—" The bird's bubbling cries ended abruptly as its rotted beak fell off.

The captain pointed a bloated arm toward a group of about ten pirates. "Yooou. Taaake theeese stooowaways tooo theee plaaank. Theee reeest ooof yooou looouts, maaan yooour staaations!"

Artek and the others watched in grisly fascination as the zombie pirates shuffled off to reenact the tasks they had performed in life. A dozen pirates climbed clumsily into the ship's rigging. Several promptly fell back down to the deck, landing with wet, nauseating thuds, then lurched to their feet to try again. Other zombies began swabbing the deck with ragged mops. They made little progress, for every time they cleaned an area to their satisfaction, a gobbet of their own putrid flesh dropped to the deck and had to be wiped up. Still other undead pirates manned the schooner's booms and lines.

"Look out!" Corin cried in terror.

They ducked just in time to avoid a whistling boom as it swung overhead. One of the nearby zombies was not so quick. The cross-mast struck it in the forehead, and its cranium burst apart like an overripe melon.

"That's got to hurt," Muragh winced.

The zombie captain shambled toward the ship's wheel. "Ooout ooof myyy waaay," it groaned to the pirate who had been piloting the ship. The sailor tried to let go of the wheel but was too slow. The captain pushed it roughly aside. With a rending sound, the sailor's arms tore off at the shoulder and dangled from the wheel by their still-gripping hands. The armless zombie tottered away, its shoulders dripping yellow ichor. Disregarding the severed limbs, the captain grabbed the wheel and began steering. The schooner lurched wildly to the left, then gave a violent jerk, hull groaning, as the keel scraped against an underwater boulder.

Beckla and Corin both grabbed hold of Artek to keep from being thrown to the deck.

"Is that thing deliberately trying to run this ship onto the rocks?" Beckla cried.

"Probably," Artek answered grimly. "But I don't think it's just the captain. Can't you hear it? The roar of the river is getting louder. I think we're approaching rapids of some sort."

"Oh, wonderful," Beckla groaned. "This creaky old ship will be dashed to bits."

"I think we have an even more immediate concern," Corin gulped.

The ten zombies that had remained surrounded them, grabbing them with cold, damp hands.

"Tooo theee plaaank," one of them moaned, its breath a fetid exhalation of rot.

"Get your clammy paws off of me!" Beckla snapped. "I'll walk on my own!" She jerked her arm away from the zombie that held her, then gagged. The zombie's hand had broken off and continued to clutch her arm. With a cry of disgust, she shook off the putrid hand. It fell to the deck and scuttled away like a drunken spider.

The zombies shoved them forward, leading them toward the port side of the ship. They stopped before a rickety wooden plank that protruded from the deck over the rushing waters of the Sargauth. Artek saw that the river was indeed giving way to rapids. The swift waters broke and frothed upon sharp spurs of stone. Once again the schooner jerked and shuddered, its timbers groaning alarmingly.

They stood in a tight knot before the plank. Behind them the zombie pirates drew corroded cutlasses, barring any avenue of escape.

"Maybe we'll be better off in the river than aboard the ship," Corin murmured hopefully.

Beckla eyed the violent waters below, then shook her head. "We'd never survive the river. If we didn't freeze to death first, we'd be dashed against the rocks."

"Excuse me," Guss whispered. "I have a plan. I know it's terribly rude of me, but would you mind if I went first to the plank? These fellows don't seem very bright, what with their rotten brains and all. I don't think they've noticed my wings."

Artek stared at Guss in astonishment. Even in an emergency, the gargoyle was exceedingly polite. However, he had time for nothing more than a nod. One of the zombies brandished its cutlass menacingly.

"Aaall riiight," the pirate droned in its mushy voice. "Whooo's fiiirst?"

Guss raised a clawed hand. "That'll be me," he said cheerfully. "Be ready," he whispered to the others, then stepped onto the plank. The undead pirate followed after him, poking him with the cutlass, urging the gargoyle on. Finally, Guss ran out of plank. With a cry, he dropped down and disappeared into the gloom below. The pirate slowly turned around, grinning. Several yellowed teeth dropped from its rotting gums. "Neeext?" the pirate asked.

Before the others could react, a dark form rose suddenly from below and struck the underside of the plank. With a look of dull surprise, the zombie pirate bounced into the air, then plunged downward to be swallowed by the roaring waters of the Sargauth. Wings beating frantically, Guss rose higher into the air.

"Now!" the gargoyle cried to the others, green eyes glowing ferally.

Artek did not need to be told twice. While the remaining zombies gaped in dim-witted astonishment, he drew his saber and leapt forward, swinging. The sharp blade bit deeply into rotten meat, cleaving a pirate in twain. The two halves of the zombie fell wetly to the deck, twitched, then ceased moving. Directly behind him, Beckla shouted a harsh word of magic. Blue energy sprang from her fingertips and engulfed one of the zombies. It let out a shrill scream as its putrid flesh sizzled and bubbled, then it exploded in a spray of foul gobbets.

"I think you overcooked that one, Beckla," Artek said in disgust, wiping bits of rotten meat from his face.

"Sorry," the wizard replied, shaking shreds of zombie from her clothes.

Though slow of thought, the seven remaining pirates had finally realized they were under attack. Raising their rusty cutlasses, they lurched forward. Artek raised the cursed saber, suddenly finding himself facing three of the creatures. Their blows were slow and clumsy, but they outnumbered him, and he was barely able to counter their swings. Two zombies trudged toward Beckla. She managed to roast one with another spell, then the other closed in. There was no more time for magic. She drew a small knife from her belt and dodged the swing of the pirate's notched blade. With a roar, Guss swooped down, plucked up one of the zombies assailing Artek, and tore it to shreds in midair. Artek momentarily froze, startled by the gargoyle's sudden ferocity.

Then a cry of fear caught his attention. Artek parried several blows, then turned his head and saw Corin backing toward the rickety railing of the deck as a pair of zombies advanced on him. Artek tried to dodge the two pirates before him, but they blocked the way. He couldn't get to Corin. If the foolish lord died, then their battle was in vain.

Corin nudged against the ship's railing and could go no farther. Leering hatefully, the two shambling corpses closed in on the nobleman. Shaking in fear, Corin thrust his rapier before him, gripping the hilt with both hands. He squeezed his eyes shut, clenched his jaw, then proceeded to wave the sword in a fancy and ridiculously embellished maneuver—no doubt learned from some foppish fencing master who had never faced a real enemy in his life. The slim rapier whistled through the air, nearly invisible as Corin slashed, circled, and thrust with a bad actor's flamboyance. Finally he lowered the sword and cracked his eyes. The zombies only grinned, apparently unaffected by his efforts. They raised their cutlasses.

As they did, the sword hand of one of the zombies fell off, sliced clean at the wrist. The undead pirate gaped at the oozing stump in mindless confusion. A moment later, its entire arm fell off at the shoulder. Then its nose slipped from its face, followed by an ear. Then all at once, the zombie fell apart into a score of neatly sliced pieces that tumbled quivering to the deck. Corin stared at his rapier in amazement.

Though only four zombies remained, things still looked ill. Corin's second foe was too close for the nobleman to try another fancy maneuver. Beckla's knife was proving to be no match for the cutlass of the pirate who faced her. Still fending off the blows of a zombie on either side, Artek was unable to make headway against either. Guss hovered in midair, uncertain which of his companions most needed his help. There was time to aid only one.

At that moment the schooner was swept into churning rapids. The ship lurched violently toward starboard, then a half-second later tilted toward the port side again. Corin fell sprawling on all fours. His foe clumsily tripped over him, flipped head over heels, broke through the railing, and tumbled overboard. The zombie facing Beckla lurched forward, impaling itself on her outthrust knife. She spun to the side, jerking her blade out of its body, and the pirate fell flailing over the side of the ship. Artek managed to keep his feet planted on the heaving deck and took advantage of the confusion, severing the head from one of his flailing opponents.

Now that only one zombie remained, Guss did not hesitate. The gargoyle swooped down from above and plucked up the last of the ten pirates. Clutching the creature in midair, he raked the pirate's belly with his hind claws. Entrails spilled out like dark snakes, but the zombie was not defeated. It swung its cutlass blindly. The rusted metal bit into the flesh of Guss's shoulder, then shattered. Guss let out a cry of pain as brilliant green blood streamed down his arm. He clenched his clawed hands, rending the zombie in two, then flung the still-squirming halves into the raging waters of the river.

Breathing hard, Artek looked around. The rest of the zombie crew still went mindlessly about their various tasks, taking no notice that their undead shipmates had been destroyed, or that the prisoners were now free. The cursed saber jerked in his hands, tugging him toward the nearest zombies. Forcibly, he tried to sheathe the magical blade, his face twisting with effort. The muscles of his arms rippled and bulged, but it was no use—he could not release the saber. As long as there were zombies remaining, the cursed blade would force him to fight. The sword pulled him another step toward the nearest pirates.

"I can't resist the saber much longer," he said through clenched teeth. "And I have a bad feeling that as soon as I attack one of the zombies, the rest of them will come after us."

"You're probably right," Beckla agreed somberly, slipping her bloody knife beneath her belt. "I'll help you keep your ground."

"No, stay back!" cried Artek. "I might hit you with the saber. That goes for all of you—keep away!"

"Where's Guss?" Corin asked as he climbed to his feet.

"Here I am!" a rumbling voice called from above. Stubby wings beating up a stiff breeze, Guss dropped down from the darkness and settled onto the rolling deck.

Beckla moved quickly toward him, concern in her brown eyes. "Guss, you're hurt!" She examined the ragged wound on his arm. Bits of dirt and rust were embedded in the cut, and it already looked as if it were beginning to fester. "We need to clean this wound now. There's no telling what filth was on that zombie's sword."

Guss wiped the sweat from his brow with a clawed

hand. "There's no time."

"What's going on?" Artek demanded, straining
against the pull of the saber. His boots skidded on
the slimy planks as he slid another foot forward.
Once again the ship tilted wildly to the side, then
slowly righted itself.

"While you were recovering, I flew ahead of the
ship to scout out the rapids," Guss explained quickly.
The others listened in growing dread as the gargoyle
described what he had seen. "We're in the worst of
the rapids now—it doesn't get any rougher than this.
I think we can make it. But up ahead, the cavern
and the river both divide. Down the right-hand passage, the waters grow calmer."

"And down the left?" Beckla asked nervously.

Guss's long pause was as terrifying as the words
that followed. "Farther down the left-hand passage,
there's a great roar. The river drops over a huge
waterfall. I don't know how high the falls are." The
gargoyle licked his scaly lips with a green tongue. "I
couldn't see the bottom in the dark."

Artek swore, still fighting the saber's pull. "The
captain has been keeping the ship to the left side of
the cavern. He must be steering *The Black Dart* toward the waterfall."

"But why?" Corin asked fearfully. "The ship will
be broken to bits."

"Why not?" Beckla replied. "The captain's already
dead. What does he have to lose?"

Artek racked his brain until he hit upon a plan. It
was not elegant—hardly the level of the crafty thieving jobs he had executed in the past—but it was all
he could come up with. He struggled against the

murderous will of the cursed saber. He had to remain in control only a few moments more, and then the blade could do its work.

"Guss," he gasped. "Fly ahead of the ship and keep watch on our progress. Call out when we're near the fork in the river. Beckla, Corin—try to find a way to distract the crew. Use your imaginations! Anything you can do to gain their attention without getting yourself killed will work."

"But what are you going to do?" Beckla asked urgently.

"I'm going to try to convince the captain to change our course."

With that, they set to their tasks. Guss rose into the air, wings flapping. He disappeared into the gloom ahead, though not before the others saw him grimace in pain and clutch at the wound on his arm. Grunting with effort, Artek managed to turn and point the quivering saber toward the prow of the ship. The zombie captain stood before the wheel, spinning it wildly as *The Black Dart* careened down the rapids.

"There," Artek whispered fiercely. "That is our enemy. That is the one we must slay."

To his wonder and relief, the saber seemed to understand his words. It jumped in his hands, ignoring the other zombies, and pulled him toward the pirate captain. This time Artek did not resist. He let the saber lead him toward the prow. It was time to stage a mutiny.

* * * * *

Beckla rummaged through a heap of crates, barrels, and assorted refuse. There had to be something here that would help them.

What are you doing, Beckla? cried a voice in her head. *This wasn't part of the deal. They're as good as dead. You should use it now!*

"There's still time," she muttered under her breath.

"Time for what, Beckla?" Corin asked. The nobleman stood nearby, wringing his hands.

Beckla swore inwardly. She was getting careless. That was the surest way to get herself killed. And getting killed was definitely not the point of this exercise.

"There's still time to help Artek," she said firmly.

Beckla flipped open the lid of an old chest. It was filled with rusted fishing gear, none of it worthwhile. She started to let the lid drop back down when two objects caught her eye. She looked up at Corin.

"Can you shoot a bow?" she asked quickly.

The young lord shrugged. "I studied archery as a lad, as all nobles do." A wan smile crossed his pale visage. "I wasn't half bad, if I do say so myself. Why do you ask?"

"This is why." Beckla pulled a short bow and a quiver of arrows from the chest and thrust them toward a surprised Corin. The weapon was old, but the bowstring had been wrapped in oiled leather and was still sound. The arrows were rusted at the tip, and their shafts were warped, but they would do.

Beckla grabbed a handful of greasy rags and handed them to the nobleman. "Tear these into strips and tie them around the tips of the arrows."

While the lord did as she instructed, Beckla pulled a small wooden cask out of the chest. Liquid sloshed within, and she hoped the brand on the side meant what she thought it did. With her knife, she pried the cork out of the top of the cask, then bent down to take a sniff. Her head reeled as a sharp, spicy warmth filled her lungs. It was rum, all right—potent stuff, by the smell of it. Taking a deep breath to clear her head, she recalled the words of a spell.

Whispering in the arcane language of magic, Beckla weaved her hands over the cask of pirate rum. A blue aura shimmered around the cask as it slowly levitated off the deck. Guided by the motions of her hands, the cask drifted through the air. A sheen of sweat broke out on Beckla's brow. This was the most difficult spell she knew, and if it failed, she could not try it again. She moved her fingers in intricate patterns, weaving invisible threads of magic. It was all she could do to keep the enchantment from unraveling.

As she concentrated, the cask floated over the head of a zombie swabbing the deck. Beckla twitched her fingers, and the cask tipped, dousing the zombie with a cupful of rum. Heedless of the liquid, the mindless creature continued to lurch about its task. Beckla weaved her hands, and the cask floated toward another zombie. Once again it tipped, pouring dark rum onto the undead pirate, soaking its rotten clothes. As she continued, Beckla tightened her control over the spell, and the cask flew more swiftly through the air, dousing zombie after zombie with the reeking spirits. Finally, the cask was empty. With a groan, Beckla released the spell. Her head throbbed with the effort, but there had been enough rum to douse only half of the zombies. She hoped it would be enough.

"Now what?" Corin asked in puzzlement. He

gripped the bow and a rag-wrapped arrow.

Beckla pointed a finger at the arrow and said, "*Urshak!*" Instantly the tip of the arrow burst into flame. Corin almost dropped the bow in shock, but a stern look from Beckla made him tighten his grip. "Start shooting," she ordered sharply.

Corin raised the bow, pulled back on the string, aimed at a zombie perched in the rigging above, and released. The flaming arrow traced a crimson arc through the air, then plunged directly into the center of the zombie's chest. For a second the pirate stared stupidly at the burning arrow embedded in its body. Then, all at once, the zombie burst into crimson flame. Limbs waving spastically, the undead pirate fell from its perch and plunged to the deck below, exploding in a spray of charred flesh.

Beckla allowed herself a smile of dark satisfaction. The pirate rum was highly flammable, and made an excellent fuel.

"Keep shooting, Corin!" she shouted.

The startled lord lifted another arrow, and Beckla set it afire with a magical command. Corin released the arrow, and another writhing zombie was engulfed in a pillar of searing flame. The bow twanged again and again as Corin released a barrage of flaming arrows. The nobleman had not exaggerated his skill. His aim was perfect, and not a single arrow missed its mark. In moments more than a dozen zombies were ablaze, stumbling around the ship, sending up pillars of black smoke like foul torches.

Many of the burning zombies tumbled overboard, just as Beckla had hoped. However, some of them ran into heaps of old crates or rotten sailcloth and set the materials alight. Other zombies moved haltingly to stamp out the new fires. However, even without being doused with rum, their dry, tattered clothes were flammable enough, and they only succeeded in setting themselves ablaze and stumbling off to start still more fires. Several burning zombies became entangled in the ship's rigging, and in moments flame licked up both of the schooner's masts.

Corin shot Beckla a look of sudden fear. "I think your plan worked better than you thought it would."

"So it seems," Beckla replied dryly. She looked at the rapidly growing fires, wondering if she had just succeeded in getting herself killed after all.

* * * * *

Gripping the tingling hilt of the cursed saber, Artek stealthily approached the undead pirate captain. The zombie stood before the wheel of the ship, steering wildly, his back to Artek. As the wheel spun, *The Black Dart* tilted alarmingly to starboard. Just when it seemed the ship would capsize, the captain spun the wheel in the opposite direction, and the ship lurched back to port, running dangerously close to the left side of the subterranean cavern. A deep, throbbing roar now mingled with the frothy voice of the river. It could be only one thing: the waterfall.

Artek continued to creep silently toward the captain. He needed just one uncontested swing to lop off the zombie's moldy head, and the ship's wheel would be free. Just a few more paces. Artek raised the cursed saber. Scarlet light flickered down its edge.

Without warning, the decomposed parrot on the

captain's shoulder turned its head. Its dead black
eyes saw Artek, and the parrot opened its beakless
mouth in a muffled squawk of alarm. Artek swore
under his breath. The blasted, worm-eaten bird! He
sprang forward, hoping to make his swing, but it was
too late.

The zombie captain turned with surprising speed
and raised its rusted cutlass, blocking Artek's blow.
Artek grunted as a jolt of pain ran up his arm. He
stumbled backward, then caught himself. The captain was stronger than the other zombies, and
seemed somewhat less decomposed. Perhaps it had
been the last to die, hoarding the ship's dwindling
food supplies while the rest of the crew perished one
by one. Regardless, Artek now stood before a foe who
would not be as easily defeated as the others.

Artek crouched warily, looking for an opening. He
feinted left, trying to draw the captain's attack in
that direction. However, such subtle moves were
quite lost upon the rotten-brained zombie. Utterly
ignoring the feint, the captain charged forward.
Artek barely managed to spin aside, avoiding the
zombie's lumbering blow. Before Artek could fully re-
cover, the undead captain charged again, cutlass
raised. The move caught Artek completely off
guard—no sensible opponent would move so madly,
leaving himself completely open. Of course, the dead
captain had no need to follow the rules of the living.

Exploiting the opening created by the captain's
upraised sword arm, Artek lashed out with his saber,
slicing through the zombie's grimy coat and carving
a deep gash across its chest. Once again he realized
his mistake. Any living opponent would have stum-

bled back in response to this grievous wound, but the zombie, oblivious to pain, did not hesitate to charge. It swung its cutlass in a wild arc. Caught by surprise, Artek tried to lunge out of the path of the blade, but he was too slow. The dirty tip of the cutlass traced a stinging line across his left side. Artek gasped, his head reeling with sudden pain. He clutched at his side with his free hand, and his fingers came away wet with blood.

Again he was forced to react as the zombie charged heedlessly at him. He parried a series of bludgeoning blows that left no chance for a counterstroke. Artek tried to reach for the wheel, but he nearly got his hand cut off. Steadily, the captain's mindless advances pushed Artek backward, away from the ship's wheel. The throbbing roar grew louder, echoing deafeningly off the rough stone walls of the cavern.

"Artek!" came Guss's voice from above, his shout barely audible over the watery din. "The ship is almost to the fork in the river. You've got to steer it to starboard or it'll head down the left-hand passage, toward the waterfall!"

"Thanks for the reminder," Artek grunted as he dodged the captain's whistling cutlass.

Movement caught the corner of his eye, and Artek risked a hurried glance over his shoulder. New fear spilled into his stomach—a dozen bloated forms shambled toward him. With the attack on their captain, the zombie pirates finally took notice of Artek. With scurvy grins, they drew their cutlasses.

Artek had to turn his head back to the captain, or lose it. With renewed urgency, he fended off the zombie's attacks and even gained some ground. However, he knew it was only a matter of moments until the other undead pirates reached him, at which time he would join the crew of *The Black Dart* in death.

Without warning, crimson light flared behind him. Artek risked a second glance over his shoulder, and what he saw almost made him drop his sword in surprise. One of the approaching zombies had burst into flame. Writhing and burning, it stumbled away. Even as he watched, scarlet fire engulfed another zombie. All over the ship, pirates were being transformed into undead torches. The remaining zombies hesitated, then turned to try to stamp out the resultant fires with their clammy feet. Despite his predicament, Artek could not suppress a sharp-toothed smile— Beckla and Corin had done their work.

Once again Guss's voice called from above. "Artek, you're almost out of time! The fork in the river is just ahead!"

Ignoring the searing pain in his side, Artek attacked the captain with redoubled vigor, driving the zombie back toward the wheel. The schooner's keel grated against a submerged rock, and the ship gave a jarring shudder. Somewhere timbers cracked like old bones. Decayed limbs unable to keep their balance, the zombie captain stumbled backward against the ship's wheel. It was now or never.

Artek sprang forward, letting the cursed saber have free rein. The blade struck once, hewing off the captain's sword arm. Then it swung again, severing the zombie's other arm. Finally, the magical saber pulled Artek forward in a mighty thrust. The blade pierced the pirate captain's heart, pinning the zombie to the center of the ship's wheel.

"Artek, now!" Guss cried out from above.

With all his strength, Artek grabbed the ship's wheel and spun it—along with the feebly flopping zombie captain—to the right. At the same moment a sharp angle of stone loomed in the darkness before the schooner. The dark waters of the Sargauth broke and divided upon the rocky wedge, half going right, and half going left.

With a shout, Artek turned the wheel farther. For a terrified moment he thought the schooner was going to run directly into the sharp wedge of stone before them. Then, at the last moment, the rushing waters swept the schooner into the right-hand passage. There was a horrible splintering sound as the port side of the hull grated against the rough stone wall. Artek was tossed to his knees as the ship convulsed violently. Then the grating noise ceased and the shaking ended as *The Black Dart* sailed down calmer waters. Artek climbed to his feet, gazing in amazement at the placid river ahead. They had done it.

"Ar'talen!" Corin cried behind him. "I think that we're in a spot of trouble."

Artek turned to see Corin and Beckla hurrying toward him. Behind them, the entire aft section of the ship was in flames, thick smoke drifting in the air.

Beckla's face was smudged with soot. "All the zombies are destroyed," she said breathlessly. "But we couldn't put out the fires. The ship is going to burn up!"

"Not if it sinks first," Guss countered, landing on the deck before them. "The hull has been taking on water the whole time from the small hole in the starboard side. And when we struck the cavern wall, a large rip was torn along the port side of the prow. In a few minutes, this ship is going to be on the bottom of the river."

Artek ran a hand through his sweat-soaked hair. Death by fire *and* drowning? They had fought too hard for this victory to give up now. With an angry motion, he jammed the cursed saber into its sheath. The blade did not resist the action, confirming that, indeed, the zombies were no more.

As Artek madly considered their options, the walls of the cavern suddenly fell away. There was a queer, green-gold cast to the air, and Artek had the sense that they had just passed into some far vaster space. However, he could not see through the hazy curtain of smoke that hung above the schooner.

"We'll have to abandon ship!" he shouted. "The river is calmer here, so we should have a chance. Make for the right bank." He grinned fiercely. "I sure hope everyone knows how to swim."

"Hey, don't forget me!" a dry voice called out. As the deck listed, an off-white shape rolled toward them. It was Muragh. Guss snatched up the skull. There was a sound like thunder as the schooner's foremast cracked and fell flaming toward the deck.

"Now!" Artek shouted.

Guss flew into the air, and the others dove off the side of the flaming ship, into the frigid waters of the river below.

9

The Hunt

Artek was the first to the shore.

Dripping, he pulled himself out of the chill river and onto the sandy bank. He grimaced as he stood, immediately hunching over to clutch his injured side. The cutlass wound was not deep, but the gash burned as if someone had poured molten lead into it. Behind him, Beckla stumbled onto the shore, followed by a bedraggled Corin.

"In the name of Mystra, what is this place?" the wizard gasped in an awed voice.

"Are we dreaming?" the nobleman wondered, gazing around them.

Artek frowned at their curious words. What were

they talking about? Clenching his jaw against the searing pain, he lifted his head, and his oath of astonishment was added to theirs.

They stood on the edge of an enormous cavern. At least, it seemed like a cavern—high walls of rough stone rose all around them. Yet there was no rocky ceiling arching overhead, no dim cavern roof dripping with stalactites. Instead, there was a smooth azure dome, tinged by a faint yellowish haze. In the center of the dome hung a blazing orb of fire that filled the cavern with a warm golden light.

"Why, it's the sun," Corin breathed in astonishment.

Artek took a staggering step away from the river, toward the edge of a dense forest that filled the cavern. Tall trees danced under the touch of a soft zephyr. Of course, he realized. The blue dome was the sky, and the white puffs were clouds. Familiar as it was, the sight was so unexpected that he had not even recognized it.

"But this can't be," he murmured, shaking his head in confusion. "The River Sargauth keeps flowing from here. We haven't made it to the ocean yet. And that means we're still underground, beneath Mount Waterdeep." He shot an uncertain look at Beckla. "Aren't we?"

The wizard nodded slowly. "I think so. There's no ocean in sight. And I would have noticed if we had passed through another gate." She gazed thoughtfully at the verdant forest. "Besides, this doesn't look like any place near Waterdeep that I know."

There was a whirring of wings as a dark form swooped down from the sky. Guss landed on the pebbly bank of the river, Muragh in hand. The gargoyle staggered dizzily and dropped the skull.

"Hey!" Muragh cried indignantly. "Try to be a little more gentle next time. These old bones are very delicate, you know."

Guss paid no heed to the skull's complaints. He lifted a clawed hand, rubbing his skull.

"What's going on, Guss?" Artek asked. Pain made him limp as he approached the gargoyle, and Artek was frustrated. The cutlass wound in his side was shallow. It shouldn't be hurting so much.

"I bumped my head," Guss said in a groggy voice.

"You did *what*?" Artek demanded incredulously.

Guss swayed on his sharp-taloned feet. "When I saw all that space, I became terribly excited," the gargoyle explained. "I wanted to fly up into it, but when I got as high as the cavern's walls, I cracked my skull on something. I couldn't see it, but believe me, it was hard as stone." The gargoyle groaned, and still gripping his head, sat down hard on his tail.

Curiosity flashed in Beckla's brown eyes. She opened her mouth to ask a question but was interrupted by a loud cracking sound. They all turned around. On the river, the hull of *The Black Dart* had broken in twain. The burning halves of the ship sank swiftly into the water, hissing as they submerged. In moments the old pirate schooner vanished from sight beneath the dark surface of the river, sunk at last to its watery grave.

Artek wanted to ask Guss more about the sky, but a wave of nausea suddenly crashed over him, and he too sat hard on the ground. Both he and Guss moaned in pain. The gargoyle let go of his head and clutched the oozing wound on his arm. Concerned,

Beckla knelt beside them.

"Both of you are burning up," the wizard gasped as she felt their foreheads.

Muragh rolled toward them, coming to a halt on a small heap of gravel. "It's the zombie wounds," the skull said grimly. "It's begun."

"What's begun?" Corin asked.

"The transformation," Muragh replied, his mandible working. "A wound tainted with the filth of a zombie will fester. Gradually, the victim's body will start to die. But he won't stop moving. Instead, the victim will become a zombie himself."

The others stared at Muragh in horror. Artek shook his head weakly. All his life, he had been part monster. He had resigned himself to that fact. But to become a zombie was a fate he could not bear. "Kill me," he begged hoarsely. "Kill me before it's too late."

At last Beckla regained her senses. "Not so fast, Ar'talen," she said crisply. "I'm not going to give you two up for dead . . . er, *un*dead just yet. Where's that vial of healing potion—the one you used to cure me of the wraith spider venom?"

Artek tried to move, but he was too weak. His skin was burning as if on fire. Sweat poured down his face, but he felt terribly cold. "It's . . . it's in my pocket."

"I don't usually do this sort of thing until I've known a gent for a while, but . . ." The wizard reached into the pocket of Artek's black leather breeches, and pulled out the glass vial. It was empty except for a few purple drops at the bottom. "Corin, do you have another one of these?" she asked the nobleman.

He shook his head sadly. "I'm afraid that was the

only one I had."

Beckla tilted the vial, eyeing the residue critically. "I guess we'll just have to hope this is enough."

The wizard unstopped the vial and poured a drop of the precious fluid on the angry scratch on Guss's arm. She spread the potion over the wound with a finger, then turned to Artek. With Corin's help, she managed to pull off Artek's leather jerkin.

"Are you wearing a fur undershirt, or does all that belong to you?" she asked dryly.

"Very funny," Artek growled. "You'd be hirsute yourself if you had orc blood in you. And let me say that I think it looks a lot better on me than it would on you."

"I won't argue with you there."

Perhaps because his flesh had been forged from stone, Guss's wound had only begun to fester. Artek's looked far worse. The shallow cut ran along his left side onto his muscular chest. The center of the wound was bright red, but the edges were disturbingly dark and gray—the color of a corpse's skin. Three drops remained in the vial, and Beckla used them all on Artek, spreading them carefully to cover the entire wound.

"Now what?" Artek gasped.

"We wait," Beckla replied gravely. "If it's going to work, it shouldn't take long."

Even as she said this, Guss let out a grunt of surprise. Though still open and bleeding, the wound on his upper arm no longer oozed ichor, and the signs of festering had vanished. It appeared no more than a normal scrape.

"I think something's happening," Artek said.

A violet radiance glowed around the wound on his side, then abruptly vanished. Like Guss's injury, the scratch was not healed, and still bled freely, but the alarming grayness was gone. Artek breathed a sigh of relief. His sweating ceased, and the preternatural chill left his bones. He shrugged his jerkin back on over his broad shoulders and stood.

Corin clapped his hands together. "I'm so terribly glad that you two aren't going to become zombies," he exclaimed happily. "I believe I received my fill of battling undead on the pirate ship."

The nobleman glanced in Artek's direction, and Artek had the sudden feeling that the young man was looking at him expectantly. What in the Abyss could Corin possibly want? Artek shifted uncomfortably, searching for something to say.

"Well, you did a good job against the zombies, Corin," he muttered finally. "That was some fancy swordplay you used back on the ship."

Corin's face lit up brightly at this compliment. He puffed out his chest and opened his mouth to reply.

"Next time, you might even want to try fighting with your eyes open," Artek added sharply before the lord could speak.

Corin's mouth snapped shut and his shoulders slumped. A crestfallen expression replaced the look of pride on his boyish face. Artek swore inwardly. Once again he wondered if he had been too harsh on the nobleman, but he couldn't concern himself every moment with Corin's sensitive feelings. He had more pressing concerns. Like getting them out of this place alive. Grumbling to himself, he turned away.

"Well, we can't follow the Sargauth any longer,"

Artek said. "It loses its banks just past this shore. So we'd better start exploring," he said, leading the way toward the edge of the forest. "If we're going to find a way out of this place, we have to figure out where and what it is first."

"Maybe we could build a raft from these trees and keep sailing down the river," Beckla suggested hopefully.

"Not unless you can cast a spell and turn our hands into axes," Artek replied, eyeing the towering trees. "The only blade among us is this damned cursed saber. It would take me a year to cut down one of these trees with a sword. And in case you've forgotten, I have considerably less time than that before this thing stops my heart." He glanced down at the tattoo on his arm. After a moment, something odd struck him, and he gazed up at the sky. "That's strange," he said with a puzzled expression.

"What's strange?" Muragh piped up. "Other than myself, of course."

Artek pointed to his tattoo. The arrow was now midway along the circle between sun and moon. "According to this, it's high noon up above, on the surface. The sun should be directly overhead in Waterdeep. But here the sun is more than halfway past its zenith, and sinking. Reckoning by the sun here, it's a good four or five hours after midday."

"Maybe something's gone wrong with the tattoo," said Beckla.

"Maybe," Artek answered skeptically. "But that's not the only thing. Right now it's spring in Waterdeep, but the heat of this sun feels more like midsummer to me."

Beckla did not have a response to this, and Artek decided it did not truly matter. His life was tied to the magical tattoo, and so it was all that mattered. According to the tattoo, he had half a day and a night to live. It was time to get moving. Leading the way, he plunged into the thicket of trees.

The forest was even denser than it had looked from the outside. Trees grew close together, spreading their branches into a thick green canopy high above. In the dappled shadows below grew myriad vines and bushes, some covered with alien-looking blooms. Pale mushrooms grew from the rotting bodies of fallen trees. None of the plants were any that Artek or the others recognized. The air was damp and muggy, and soon all of the humans were sweating profusely. Tiny, bothersome insects danced in the air, flying into their ears and up their noses, making them sneeze. As always, Muragh chattered ceaselessly as they went. However, Corin was unusually silent. The young lord walked quietly at the rear of the party, eyes cast down upon the ground.

"So, tell me," Muragh went on in his reedy voice. "If we are really still underground, how is it that this forest can survive here?"

For a change, someone actually answered the skull's question. "I don't know," Beckla said, shaking her head as she lowered a glowing hand. "However, as far as I can tell with my magic, nothing about these woods is enchanted. These are all perfectly normal, mundane trees. Somehow, they must be getting all the light and water they need to—"

Artek held up a hand, silencing the wizard's words. He paused, listening with his slightly pointed ears. He heard something: a rustling, followed by the cracking of a dry twig. Something was lurking in the undergrowth just ahead. Whatever it was, Artek knew it was best to consider it dangerous. Whispering, he explained what he had heard to the others. They quickly formed a plan, and in moments were ready to act.

Beckla pointed a finger at the bushes ahead and intoned the words of a spell. Shimmering darts of energy sprang from her fingertips and struck the tops of the bushes, instantly vaporizing them. That was Guss's cue. Snarling as Artek had instructed him, the gargoyle swooped down from a high branch where he had perched, diving toward the bushes. There was a hoarse cry of fear, and a shabby form leapt out of the bushes. Artek jumped from behind a tree, tackling the running form. His quarry struggled wildly, but Artek was the stronger, and he pinned the other to the ground.

"No, don't take me to *him!*" cried a cracked and terrified voice. "Waukeen save me! I saw what happened to all the others. My heart! His tooth will pierce my heart! And his eyes. Too bright, his eyes. They burn as he crushes them in his jaws. They'll crush me, too!"

So terrified was the voice that Artek was startled and moved to pity. He loosened his grip—though not so much as to lose control—and leaned back, gazing at his quarry. It was what was left of a man. He was clad in strange, flowing clothes that might once have been fine but now were filthy and tattered. His tangled hair was matted with leaves, and a scraggly beard clung to his chin. His gaunt body was half-starved, and dark eyes stared madly from his twisted face.

Artek gazed at the broken man. "We're not going
to hurt you," he said, gripping the man's shoulders
firmly but gently.

For a moment the madman struggled, then went
limp. A look of wonder crept onto his haggard face.
"You're not on the Hunt, are you?"

Artek shook his head. "The Hunt? What do you
mean?"

"The Hunters from the Temple," the man said,
licking his lips fearfully. "Have you not seen them
yet? Ah, but you will. You will! Their god is a beast,
and a master of beasts. And beasts we are to him."
Weird laughter bubbled deep in his throat.

The others approached cautiously and gathered
around the madman. Artek allowed him to sit and
studied his twisted face. Certainly this ragged fellow
had seen something that had frightened him out of
his wits. Artek wondered what it could be, and also
how this man—and these Hunters he spoke of—had
come to be here in this strange forest. The answer
might give them a clue to a way out.

"Can you tell us more about this Hunt?" Artek
asked quietly. He gestured to the trees around them.
"Or what this place is?"

The madman looked warily from side to side.
"They'll be coming soon. We can't stay here."

"Please," Artek urged gently. "It won't take long.
And then we'll let you go free. You have my word."

The other man's dark gaze bore into Artek. He
spoke in an eerie voice. "No one is free in Wyllowwood. Not for long, anyway. I am the last. I know."

The madman then began to speak in a chantlike

voice. His tale was difficult to follow, for he spoke in disjointed sentences, and often interrupted himself with broken laughter or moaning sobs. From what Artek could piece together, the man's name was Solthar, and he had been a merchant of some sort. While Solthar was traveling, a sudden storm had come upon his caravan. Seeking shelter, he and the rest of the party had entered a cave—only to find themselves in this forest. They had searched for a means of escape, but to no avail.

"Once you find yourself in Wyllowwood, there is no escape," Solthar said. "Unless you throw yourself in the icy river. Some did. Yes, some did, and they drowned. I cannot will myself to follow them. Soon perhaps. Soon. But not yet!"

"But what about the rest of your traveling companions, Solthar?" Artek asked intently. "Did they all cast themselves into the river?"

Solthar shook his shaggy head. "Oh, no. The Hunt took most of them. The Hunters will take you, too. Into the jaws of the beast they'll throw you. And then—*snap!*" He clamped his hands together, like a mouth closing, then trembled in fear.

After this, Solthar spoke only in unintelligible fragments. They had learned all they could from the mad merchant. Knowing there was no use in keeping him, Artek told Solthar he could go. The madman shot them one last queer look, then scurried away, disappearing into the undergrowth.

Artek rubbed his chin thoughtfully. "It sounds like a gate, doesn't it?" he asked. "The cave that Solthar and the others stumbled through."

Beckla gave a vague shrug. "Maybe. It's hard to

say from his tale alone."

Yet, for some reason, Artek *was* sure. Perhaps it was thief's instinct. "I think we should at least check it out. If we can find the cave, that is."

He gazed expectantly at Beckla. Finally she sighed and nodded. "All right. If it is a gate, my magic should be able to home in on it. But if it isn't, we'll be wandering in circles, you know."

Beckla spoke in the language of magic, and once again her hand glowed with a faint blue light. For a moment she shut her eyes, letting her hand float before her. It drifted slowly toward the right. "This way," she said, walking off into the forest.

She ran headlong into a tree. "Ouch!"

"Maybe you should consider opening your eyes first," Artek suggested.

"Really, Ar'talen?" she replied acidly. "Why, you're absolutely brilliant." The wizard opened her eyes and, muttering under her breath, marched onward—this time avoiding the trees in their path.

The sun above had sunk only a short way more in the sky when the trees thinned, and they found themselves on the edge of a glade. The short hairs on the back of Artek's hands and neck prickled. There was danger here. With a quick gesture he brought the others to a halt. Cautiously, he peered through a tangle of branches into the glade beyond.

In the center, next to a small lake, was a compound of low buildings ringed by a wall of ruddy stone. Soaring above the other structures was a great dome painted bright crimson. Dark smoke rose from within the compound, and the reek of charred meat drifted in the air. It was an evil smell. Artek realized this place could only be the temple of which Solthar had spoken in dread.

Artek watched men enter from the opposite side of the glade. They wore crimson cloaks and rode toward the temple on black horses. They passed through an archway in the wall and vanished within.

"I think we would do well to circle around this place," Artek whispered to the others.

Plunging back into the depths of the forest, they gave the temple a wide berth. The trees drew nearer together, and the undergrowth thickened. Cruel thorns tore at their clothes and scratched their skin. Finally, because his stony hide was immune to the thorns, Guss was forced to lead the way, hacking out a path with his sharp onyx talons. Sweating and bleeding, the humans followed behind. Only Muragh was not bothered by the journey, tucked as he was in Beckla's pack, and his constant chattering was almost as tortuous as the march. Just when Artek was ready to give up in exhaustion and turn back, the trees came to an abrupt end. Before them rose a high wall of jagged rock. They had reached the edge of the vast cavern. In the wall was a narrow gap.

Beckla's hand glowed bright blue as she stretched it out toward the opening. She nodded gravely. "There's magic in there, all right."

Keeping together in a tight knot, they entered the mouth of the cave. The floor was dry and sandy, and the walls oddly smooth, as if scoured and polished by some ceaseless force over long years. They rounded a sharp bend and found themselves at the end of the narrow passage, which opened into a landscape beyond.

It was a desert. The golden sun beat down upon

wave after wave of sand. Dunes stretched like a great yellow ocean to a distant horizon. A parched, gritty wind blew into the fissure, chafing their skin even as it did the stone walls. Artek shook his head in awe and confusion. As far as he knew, the closest desert to Waterdeep was hundreds upon hundreds of leagues away. Wherever this place was, it was nowhere near the city.

Beckla raised her glowing hand. A matching blue aura glimmered across the opening before them, almost like a thin pane of glass. "I think I understand now," Beckla said in amazement. She turned to the others. "This opening is a gate. And see? The sky here has the same yellowish tinge as the sky above the forest."

Artek frowned in puzzlement. "But what does it mean?"

"I know it's hard, but do try not to be so dense, Ar'talen," Beckla said with a scowl. "Don't you see? The entire roof of the cavern is a gate. The gate opens onto this desert. That's how the forest gets the light it needs to survive so far below ground. I suppose the necessary water comes from the river and the lake."

Guss scratched his head. "So when I cracked my skull on the sky, that was really the cavern roof?"

Beckla nodded in agreement. "That's right."

"Wait a minute," Artek protested. "This doesn't make any sense. If the entire sky is a gate that lets through sunlight, why didn't Guss simply fly through into the desert beyond?"

The wizard tapped her cheek with a finger. "I think I know the answer to that," she said finally. "Guss, why don't you try to step through the gate here?"

"Oh, after you," the gargoyle said hurriedly.

Beckla sighed in exasperation. "This is just a test, Guss. You don't have to be polite, you know."

"Oh," the gargoyle said sheepishly. He shrugged his massive shoulders, then stepped through the gap. At least, he *tried* to step through. There was a blue flash, and he was roughly thrown backward into the others.

"That's what I was afraid of," Beckla said glumly.

"What?" Artek grunted. "That I would get crushed by a gargoyle?"

"Sorry!" Guss apologized, leaping off Artek and helping him to his feet.

"Not you, Ar'talen," Beckla said in annoyance. "The gate. It obviously works in only one direction. People—and sunlight—can pass through to the forest. But they can't go back out. Just like Solthar said."

Artek felt his hopes evaporate like water in the hot desert sun. "It doesn't really matter. This gate couldn't have helped me. Or Corin. Wherever this desert is, it's certainly more than a day's journey back to Waterdeep. And less than a day is all both of us have to get back." He laid a big hand on Beckla's shoulder. "But this could have given you a way out of Undermountain. I'm sorry."

For a moment her brown eyes were troubled, then she shook off his hand. "I'll survive."

Leaving the fissure, they returned to the edge of the forest. However, Artek had no idea where they should try to go. He was out of ideas.

"Shall I lead the way this time?" Corin asked. Before anyone could answer, he drew his rapier and began hacking at the tangle of branches and vines before them. However, the thin blade merely bounced off the dense foliage. It flew from the nobleman's grip and landed quivering in the ground directly between Artek's legs.

Corin's face blanched. Artek gripped the rapier and jerked it out of the ground. He did not have the time to deal with Corin's foolishness. His blood began to boil. He couldn't suppress his orcish rage.

"I could try again," Corin said hopefully, reaching for his rapier.

Artek did not hand the blade to him. "No, Corin," he growled. "Don't try again. In fact, don't try anything again." Baring his pointed teeth, he advanced on the startled lord. "Don't *do* anything, don't *say* anything—don't even *think* anything. Understand?"

"But I—"

Artek interrupted him. "No buts, Corin," he snarled viciously. "You've landed us in enough trouble already. Escaping is going to be hard enough without you getting us into worse straits with your antics. Haven't you gotten it though your silly noble head yet that you're—"

Despite his anger, Artek clamped his mouth shut on the hurtful words he'd nearly uttered. It was too late. The damage had been done. Corin gazed at him with wounded eyes.

"That I'm what?" the nobleman asked quietly. "Go ahead, Ar'talen. You can say it. After all, I've heard it often enough." Artek gazed at him in silence, while the others looked on in concern. Corin shook his head ruefully. "Fine, then. I'll say it myself. I'm worthless. That's what you were going to say, wasn't it? That I'm stupid, and soft, and utterly worthless."

A look of defiance colored his pale visage. "Well, maybe you're right," he went on bitterly. "Maybe I am worthless. My father certainly would have agreed with you. Then again, you don't know me any better than he did. You don't know what my life has been like." He clenched his hand into a fist. "You don't know the first thing about me!"

Corin drew a deep breath, forcing his fingers to unclench. A fey light crept into his blue eyes. "Well," he said calmly, "I won't trouble you any further. I'm sure you'll fare far better without my presence to hinder you. I wish you all the best of luck. Good-bye."

With that, the young lord plucked the rapier from Artek's surprised hand, then turned and plunged into the forest. Artek started to lunge after him, but a hand on his shoulder halted him. It was Beckla.

"Let him go," the wizard said softly. "Give him a little time to himself."

Artek glared at her. "A little time to get himself killed, you mean? In case you'd forgotten, that foolish young noble is the reason I'm here in the first place! He'll owe me big when we finally get out of here."

Beckla thrust her hands on her hips, her brown eyes flashing with fire. "And in case *you'd* forgotten, it's because of your idiotic talk that he's run off into the forest."

Artek opened his mouth, but he had no reply to her stinging words. She was right.

"Well, you've botched things up rather nicely," Muragh said.

"Don't worry," Guss said, his gruff voice reassuring. "We won't let him get too far ahead."

Artek nodded silently. He moved a short distance from the others to think. Why had he said those harsh things to Corin? They sounded *exactly* like the sort of things his father had said to him when he was just a child. Arturg had been a hard teacher, and it had seemed Artek's thieving skills had never lived up to his father's expectations. Even when he had grown into a man, and his abilities had far surpassed those of his father, Arturg's voice had still echoed stingingly in his mind. As a child, Artek had vowed never to speak cruelly to another as Arturg had to him. Yet he had broken that vow with Corin, hadn't he? Like father, like son. *Arturg would be proud of you*, he told himself bitterly. He hung his head in shame.

In the distance, an eerie sound echoed through the forest. Artek looked up. The sound came again—high, clear, and menacing. It sounded like the call of a hunting horn.

"Did you hear that?" he asked the others. By their fearful expressions, they had. Dread growing, Artek gazed into the trees where the nobleman had disappeared. The sound of the horn had come from the same direction. "Corin."

With a cry, Artek leapt forward and ran swiftly through the entangling forest. Beckla and Guss followed him as quickly as they could manage, but Artek moved with the strength and grace of a wild animal, ducking beneath low branches and leaping over fallen tree trunks. He soon outpaced the others. His nostrils flared as they caught a familiar, rusty scent—blood. He pushed through a thick curtain of vines, then skidded to a halt.

It was Solthar. A long spear, decorated with crimson feathers, had pierced his chest, pinning his body to the trunk of a tall tree. His feet dangled limply a foot above the ground, and his head lolled forward, staring with blank eyes. He was dead.

The vines rustled and parted as Guss and Beckla caught up with Artek. Both gaped in shock when they saw Solthar dangling from the tree.

"He was right," Beckla said. "The Hunt did find him in the end."

Something in the leaf litter caught Artek's eye. He bent down and picked it up. It was a small square of grimy silk. He swore under his breath.

"This is Corin's handkerchief," he said grimly. He looked up at the suspended body of the madman. "The hunters Solthar talked about must have come upon Corin. The old man must have actually tried to help him."

"I don't think it worked," Muragh said.

Artek dug in the pocket of his breeches and pulled out a small blue stone—the heart jewel he had used to find the lost lord in the lair of the Outcasts. Blue light pulsed rapidly in the center of the crystal. Corin was still alive, but he was terrified.

"Come on!" Artek growled. "We have to find Corin."

Artek dashed through the forest again, running in the direction in which the gem's light was strongest. As he ran, he tried to recall what Solthar had said about these strange Hunters. "Their god is a beast, and a master of beasts. And beasts we are to him. His eyes. Too bright, his eyes. They burn as he crushes them in his jaws." Artek was filled with a deep sense of foreboding. He tightened his grip on the jewel. Instinct burned in his brain, urging him to hurry.

Without warning, the trees gave way to grass. Artek stumbled to a halt, chest heaving. He blinked and realized that once again he stood on the edge of the large clearing by the lake. In the distance lay the walled temple, its crimson dome gleaming like blood. A moment later, Beckla and Guss crashed out of the underbrush to stand beside him. As one, they stared in horror at the scene before them.

Far across the green field, a gangly form ran desperately while three crimson-cloaked men on dark horses rode swiftly behind. It was Corin. The lord stumbled and fell sprawling on the grass. The horses leapt over him, then circled around as their riders laughed. Corin lurched to his feet and stumbled on. The hunters blew their horns and spurred their mounts after him. The bastards, Artek thought with a snarl. They were toying with the nobleman.

Artek lunged into a run, racing across the field. He was far too slow. He was less than halfway there when the hunters tired of their game. One scooped up Corin, flinging the lord over his saddle, and the three riders rode through the archway in the temple's wall, disappearing inside. There was a distant but audible *boom!* as an iron door shut, sealing the opening. Artek stumbled and fell to the ground, utterly exhausted.

Corin was alive, but Artek had lost him.

Jaws of the Wolf

It was going to be just another job.

Artek had pulled off dozens of capers like it—more than he could count. This would not be the easiest stronghold he had ever broken into, but he did not think it would be the hardest. There was only one difference. It was not gold he planned to steal, nor jewels, nor pearls. This time he was going to steal a nobleman.

"We're going with you," Beckla said grimly, crossing her arms over her flowing shirt and gray vest.

Behind her, in the thicket in which they had hidden themselves, Guss nodded solemnly. Muragh bounced up and down in the gargoyle's clawed hands to signal his agreement.

"It's my fault he was captured," Artek growled. "Don't you see? It's because of my blasted orcish side that he's in trouble. So it's up to my other side to get him out." He turned his back on the others, not wanting them to see the pain that twisted his face. Why did he always have to war against himself like this? Even as he posed the question, he knew the answer. When he suppressed the orcish part of him, he became an overly idealistic fool, someone who stupidly trusted that others would believe his innocence without proof of his guilt. Yet when he allowed the orc in him to reign free, he was brutish and violent— a cretin who drove a young man to danger with his insensitive words. Fool or brute, he could be one or the other. But he could never be whole.

Damn you, Artek, he cursed inwardly. *Damn you, Arturg, and Arthaug before you. Yes, damn us all to the Abyss. The whole wretched family. I am what you made me, and I hate you for it.*

"I know this seems horribly rude," Guss said in a serious but polite tone, "but you'll have to stop us from coming with you."

Artek let out an animalistic snarl. He did not have time for this! Hadn't they heard the ominous words of the madman? He glanced at the heart jewel; blue light still pulsed rapidly in the center, but that could change at any second.

"Suit yourself," Artek growled finally. "But don't get in my way. The dark gods know I can't say what will happen if you do." Artek then began to move through the trees, keeping to the shadowed edge of the clearing as he circled around the temple. Beckla and Guss followed quickly after him.

Finally, they reached the shore of the lake. Here the trees drew near to the temple—no more than thirty paces of grass lay between woods and walls. The gate was on the far side of the compound, and there were no watchtowers on this side. It seemed the priests were confident within their walled stronghold and that was well. Confidence led to conceit, which in turn led to carelessness.

Artek squatted, leather creaking, and considered the best way to gain entrance to the temple.

"I could fly over the walls," Guss suggested, sensing his train of thought.

Artek let out a derisive snort. "And why not carry a gong with you so you can announce to all the priests that you're dropping in?"

Guss's wings drooped and his toothy smile turned to a look of chagrin.

"What about you, wizard?" Artek whispered acidly. "Do you know any spells that can whisk us inside the temple?"

She fixed him with a sharp look. "I can cast a spell of teleportation. But you know as well as I that only a great mage could transport the three of us. Given my level of ability, I could probably teleport a dead vole into the temple. Would that be a help?"

That last question hardly needed the caustic irony she lavished upon it. Artek grunted. He had thought as much.

The temple stood directly on the edge of the lake, and water lapped against the rear wall of the compound. Artek made a decision. Without warning the others of his intention, he moved swiftly through the trees to the shore and dove into the icy lake. With swift, strong strokes he swam underwater until surfacing before the pinkish stone wall. Moments later, Beckla and Guss rose from the lake beside him. Both gasped for breath, though Muragh seemed unfazed. Of course, the skull was used to long submersion. Not needing to breathe helped, too.

Gritting his teeth, Artek began pulling himself up the wall. Guss gripped Beckla, who in turn held on to Muragh. Wings straining, the gargoyle rose into the air, keeping pace with Artek until they reached the top together. Clutching the edge of the wall, the four cautiously peered into the temple compound below.

Below them was a series of low buildings constructed of the same rose-colored stone as the walls. The buildings were arranged symmetrically around a circular structure that dominated the center of the compound—the high crimson dome they had glimpsed earlier, supported by fluted stone columns. Evidently it was the main temple. Artek could see between the columns into the dusky interior of the temple, but glimpsed only dark figures moving around a flickering red glow. Whether it was shadows or smoke, the inner temple was filled with a gloom that even his eyes could not penetrate. Thief's instinct told him they would find Corin there.

They froze at the sound of voices below.

"With the new sacrifice, M'kar's count in the Hunt now rises to seventeen," said a deep voice.

"I wouldn't count M'tureth out yet, M'ordil," a second voice replied.

"M'tureth has captured but thirteen in the Hunt," a third voice said hotly. "Clearly M'kar has the favor of Malar."

Artek drew in a hissing breath. Malar. So that was who these priests worshiped—they were disciples of the Beast God. This was worse than he had feared. The Magisters had outlawed the Cult of Malar years ago in Waterdeep because theirs was a bloody and violent religion. Malar was held to be the master of all beasts, but he did not love them. Rather, he considered them tools to be used as he wished in order to further his evil machinations. And, to Malar, humans were just another kind of beast. Banished from the city above, the priests must have found their way into Undermountain and continued their worship in secret.

Just below them, three menacing figures came into view. They were clad in leather armor trimmed with bronze and had crimson cloaks about their shoulders. Feral beast masks of beaten bronze covered their faces. Each wore a mace at the hip, tipped with a heavy bronze claw, and white animal skulls dangled from their belts. One of the priests was enormous, the second of middle height but broad-shouldered, and the third tall but thin. An idea struck Artek. He looked at Beckla and Guss and saw that they were turning to look at him. Apparently they all had the same idea.

They waited for precisely the right moment, then as one they heaved themselves over the top of the wall and dropped down. The three priests never knew what struck them. Artek dispatched his target with a sharp blow to the base of the skull, while Guss employed a crackling neck-twist and Beckla a heart-stopping jolt of magic. They quickly dragged the three bodies behind one of the low buildings.

Moments later, three priests strode from behind the building: one short but broad, one tall and lean, and one large all over. A human skull now dangled among the animal skulls attached to the shorter priest's belt.

"Hee, hee!" Muragh giggled. "This is fun!"

"Be quiet!" Artek hissed. He adjusted his bronze mask, making certain it covered his face. While he knew little of the Cult of Malar, he did know one thing—the penalty for desecrating a temple was death. It would not do to be discovered. His anger had cooled in the face of danger, and Artek found he was now glad for the presence of the others.

Walking slowly but boldly, so as not to attract undue notice, the three wended their way among the stone buildings toward the crimson dome. As they went, they passed several other priests. Each time Artek's heart lurched in his chest, fearing discovery. However, each time the other priests merely saluted with a fist as they passed. The three impostors mimicked the action and continued on.

Rounding a corner, they found themselves on the edge of an open square. Acrid smoke drifted in the air, along with the clang of hammers on metal. It was difficult to make out what was going on through the choking haze. Crimson fire glowed in what seemed to be forges, and hissing steam rose from bubbling vats. Artek suspected this was the smithy where the priests forged their masks and clawed maces. In the center of the foundry was a dark, gaping pit. From time to time, one of the workers approached the hole and tossed in an unwanted piece of refuse. Apparently, it was a garbage pit, and a deep one at that, for Artek never heard anything thrown into it strike bottom.

Clutching their hands to the mouths of their masks so as not to breathe the noxious fumes, they hurried on. At last the crimson-domed temple rose before them. To Artek's surprise, no sentries stood watch around the column-lined pavilion. Apparently, here within the high walls of their stronghold, the priests of Malar expected no interruptions. Artek grinned fiercely behind his mask. It was going to be rather fun to rattle those expectations.

Quietly ascending the marble steps that surrounded the temple each of the three stood behind a column and peered into the smoky dimness beyond.

"The favor of Malar has shone upon the Hunt!" a majestic voice echoed from inside the dome.

Artek's dark eyes gradually adjusted to the murk, and he bit his lip to keep from swearing at what he saw. In the center of the temple was a hideous statue wrought of black metal. The priests apparently created more than just masks and maces in their foul smithy. The statue had been crudely forged in the shape of a grotesque, gigantic wolf. Bloody light flickered in its slanted eyes, and rancid smoke poured from its gaping maw, as if some terrible fire burned in the pit of its belly.

A dozen priests stood around the idol. Huddled at the statue's feet were two bound prisoners. Their faces were covered by bronze masks molded into expressions of terror. One of them was a man whose ragged clothes and scraggly hair recalled Solthar. The other was a slender man with long golden hair. Artek clenched his hands into fists—it was Corin.

The priest who had spoken before wore a mask with a haughty expression. He gestured to the two prisoners. "Behold! I, M'kar, bring not one, but *two* beasts as gifts for the jaws of our lord, Malar!"

The gathered priests murmured in appreciation. All, that is, except for one who stood slightly apart from the others. Somehow, his bronze mask seemed to frown. Artek guessed that had to be M'tureth—M'kar's rival.

"Let the feeding begin!" M'kar thundered.

Two priests gripped the bedraggled man. He struggled against them, but his bonds held his arms and legs fast. It was no use. Together, the two priests lifted the man into the open jaws of the statue. There he lay, eyes wide with terror behind his mask, wondering what was to come. He did not have long to wait.

"Is Malar hungry?" M'kar asked in a sinister voice. "Is he pleased with the gift?"

One of the other priests reached into a bronze basin and drew out a handful of slimy, ropelike strands. With a queasy grimace, Artek recognized what they were—animal entrails. The priest flung the entrails onto the stone floor, then studied the patterns they formed. After a moment, he nodded. "The augury speaks clearly. Malar is pleased. Let the feeding begin!"

With his clawed mace, M'kar tapped the statue's brow. A rumbling almost like a growl emanated from the statue, along with a hiss of steam, and then the jaws began to close. The prisoner screamed, straining against his bonds in vain. His screams were cut short as the wolf's iron jaws clamped shut. A moment later, the beast's maw opened slowly once more. The jaws were empty, save for foul smoke. The sacrifice had been accepted. Now all eyes turned to the other prisoner before the statue.

Artek quickly backed away. They had only seconds to rescue Corin. He had an idea, but whether it would work or not was another matter.

"Beckla, I could use that dead vole trick of yours now," he whispered.

She stared at him in confusion. "The teleport spell, you mean?"

"Yes. Only we need something for you to teleport. An animal of some sort. It doesn't have to be alive. In fact, it really shouldn't be."

Guss let out a dejected sigh. "I found this a little way back. I was saving it for my lunch, but as long as it's an emergency . . ." He pulled a very dead rat from beneath his cloak, its limbs curled with rigor mortis.

"That was going to be your lunch?" Beckla gagged, staring at the rat.

"This is not the time to discuss gargoyle eating habits," Artek hissed in annoyance. "Now here's my plan. Listen close, Muragh. I'm going to need your help."

Moments later, Artek boldly strode into the temple, leaving the others outside. The priests looked up at him in surprise. Corin lay within the jaws of the wolf, his blue eyes nearly mad with fear behind his mask. The augur held a handful of dripping entrails, ready to cast them onto the floor.

"What is the meaning of this?" M'kar demanded. "You are not of the Inner Circle. I should have you fed to Malar for this insolence!"

"It is no insolence," Artek said in a deep voice from behind his mask. He gestured to Muragh, who hung from his belt. "Malar has spoken to me through this skull. He does not care for you or your gifts, M'kar."

Fury blazed in M'kar's eyes. However, behind M'tureth's mask, interest flickered in the cool gaze of the rival priest.

Artek did not give M'kar a chance to respond. He lifted his hands above his head. "Give us a sign, Malar! Tell us what you think of M'kar's desire to rule us all!"

A small object dropped out of the shadows above, landing with a *plop* on the stones—Guss's dead rat. Beckla had been right on cue.

"Malar has spoken," the skull intoned in an eerie voice. "Heed the sign! Malar has spoken!"

The priests gaped in horror at the skull. "Behold, it is a rat," Artek intoned while he had their rapt attention. "So that is what Malar thinks of you, M'kar."

Murmurs of shock rose from the gathered priests, while wicked chuckles issued from M'tureth's bronze mask. M'kar glared at the laughing priest. "Did you arrange this little travesty, M'tureth?" he demanded in rage.

"No, M'kar," M'tureth crooned. "It seems Malar has found a way to ridicule you himself. Clearly, your gifts have won you no favor."

"We shall see," M'kar spat.

The priest moved faster than Artek had thought possible. Before Artek could spring away, M'kar swung his clawed mace and roughly knocked aside Artek's mask. The mask clattered to the floor, spinning away. The priests stared at Artek in astonishment.

"An impostor!" M'kar cried.

"Now!" Artek shouted.

At that signal, a winged form flew between two columns, crimson cloak fluttering, snatching Corin from the jaws of the wolf. Guss flew back out while the priests stared in confusion.

"Kill him!" M'kar screamed in rage.

His words propelled the priests into action. As one, they lunged for Artek. In desperation, he grabbed the bronze vessel filled with entrails and heaved it toward the feet of the oncoming priests, spilling the contents of the bowl across the floor. The priests skidded upon the slimy entrails and went down in a tangled heap.

Artek did not waste the chance. He ran out of the temple, and the others met him on the steps. Guss slashed Corin's bonds with his sharp talons.

"That was fun!" Muragh giggled. "I like being a prophet of Malar."

"You're going to be a *snack* of Malar if we don't get out of here," Beckla said breathlessly.

"May I suggest that we run for it?" Guss proposed.

"You may," Corin agreed weakly.

A deafening noise rose from the temple. Someone was beating a gong of alarm. "Come on!" Artek yelled.

They dashed in the direction of the gate but were brought up short by a dozen priests who had answered the alarm. Hastily they turned and ran in the other direction with the disciples of Malar on their heels. They careened into the smoke-filled foundry and abruptly came to a halt. On the far side of the square stood a score of priests, all gripping clawed maces. Behind them the other priests approached at a run. They were surrounded.

"There's nowhere left to go!" Beckla cried.

Artek's eyes locked on something in the center of the smithy. "Yes, there is!" he shouted. Grabbing the others, he lunged for the open garbage pit. The priests swung their clawed maces, but the weapons only whistled through empty air. Artek leapt into the hole, pulling the others along with him. He could only hope that the pit was as deep as he had thought it was.

As it turned out, it was deeper.

* * * * *

Artek sat up with a groan. Bits of garbage tumbled from his shoulders. It felt as if his body had been trampled by a stampeding herd of Vaasan thunderhooves.

"Where . . . where are we?" asked a tremulous voice. It was Muragh. The skull still dangled from the belt of Artek's priestly garb.

"Good question," Artek said hoarsely. His darkvision adjusted, piercing the perfect blackness around them. They were in a small, rough-hewn cave. Beneath them was a heap of rotting refuse and rusting junk that had been tossed into the garbage pit so far above. Sudden panic clutched his heart. Where were the others?

He shook his head, trying to clear away the disorientation of the nightmarish fall. Then he remembered. After they had leapt into the pit, leaving behind the bloodthirsty priests of Malar, the hole had angled, and they had slid wildly down a steep stone slope, unable to stop their descent. Once again, Undermountain had pulled them deeper. Even Guss had been trapped, for the passage was too narrow for him to spread his leathery wings.

It seemed they had slid for hours, plunging ever deeper into the bowels of the world. Then, without warning, the tunnel had divided. Beckla, Corin, and Guss had fallen to the left, while Artek and Muragh had bounced to the right. The screams of the others had vanished in an instant. A few moments later, the harrowing ride had come to a jarring end. The tunnel had ended, and for a moment Artek had fallen through empty air. Then he had landed atop the garbage heap. Foul as the refuse was, he knew he should be grateful, for it had cushioned his fall, leaving him with bruises instead of broken bones.

Artek half-climbed, half-slid off the midden heap and stood stiffly. Sweat beaded on his brow. The darkness was hot and oppressive here. The weight of countless tons of rock pressed heavily from above. A sharp metallic odor hung upon the air, stinging his nostrils and burning inside his lungs. Then he heard a weird clicking sound that drew closer as he listened. He saw a dark opening in the far wall of the chamber—the source of the sound.

"Do you hear that?" Muragh asked nervously.

Artek nodded grimly. "Something is coming."

"Quick!" the skull whined in terror. "Hide us!"

"Wait a minute," Artek muttered. "I'm the one who should be afraid. You're already dead, you know."

"And it's an experience I don't care to repeat," Muragh replied with a shudder. "Now move it!"

Much as Artek would have liked, there was no time to reproach the imperious skull. Moving silently, he padded toward the cave's wall and pressed his body into a shadow-filled fissure. The eerie clicking noise drew nearer. A red glow appeared in the opening in the far wall. A moment later, two creatures scuttled into the chamber.

Bugs—that was Artek's first thought. But they were like no insects he had ever seen. They were easily as large as a man, but flat and round, with small heads and eight appendages, two of which ended in strangely shaped claws. Each seemed to have a lantern attached to the back of its head, and it was from these that the ruddy light issued. In all, they looked like weirdly distorted sea crabs. The blotchy carapaces that covered their backs were the exact color of rusted iron.

No, Artek realized in shock, their shells didn't simply look like iron. They *were* iron. And so was the rest of them. There was no doubt. His heat-sensing darkvision could discern the difference between living tissue and dead metal. Whatever these creatures were, they weren't alive at all, but some sort of mechanical devices. Yet they seemed to move with a rudimentary intelligence as they made for the garbage heap.

To Artek's further surprise, a tinny voice emanated from the pincer mouth of one of the creatures.

"*Whrrr*. Ferragans search for metal," it droned. "Good ferragans. *Clkkk*."

"Yes, search fallings from above," the other creature echoed in a metallic buzz. "*Scrrr*. Find metal. Squch be happy. *Bzzzt*. Good, good ferragans."

The crablike creatures—which were evidently called ferragans—scrabbled onto the garbage pile. Artek now saw that each bore two different types of claws: one shaped like a broad hammerhead, the other like a pincer with three multijointed prongs. With this latter claw, obviously designed for gripping, the ferragans began picking through the rubbish heap. When one found a piece of scrap metal, it reached back and placed it in a wire basket attached to its carapace, emitted a high-pitched clicking that sounded almost like gleeful laughter and then continued searching. Finally, their baskets full, the two creatures clambered off the pile.

"*Clkkk*. Good ferragans," they droned in mindless monotones. "Found metal. *Whrrr*. Good, good ferragans." The creatures scuttled from the chamber and were gone.

Artek crept from his hiding place. He considered following the ferragans, then decided against it. What would be the point? Where could they lead him that would be any better than this pit? Either way, he had lost the others—and himself. There was no telling how deep below the surface they were now. The darkness seemed to creep into his heart, snuffing out his wan hopes. He would never get back to the city in time now. In disgust, he cast off the priestly garb of Malar. With a desolate sigh, he sat down on the foot of the garbage heap, setting Muragh beside him.

"Why are you just sitting here, Artek?" Muragh said in puzzlement. "What's the matter with you?"

He did not answer the skull. Instead he stared at the tattoo on his arm. The sun had just passed the arrow. In the world above, night had fallen. Just twelve more hours, and all of this would be over.

"I wish it would just happen now, so I could get it over with," he whispered bitterly.

"You wish *what* would happen now?" Muragh asked.

"This," Artek growled, striking the tattoo with his opposite hand. "What's the point in waiting to die?" He shook his head grimly. "I wish I were already dead."

"Don't say that."

Artek stared at the skull in surprise. Muragh's reedy voice had dropped to a grim whisper. His lipless mouth no longer seemed to be grinning, but clenched in anger. His orbless eyes bore into Artek.

"Don't ever say that," Muragh repeated darkly. "You don't know what it's like. You can't know. You *can't*." The skull shuddered, though whether in terror or rage—or perhaps both—Artek could not tell. He shook his head, unsure what to say.

"Isn't this just perfect?" Muragh asked with bitter mirth. "Here you want to throw away your life, and I would give anything to have mine back. Even for just twelve hours. Whatever time I had left, even if it was only a *minute*, I wouldn't squander it. I would enjoy every second of it, and be grateful for what I had." Despite his lack of flesh, Muragh's expression was somehow rueful. "Life is always most wasted upon the living. The gods sure have a twisted sense of humor."

Shamed, Artek hung his head. Again, he had proven himself utterly thoughtless. He might as well have been a rich man throwing away a loaf of bread in front of a starving beggar. Finally he looked at the skull. "What is . . . what is it like to . . . ?"

"What is it like to be dead?" the skull finished for him. "Is that what you want to know?"

Artek nodded. For a long moment, he thought Muragh was not going to answer. Then the enchanted skull spoke in a low, eerie voice.

"It's horrible, that's what it's like. It's cold, and dark, and empty, utterly empty. Maybe it's better for those who have truly departed. Maybe they manage to find some kind of peace. I wouldn't know. I'm half in the world of the dead and half out of it. I dwell in the chill of the grave, but I still gaze upon the land of the living. It's torture. I can see the light and warmth that I can never feel again."

Sighing, Muragh whistled through his broken teeth and his few remaining wisps of rotting hair moved in the slight breeze. At last he went on.

"The worst of it is the loneliness. I could bear it all if it weren't for that. Death is lonely. So terribly lonely. I know I can never be alive again. It's just a dream. But I wish . . ." It seemed impossible, but Artek thought he saw a bead of moisture trickle from Muragh's empty eye socket and run down his cheek.

Artek gazed at the skull with troubled eyes. All this time he had been wallowing in his own self-pity, cursing the lot fate had drawn for him. Yet here was one to whom fate had dealt a far crueler hand, and he bore it far more stoically than Artek ever had. Artek felt ashamed, and knew he should. He could learn a lesson from the skull. Even if he had only a short time left, he would not simply throw it away.

"I can't pretend to know what you've gone through, Muragh," Artek said. He laid a hand gently on the skull's yellowed cranium. "But I want you to know that you aren't alone. Not anymore."

Muragh worked his fleshless jaw, but for once the enchanted skull was speechless. Artek laughed softly, then scooped up the skull. "Come on. I don't know how far away the others are, but they had to land somewhere. No matter how far it is, we'll find them." His orcish eyes piercing the gloom, he moved stealthily through the opening through which the ferragans had disappeared and into a twisting tunnel beyond.

He had gone only a short distance down the passage when Muragh found his voice. "Wait a minute, Artek!" the skull said. "There's something I need to tell you. I think I know where we are."

Artek stopped and stared at the skull. "Well, why didn't you say so before?"

"I didn't want to interrupt our touching moment," Muragh quipped.

Artek had no reply.

"Anyway," the skull went on, "I've never been here before, but if the rumors I've heard are even half true, then the name of this place is almost certainly Trobriand's Graveyard."

Artek sighed, hoping this wasn't a waste of time. Now that he had shaken off his despair, every second counted. "And just who is this Trobriand person?"

"He's one of Halaster's apprentices."

Artek swore.

"Didn't your father ever teach you a lesson about using foul language?" Muragh asked dryly.

"Of course," Artek replied. "Where do you think I learned all these curses?"

Ignoring the skull's groans, he thought about the implications of this new knowledge. Between the mad voyage of the pirate ship and the perils of the Hunt in Wyllowwood, he had all but forgotten their quest to locate one of Halaster's apprentices. If they could find Trobriand, maybe they could convince him to show them a gate out of Undermountain.

"Tell me more," Artek said, his excitement growing.

In the darkness, he listened as Muragh told all that he knew of Trobriand. There was not much. Trobriand was also called the Metal Mage, for his ultimate goal was to create mechanical beings that were stronger, faster, and smarter than any living creature. Over the centuries, this pursuit had both consumed and eluded him. While he constructed countless metal horrors that were swift and power-ful, none approached the level of intelligence he de-sired. According to the rumors, the Metal Mage cast the failed results of his experiments down into a pit deep in Undermountain—a place thus known as Trobriand's Graveyard.

"It doesn't sound hopeful," Artek said when Muragh finished. "But there must be some way we can contact Trobriand. I can't believe that he doesn't keep an eye on his old creations, just to see what they're up to down here. But first we must find the others."

Gripping Muragh, he continued down the tunnel. Before long, a ruddy glow crept into the air. Clanging sounds echoed off the stone walls. Finally, Artek came upon an opening in the left side of the passage, and cautiously peered within.

In the chamber beyond, a pair of ferragans was busily at work. Artek could not tell if they were the same two he had seen earlier. They all seemed to look the same. One operated the bellows of a glowing forge, while the other hammered pieces of red-hot metal with its claw. In the corner sat a third ferra-gan who was missing several of its legs.

"*Clkkk*," emanated a sound from the broken ferra-gan's pincer mouth. "New legs good. *Scrrr*."

Evidently Artek was witnessing a repair job in action. He moved quickly past the opening. No alarm went up. No ferragans scuttled in pursuit. They had not seen him. He continued soundlessly down the tun-nel. More chambers opened up to either side, and in several others ferragans went about their tasks: un-loading wire baskets of junk, sorting through stray bits of metal, and forging new body parts. What these mechanical creatures lacked in wits they certainly made up for in industriousness.

A shout suddenly echoed down the tunnel. It was not the drone of a ferragan, but a human voice.

"Get your rusty hands off me!"

Artek would recognize that tone of cutting indignation anywhere. It was Beckla.

He sprang into motion and dashed down the tunnel. The walls fell away, and he found himself in a large cavern, its stony ceiling lit by a flickering crimson glow. A fierce heat wavered in the air, created by a bubbling pit of molten metal in the center of the chamber. Even as Artek watched, a ferragan dropped a chunk of iron into the pit. It melted and sank into the glowing pool. Then another sight caught his eyes, and his heart lurched in his chest.

Three ferragans each dragged a struggling form toward the smoking pit. Two of the forms wore crimson cloaks, and all three wore masks of beaten bronze. Artek was surprised that the masks had not come loose in the fall down the pit.

"Unhand us immediately!" the figure without a cloak cried imperiously. Corin.

"*Chhhk*," one of the ferragans said. "This metal is reluctant."

"Must not resist," another iron creature droned. "All metal must be melted. *Vrrrt*. That is Squch's rule."

Dark realization struck Artek. Seeing their bronze masks, the dull-witted ferragans must have mistaken Beckla, Corin, and Guss for pieces of scrap metal. And now the creatures were going to melt them down.

11

Specimens

Wizard, noble, and gargoyle fought against the pincers that held them, but living muscles—even those forged from stone—were of no use against hard iron. The ferragans clambered near the bubbling pit and raised their jointed appendages, preparing to cast their struggling burdens toward the vat of molten liquid. Beckla, Corin, and Guss would be burned alive. Artek had to do something. But what?

Before he could think of an answer, a piercing sound—high and keening, like an alarm—filled the air of the cavern. The ferragans abruptly froze. In what seemed like terror, they stared at an opening in

the far wall of the chamber, their glass eyes bobbing
on the ends of wiry stalks.

Clanking, a half-dozen hulking forms appeared in
the far opening and scuttled into the cavern on mul-
tiple legs. Their shells were as bright as polished
steel, and they waved great serrated claws before
them and dragged flat, razor-sharp tails behind. To
Artek, they looked for all the world like gigantic
steel lobsters. They surrounded the three ferragans
cowering near the pit of liquid metal.

"HALT!" one of the creatures ordered in a thrum-
ming monotone.

"DROP!" commanded another.

Clicking in fear, the ferragans opened their pincers, releasing Beckla, Corin, and Guss. The three
fell to the floor mere inches from the edge of the fiery
pit. They tried to crawl away but were stopped by
the impenetrable line of lobster-creatures.

"PRISONERS!" said one of the steel-shelled new-
comers. "OURS!"

Beckla tore off her bronze mask, and Guss and
Corin did the same, staring at the creatures in horror. As they revealed their faces, pitiful squeaks and
rattles rose from the three ferragans.

"*Clkkk!* Not metal!" they wailed in their buzzing
voices. "Bad ferragans! *Whrrr!* Prisoners for
thanatars only! Not for ferragans! *Scrrr!* Must re-
forge ferragans! Bad, bad!"

Evidently consumed by remorse at their mistake—and their apparent failure to be good ferragans—the three crablike creatures lurched forward
and heaved their rusty iron bodies into the pit of
molten metal. They clicked and squealed, pincers

waving, as their carapaces began to glow: first red, then orange, then white-hot. Melting, they sank into the pit and were gone. The remaining ferragans kept their distance, staring submissively at the lobster-like creatures that the others had called thanatars. While the ferragans were workers, the thanatars were obviously the police.

"TAKE!" one thanatar commanded, and several others reached their serrated claws toward the three captives near the pit.

Artek gripped the hilt of the cursed saber at his hip, but he resisted the urge to leap into the room swinging. He wasn't certain he could kill—disassemble?—even one of the steel-shelled thanatars, let alone six of the things. Yet he couldn't let them simply drag the others off to some dark prison.

Once again Artek's dilemma was resolved as several more mechanical forms slithered into the chamber. *Things are getting stranger by the second,* he thought. The new creatures were sleeker than the others, as dark as polished jet, with sinuous, many-sectioned bodies and countless undulating legs. If the ferragans were crabs and the thanatars lobsters, then these new metallic monsters were giant silverfish. They had no eyes, but dozens of wiry antennae sprouted from their heads, waving before them. Clearly, the antennae were their primary sensing organs.

"SILVERSANNS!" one of the thanatars intoned. Somehow the word resonated with derision.

"Not are thessse prisssoners, yesss?" one silversann said, in a hissing voice.

"Ssspecimens are they," added another. "Ssstudy them we will. Take them not to prissson, yesss?"

The thanatars glared at the silversanns, but they hesitated, their claws hovering over the prisoners. Artek sensed a rivalry between the strong-bodied thanatars and the obviously more intelligent silversanns. And right now that rivalry was the only thing keeping the others alive.

The largest of the thanatars—and evidently their leader—advanced on the silversanns. "PRISONERS!" the creature said again. "OURS!"

"Have them when done with our ssstudies you may, yesss?" a silversann replied.

"Ssstudy, yesss?" echoed another. It stroked Beckla with its feelers. The wizard recoiled in disgust.

"SQUCH!" the lead thanatar said in protest. "PRISONERS. OURS!"

Squch. Artek had heard the ferragans utter that word earlier. It almost seemed like a name of some sort. It was as if the thanatar were saying that this Squch had granted them all prisoners.

"But to usss ssspecimens Sssquch gave, yesss?" the leader of the silversanns countered. "Oursss ssspecimens are. Yesss, yesss?"

Artek shook his head. Evidently, the silversanns thought this Squch person had given the captives to *them*. While he couldn't be sure, he guessed that Squch was the leader of all of the mechanical creatures. They certainly seemed to speak his name with reverence and fear.

The thanatars waved their claws menacingly at the silversanns. The slinky mechanicals cowered—clearly they were not created for battle like the lobster-creatures—but they did not give any ground. Fear rose in Artek's throat. If there was a fight, Beckla,

Corin, and Guss would be caught in the middle—and likely torn apart.

"Quick!" Muragh hissed. "Do something!"

"I'm thinking!" Artek muttered back. Then an idea struck him. There was no time to decide whether it was good or bad. Taking a deep breath, he left the safety of the tunnel and ran into the cavern. "Greetings!" he shouted at the top of his lungs.

As one, all the mechanicals turned in his direction.

"Great," Muragh mumbled. "You've got their attention. Now what?"

Artek swallowed hard. "It seems that you're at a bit of an impasse," he said loudly. "Perhaps your leader, this Squch of yours, could help you resolve it. Why don't you ask him what to do?"

The metallic creatures stared dumbly at Artek. His words were lost entirely upon them. Only the silversanns seemed to grasp part of what he had said, their supple antennae waving uncertainly.

"You'd better speak to them in a language they can comprehend," Muragh whispered.

Artek nodded. He tried again, choosing his words carefully and speaking in his best imitation of their tinny voices. "Prisoners?" he asked, pointing to his companions and then himself. "Specimens?" He shook his head and shrugged his shoulders. "Ask Squch. Squch knows."

These words seemed to excite the mechanicals. The thanatars emitted high-pitched whistles, clacking their claws. The silversanns hissed sibilantly, feelers whipping back and forth. Artek watched in growing alarm, wondering if he had angered them.

"SQUCH!" the thanatars uttered. They seemed to

nod their small steel heads. "SQUCH! TELL!"

The silversanns rippled their sleek bodies. "Yesss. Asssk mussst we Sssquch, yesss. Tell usss will Sssquch what to do ssshould we. Yesss, yesss."

Three thanatars picked up Beckla, Corin, and Guss, holding them securely—but not ungently—in their clawed appendages. Another thanatar moved toward Artek, and he suppressed the instinct to run as it reached out and lifted him off the floor. The ferragans clicked submissively, scuttling out of the way as the thanatars marched toward the opening through which they had entered. Antennae waving, the silversanns slithered behind.

"It's good to see you, Ar'talen," Beckla said, her face drawn with fear. "But I sure hope you know what you're doing."

Artek did not answer. He hoped he did as well. Either way, it was a gamble. But if anyone knew how to contact Trobriand, it would probably be the leader of these creatures. And that was Squch.

The thanatars carried them through a winding labyrinth of rough-walled tunnels and irregular chambers. Here and there, thin veins of silvery metal marbled the stone walls. Artek guessed that this place had been a mine once, perhaps constructed by the same dwarves—the Melairkyn clan—who had built the vast city of Underhall eons ago. Artek shuddered. They must be far below Waterdeep indeed. Yet, remembering Muragh's words, he hardened his will. He would not give up—at least, not until the very end.

At last they passed through a rough archway into a large natural cavern. Here the stone walls were riddled with serpentine veins of silver metal. Lanterns like those that were attached to the heads of the ferragans lined the perimeter of the cavern. Their light was reflected and somehow amplified by the thin veins of metal, filling the air with a dazzling silver glow. It was breathtaking.

The thanatars came to a halt in the center of the cavern, the silversanns just behind. Opening their claws, the steely creatures dropped their burdens. The three humans, the gargoyle, and the skull dropped to the floor with various exclamations of discomfort and indignation. Before them was a shadowed hole in the floor that filled Artek with a sense of dread. Behind them, the thanatars and silversanns formed a half-circle, falling into an expectant silence.

Without warning, two red-hot pinpricks appeared in the dark circle of the hole. A shadow stirred within, and an eerie rattling emanated from the depths. Then, with menacing speed, something climbed out.

It was silver—as silver as the brilliant metal that snaked through the walls of the cavern. It was not unlike the thanatars, yet it was smaller, sleeker. And, Artek sensed, it was far more deadly. Its two clawed appendages were slender, even delicate, but gleamed sharply like polished knives. Six legs supported its shiny, multiplated abdomen. An armored tail curled up and over its back, ending in a cruelly barbed point. It was a scorpion, a gigantic silver scorpion.

The thanatars lowered their claws and the silversanns drooped their antennae in gestures of submission. "SQUCH!" they spoke in reverence. "Sssquch, yesss. Sssquch!"

"What have you brought me?" Squch demanded, pincer mouth moving. Unlike that of the others, the scorpion's speech was surprisingly intelligible, though clearly inhuman.

"PRISONERS!" the thanatars intoned.

"Ssspecimens are they, yesss?" the silversanns contradicted.

"I will be the judge of that," Squch snapped.

Legs moving swiftly, the metallic scorpion scrambled forward. Artek reached out his arms, keeping the others from trying to get up and run.

"Yes, you are wise, soft one," Squch said with a weird rattling that was almost like laughter. "I am a scaladar. To flee from me is a grave error." The scaladar lowered its barbed stinger, brushing the point softly across Artek's cheek. The reek of venom filled his nose. He clenched his jaw to keep from flinching—to move was to die. The scaladar laughed again and raised its stinger.

"We won't flee," Artek said gravely. "You have my word."

"Why have you intruded upon my domain?" Squch demanded, crimson eyes flaring.

Artek licked his lips nervously. It was now or never. "We come seeking the wizard Trobriand."

The silversanns hissed in terror, and the thanatars clacked their claws in agitation. Squch's stinger flicked forward, and the din instantly fell into silence. The scaladar loomed threateningly above Artek. "You dare to speak that name in my presence, soft one?"

Artek exchanged uncertain looks with the others, then slowly rose to his feet. What did they have to lose? Gazing into the burning eyes of the scaladar, he told of their search for one of Halaster's apprentices and a gate out of Undermountain. When he finished, the scaladar laughed its brittle laughter again.

"You are a fool, soft one," Squch replied. "Trobriand cares nothing for nonmetal creatures such as you. You would gain no help from him."

Artek was not going to give up so easily. "You may be right, Squch. But with all due respect, I'd like to try just the same. Please—do you know where we can find your maker, Trobriand?"

The scaladar's stinger trembled in sudden rage. A drop of venom fell from the barbed tip. It hissed and smoked as it struck the floor, burning a pit into the stone. "Do I know where you can find Trobriand? *Do I know where you can find Trobriand?*" Squch's silver armor rattled in fury. "If I possessed such knowledge, do you believe that I would still be here, existing in this wretched hole in the ground?"

Artek backed away, shaking his head in confusion. The scaladar advanced on him.

"Do you know what we are to Trobriand?" Squch droned furiously. "Trash! Refuse! Garbage! He created us. He forged our bodies. He gave us thoughts. Yet when he grew tired of us, he cast us down into this pit!"

The scaladar waved a claw at the fearful thanatars and silversanns. "The Metal Mage discarded most of these walking scrap heaps for their stupidity. Oh, but not I! I was too clever, you see. That was my flaw. Trobriand feared my intelligence, feared that I would usurp his power. And he was right. I would have. And I will do so yet. Then I will rise from the ground, and lay eyes upon this city I have heard of in rumor, a city which has no stone above it, but only air, a city filled with foolish, pliable soft ones. Yes, I will gaze upon this city. Then I will make it my own."

The scaladar's crimson eyes bore into Artek. "You come from this place, do you not, soft one?" the silver creature crooned in sudden interest. "Come, tell me about it. Tell me all that you know, and perhaps I will not kill you."

Artek did not know what to say. It was clear that this creature was utterly mad—no wonder Trobriand had discarded it. Yet Artek sensed that there were some kernels of truth in the scaladar's ravings. Instinct told him that Squch had not exaggerated Trobriand's dislike for living creatures. Even if they could find the Metal Mage, Artek knew that Trobriand would not help them.

"I'm sorry, Squch," Artek said carefully. "I'd like to help you, but we don't have time right now. If you let us go, we'll come back later and—"

"Stop!" the scaladar cried. "You underestimate my intelligence, soft one. You cannot deceive me with your transparent lies. If you will not freely tell me what you know, I will find another way to learn it." Squch waved a claw at the silversanns. "Take these foolish soft ones to your laboratory. Extract what knowledge you can from their heads. Once you have it, you may do whatever you wish with the rest of them."

The silversanns chittered excitedly at this news.

They snaked past the glowering thanatars and coiled their smooth antennae around the prisoners. Before Artek could protest to Squch, the silversanns dragged him and the others out of the cavern and down a dark tunnel. The prisoners tried to break free of the metallic strands that gripped them, but it was no use. The antennae were as strong as steel wire.

The silversanns took them to a dim chamber and dropped them on the floor. One of the creatures shut and locked a heavy iron door—so much for the only visible route of escape.

The chamber of the silversanns was filled with all manner of clutter: clay pots, cracked vials, broken staves, moldering books, and countless metal tools of inexplicable function. All lay carelessly strewn about or heaped into haphazard piles that seemed to have no obvious rhyme or reason. The silversanns gathered at one end of the chamber, speaking in sibilant whispers. Evidently, they were trying to decide how to extract the knowledge of their new *ssspecimens*, Artek thought grimly.

Corin sighed glumly, sitting slump-shouldered on the cold stone floor. "I'm sorry, everyone," the young lord said ruefully. "This is all my fault. We wouldn't be in this scrape if I hadn't gone and dashed off into the forest like such a dolt." He looked up at Artek with sad blue eyes. "You were right, you know. And so was my father. I can't do anything well. But you needn't worry. I've learned my lesson. I won't try to help ever again." He sighed deeply. "I apologize for getting you into this, Ar'talen. For your sake, I hope you can get me to Darien Thal and force him to have that tattoo fixed. But for my part, I don't care if I ever see the surface again."

The nobleman hung his head and fell silent. Guss gazed at him with worried green eyes, cradling Muragh in his clawed hands. Beckla shot a sharp look at Artek. It was clear she wanted him to say something. Artek just shook his head. Everything he had said before had been thoughtless and cruel. What could he say now that wouldn't simply cause more damage? It was better if he simply remained silent.

With a sound of exasperation, Beckla stood up. The silversanns were still engaged in a secret debate, and the wizard took the opportunity to poke around in the heaps of clutter surrounding them.

"Look at all this stuff," she said in sudden amazement.

"What is it?" Muragh asked.

She rummaged through one of the piles. "Broken wizard staves. Shattered wands. Cracked potion vials. Old spellbooks." The wizard looked up in wonder. "It's all magical paraphernalia."

Artek quickly stood. "Is there something that might be able to help us?"

Beckla frowned. "I'm not sure. Pretty much all of it seems to be broken or damaged. But there might be something of interest here . . ."

She kept searching, and the others joined her. As far as Artek could tell, all of the items—staves, rods, magical crystals—seemed to have been deliberately smashed. Perhaps the silversanns had damaged the objects while trying to study them. Even a roomful of magical artifacts would do them no good if all were broken.

Just then, Guss let out a grunt of surprise. With a claw, he plucked something gold and glittering from one of the piles. "Beckla, take a look at this. I'm not sure, but it looks to me as if it's—"

At that moment, the silversanns ended their debate and slithered toward them. Guss cut his words short, thrusting the object behind his back. The five prisoners stared apprehensively as the metallic creatures drew near.

"Decided then are we, yesss?" one of the silversanns asked the others, the small pit of its mouth dilating and contracting to form the syllables.

"Yesss, yesss," answered another. "More learn we mussst, before gain can we knowledge theirsss."

The first silversann undulated forward, brushing Artek with its cold antennae. "Let usss then apart take them, yesss? Sssee we can how work they. Yesss, yesss?"

Artek glared at them warily. "What do you mean, 'take us apart'?"

"Take apart mean we, yesss?" the silversann answered blithely. "Disssasssemble your pieces. Mind you not, yesss?"

Several silversanns pressed forward, each bearing weirdly shaped, sharp-edged tools in their antennae. Artek and the others exchanged looks of horror. They slowly backed away from the creatures. "We most certainly *do* mind," Artek countered nervously.

"Worry not, yesss?" the leader of the silversanns hissed reassuringly. "Put we together back your bodiesss when done we are. Yesss, yesss?"

The silversanns continued to close in, steel tools

raised. Apparently they didn't understand that living creatures couldn't simply be taken apart like machines. And once they discovered that they couldn't just put their *ssspecimens* back together, it would be far too late. Artek gripped the hilt of his saber, wondering if the blade would have any effect against the hard plates that armored the creatures.

One of the silversanns stretched a wicked-looking probe toward Beckla.

"Get back, you metal worm!" the wizard cried. She shouted several arcane words, and blue magic crackled between her outstretched fingers. "Get back, or I'll melt you!"

The silversanns let out a chorus of shrill shrieks. For a second, Artek thought Beckla's threat had terrified them. Then, in astonishment, he realized that their shrieks were sounds of delight, not fear.

"Magic, yesss?" they cried excitedly, clustering around the wizard. "How cassst you did magic? Ssshow usss, yesss? Ssshow usss!"

The silversanns continued to babble, but Artek could catch little of what the creatures said in their hissing voices. However, Beckla bent toward them, cocking an ear. As she listened, a smile gradually spread across her face. Finally she said something to the silversanns and they let out piercing squeaks of joy. They scuttled a short distance back, then waited expectantly.

Artek leaned over to murmur in her ear. "What in the world did you say to them?"

"I told them I'd teach them how to do magic," she whispered back.

"You *what*?"

"You heard me, Ar'talen."

"I heard you, but I don't understand. I'm no wizard, but even I know that only living beings can wield magic."

Beckla nodded. "I know that, and you know that. But *they* don't know that." Her smile broadened into a grin. "As it turns out, the silversanns are absolutely fascinated by magic. It's their favorite area of research. They've seen some of the thanatars' prisoners work it before, and they want more than anything to learn it themselves. Of course, no matter how faithfully they duplicate the words and movements of a spell, it will never work for them. It can't. They're not alive."

Beckla gestured subtly toward the heaps of broken artifacts. "That's what all this stuff is for. Somewhere along the line, they developed a crazy notion that when magical objects are broken, their magic is released. They sleep near these heaps of junk in the belief that, over time, they'll absorb some of that magic."

Artek shook his head at this absurdity. "So what are you going to do?"

"You'll see," she replied mysteriously. She approached the waiting silversanns.

Corin, Guss, and Muragh looked at Artek questioningly, but he only shrugged his broad shoulders. He had no idea what the wizard intended to do.

"All right, then," Beckla said crisply, addressing the mechanicals as she might a class of new apprentices at a school for mages. "Casting magic really isn't all that difficult. It's simply a matter of using the proper inflection. Now, follow my movements as best you can, and repeat after me."

She weaved her arms in a complex pattern while uttering a string of words that, to Artek, sounded far more like nonsense than they did magic. The silversanns made a comic effort to mimic her hand movements with their whiplike antennae. A buzz rose from them as they repeated her words dutifully and, unfortunately, quite erroneously.

"K'hal sith mara!" Beckla shouted in finish, raising her arms above her head.

"G'sssar ziph mooli!" the silversanns repeated happily, waving their wiry sensory organs.

A shimmering aura of sapphire light sprang into being around Beckla's body. Artek thought he saw the wizard wiggle her fingers. A fraction of a second later, a blue aura surrounded each of the silversanns. The creatures shrieked in glee, their countless legs wriggling in abject ecstasy.

"Magic do usss, yesss?" they cried. "Wizardsss now we are, yesss? Ssspells cassst we! Yesss, yesss?"

As the silversanns continued their jubilation, Beckla pulled the others some distance away.

"What did you do to them?" Artek asked, staring at the creatures in disbelief. "Did you really teach them to cast a spell?"

"Don't be a ninny, Ar'talen," she replied smoothly. "Of course not. That would be completely impossible. While I was having them repeat all that mumbo-jumbo, I worked in the words and movements of a real spell. It's just a simple aura of light. It'll fade in an hour or so. But it should keep them occupied until then."

Artek laughed, clapping the wizard on the back.

"Nicely done, Beckla," he said. The back of his neck suddenly prickled. He looked around just in time to see Corin abruptly turn away. Artek sighed, his high spirits quickly sinking. They still had to find a way out of this place, he reminded himself.

Beckla moved over to see Guss and examine the object he had found earlier. Artek stooped to pick up Muragh and approached the wizard and the gargoyle.

"It's a ring," Guss said, his green eyes glowing with excitement.

"Are you two getting married?" Artek asked dryly.

"No, not that sort of ring," Beckla scowled. "It's a magical ring." She held up a small circle of polished gold. "And it's not broken."

Artek gazed at the ring, his own excitement rapidly growing. The ring was so small that the silversanns must have misplaced it among all the clutter before they could break it. "What do you think it is?" he asked.

"I'm not sure," Beckla replied. "But I think I can find out."

"It's awfully plain-looking," Muragh said critically. "I can't imagine it does much."

Beckla gave the skull a curious look. "Maybe. Then again, sometimes appearances can be deceiving."

As the silversanns chattered among themselves about their new magical "powers," the wizard sat cross-legged on the floor. She pulled out a grimy blue cloth from a pocket and spread it before her, placing the ring on it. Next, she drew out a small vial filled with yellow sand. She unstopped the vial and carefully poured out the sand, tracing a circle around the ring. Closing her eyes, she held her hands over the cloth.

"Circles within circles," she chanted softly. "Meanings within meanings. Grant me your guidance, Mystra, Lady of Mysteries, Goddess of Magic. Help me understand the nature of the enchantment that lies before me."

As the others watched in fascination, Beckla continued to chant, now in the ancient tongue of magic. After a moment, sparks of sapphire fell from her hands. They traced a slow spiral to the ring below, imbuing it with pale blue radiance. Lines of concentration furrowed the wizard's brow. Her hands began to tremble. Suddenly, her brown eyes flew open, and the blue sparks vanished.

"Oh!" she gasped.

"What is it?" Artek asked in alarm.

Beckla shook her head slowly. "She usually doesn't answer when I ask her questions like that. At least not so clearly."

"Who are you talking about?" Artek demanded.

"Mystra," Beckla replied.

Artek slapped a hand to his forehead in incredulity. "*What?* You're telling me that the goddess Mystra just spoke to you? She told you what this ring is?"

The wizard nodded solemnly. "That's right. She *is* the patron goddess of wizards, after all."

"I know that," Artek sputtered in disbelief. "But the gods don't just answer every little question you put to them."

"Apparently, sometimes they do," Muragh quipped. The skull addressed Beckla. "It seems Artek here is having a little problem with the matter of his faith. But I'm sure the rest of us would very much like to know what Mystra told you."

Beckla picked up the ring and held it gingerly in her hand. "It's a wishing ring," she murmured. The wizard's face suddenly seemed strangely troubled.

"A wishing ring?" Muragh exclaimed. "But that's wonderful! It means we can wish our way right out of this dump. Come on! What are you waiting for?"

"Not so fast, Muragh," Beckla countered. "It doesn't work that way. Remember those enchantments that Halaster bound into the walls of Undermountain, the ones that keep anyone from magically transporting out? Well, that goes for wishes, too. If we try to wish our way out of here, we'll probably find ourselves in some random part of Undermountain, and our wish wasted to boot." She lifted the ring, gazing through its open center. "There's only one wish left in this thing. We have to use it wisely."

Artek scratched the dark stubble on his chin. He was still skeptical that the goddess Mystra had truly spoken to Beckla. But even if the wizard was wrong about the ring, it couldn't hurt to make a wish on it. And if she was right . . .

He glanced at the silversanns at the far end of the chamber. The glowing creatures still slithered and undulated in ecstasy, completely oblivious to their *ssspecimens*.

Artek turned back to the others. Then he had it. "The last apprentice!" he said, snapping his fingers. "The ring can't transport us out of Undermountain. But it *can* take us to the last of Halaster's apprentices! It's our only hope."

Beckla arched a single eyebrow. "I thought you didn't believe that this is really a wishing ring. Have you changed your mind so soon?"

He glared darkly at her. "You're not making this faith thing any easier, you know. How will the ring work if we don't even know *who* or *where* the apprentice is?"

Beckla smiled smugly. "The ring knows."

"All right, we'll give it a try," he growled. "Beckla, you put on the ring. Now, let's all gather close so—"

His words were cut short as the chamber's iron door burst open with a thunderous *boom!* It flew through the air and struck one of the silversanns, crushing the hapless creature against a stone wall. For a moment, its antennae twitched jerkily, then went still.

A half-dozen steely forms lumbered through the gaping doorway, serrated claws waving menacingly.

"SQUCH! WRONG!" one of the thanatars droned angrily.

"PRISONERS! OURS!" intoned another.

Razor-sharp tails swiping wickedly, the thanatars charged the silversanns. Apparently, the lobster-creatures had decided they did not care for Squch's decision concerning Artek and the others. The silversanns screeched in terror, waving their feelers wildly as they tried to slither out of the reach of the larger mechanicals. Several were too slow, and the thanatars caught them in their pincers and squeezed, cleaving their sinuous, metallic bodies in two. The halves fell to the floor, twitching feebly. The thanatars droned in what seemed like satisfaction. Then one of the lobster-creatures caught sight of the adventurers.

"PRISONERS!" it droned. "GET!"

The thanatars lunged forward, and the five companions gaped in horror.

"Now, Beckla!" Artek cried.

Jamming the ring on a finger of her left hand, the wizard opened her mouth. At first nothing came out but a fearful croak. She took a deep breath, then tried again. This time, faint words escaped her lips.

"I wish . . . I wish we were in the lair of the last of Halaster's apprentices," she gasped.

The thanatars opened their jagged pincers, ready to snatch up the prisoners. But a sudden, brilliant flash of azure light sundered space. In an instant, the stony chamber, the writhing silversanns, and the violent thanatars vanished. For a single moment, humans, gargoyle, and skull were neither *here* nor *there*. Then came another blinding flash, and a new reality abruptly coalesced around them.

12

Fatal Game

"Now where are we?" Beckla asked in amazement.

"Near the end of our journey," Artek answered solemnly.

They stood beneath a high stone archway. Behind them, a corridor stretched into endless shadow. Before them lay their goal—the lair of the last apprentice still in Undermountain.

It was glorious. Walls of pale marble flecked with gold soared upward in vault after dizzying vault. An intricate mosaic adorned the lofty ceiling, depicting a fantastic sky: radiant day shone brilliantly upon one side, while night glittered with jewel-like stars upon the other. Light streamed down from the mosaic above—part of it sun-gold, part moon-pearl—refracting off the polished walls. It filled the chamber with shimmering luminescence.

In keeping with the ceiling, the chamber's expansive floor was a patchwork of marble squares, alternating in a checked pattern between white-gold noon and onyx midnight. Each of the squares was perhaps three paces across, and the floor was bordered on all sides by a swath of mottled green marble. On the far side of the hall, set into a shallow nave, was a door of gold. Instinct told Artek that, for good or for ill, they would find the last apprentice beyond it.

Tucked in the crook of Artek's arm, Muragh let out a reedy whistle. "I'll say one thing," the skull murmured in awe. "Whoever this apprentice is, he certainly has a flair for decorating."

Over the centuries, no visible signs of age or decay had touched the grand hall, which seemed to indicate that it had not been abandoned. This, in addition to the sheer beauty of the chamber, boded well for their chances. Or at least, so it seemed to Artek. Together they conferred on a course of action—all except for Corin.

"I'll just try to stay out of your way," the lord said meekly. He huddled just inside the stone archway, his back to the wall, staring down at his scuffed shoes. Artek sighed quietly, but he reminded himself that there was nothing he could do.

They had come here to seek the help of Halaster's apprentice, so it seemed best to approach the wizard's door directly, without stealth. However, so as not to alarm the apprentice, they decided Artek should go alone at first. Then he would signal the others when he deemed it appropriate for them to follow.

"Wish me luck," he said nervously.

The others all did so—except for Corin. Taking a deep breath, Artek turned to stride boldly toward the golden door across the room. As he left behind the strip of mottled green marble where the others were gathered, his boot stepped first upon a square of black. He took another step forward, onto a square of white.

Then he ran face first into some sort of a wall.

Like sunlight glancing off a clear window, a plane of white radiance flashed momentarily in front of him. With a cry of pain he stumbled backward, onto the black square.

"What in the Abyss was that?" he muttered in confusion, rubbing his throbbing nose. Whatever it was, it had *hurt*.

Beckla stood up, a curious frown on her broad face. "It looked like a magical barrier blocked your way," she said.

Artek tried moving onto the white square to his left. Once again a thin plane of white energy sprang into existence before him, blocking the way. The same thing happened when he tried to move to his right. Knowing what to expect, he did not smash his face against the magical barriers. Perplexed, he turned around and stepped back onto the swath of green marble that bordered the floor.

"Something very strange is going on here," he grumbled in annoyance.

Beckla's eyes suddenly went wide with surprise, and Guss let out a low growl of shock.

"You aren't kidding," Muragh said with a low whistle.

Artek turned back around, and an oath escaped his lips. As he watched, something appeared out of thin air on the far side of the room. Images flickered into existence, wavered like desert mirages, then grew solid. No, not *solid*, for Artek could still see dimly through their ghostly forms. They stood in two straight lines upon the two farthest rows of black and white squares, one creature per square, sixteen in all.

The eight in the first rank looked to be dwarven soldiers of some sort: long-bearded, horn-helmed, mail-clad, and bearing shimmering half-moon axes. Standing behind them in the rear row—one to each side—were two tusked, long-armed ogres; two silvery knights mounted upon black steeds and bearing gleaming lances; and a pair of stern-faced sorcerers in pointed hats. These six flanked two tall, imposing figures in the center of the back row. Flowing mantles fell from wide shoulders; glimmering crowns rested upon high brows; pale eyes gazed forward in steely authority. Proud they were, and cruel: a king and a queen.

With terrible certainty, Artek knew it was going to be no easy task getting to the gold door across the room. Even if he could find a way to avoid the glowing magical barriers between white and black squares, he now had an eerie army to contend with. At the moment, the ethereal figures stood motionless, gazing forward with impassive, unblinking eyes. Yet Artek suspected this would rapidly change if he drew near.

He fixed Beckla with a piercing look. "You had to wish us to the apprentice's lair, rather than to the apprentice himself."

She shrugged her shoulders sheepishly. "Oops."

Artek let out a groan of exasperation. "How did I know you were going to say that?"

Beckla drew her eyebrows together in a scowl. "Look, Ar'talen. I was a little pressed for time. The thanatars were about to chop us to bits, if you recall. We really didn't have the opportunity to debate whether I should wish for *this* or *that*. We're lucky we made it out of there at all." She gestured toward the phantasmal army. "I think it would be more productive if we all directed our energy to the problem at hand."

The wizard was right, but Artek shot her a nasty look all the same, just to let her know he was not happy. He crossed his thick arms across his black leather jerkin and studied the scene before him with dark eyes. "It's like some game the apprentice has prepared for us," he murmured to himself.

To his surprise, someone answered him. "It's not just some game," said a quiet voice. "It's lanceboard."

Artek turned around. It was Corin. The young lord gazed with his clear blue eyes at the eerie figures across the room. "Don't you see?" Corin went on timidly. "With those black and white checks, the entire floor serves as the playing board. And those figures over there are the opponent's playing pieces."

Artek turned back toward the gigantic lanceboard. It made sense—the apprentice would not let just anyone enter his domain. They had to best the wizard at a game of lanceboard first. If they could do

so, it was likely the apprentice would view them fa-
vorably. But something odd struck Artek. "If those
are our opponent's playing pieces, then where are
ours?"

Beckla swallowed hard. "I think we're them."

Even as her words chilled him, Artek knew they
were right. No ghostly army had appeared on their
side of the marble gameboard. They themselves were
the only playing pieces they were going to get.

"Why don't I just fly across the room?" Guss
asked.

Wings flapping, the gargoyle rose into the air. He
was no more than three feet off the floor when a
plane of white magic flashed above him. He fell back
to the green marble, landing with a grunt.

"Oh, I suppose *that's* why," he winced, rubbing his
scaly tail.

"Well, this is just wonderful," Artek growled in
disgust, running a hand through his short black
hair. "I've never played a game of lanceboard in my
life. I don't even have the foggiest notion of the
rules."

He looked to Beckla, but the wizard shook her
head. So did Guss. Neither knew how to play the
game. Artek's gaze drifted toward the yellowed skull
he had set down on the green marble.

"Well, don't look at me," Muragh said defensively.
"I was just a lowly priest of Lathander in life."

The others turned their eyes toward Corin. The
young lord looked up in shock, his face drawn.

"No," he whispered hoarsely, slowly shaking his
head back and forth. "Not me . . ."

Artek quickly moved forward and knelt beside

Corin. "You know how to play lanceboard, don't you?" he asked intently.

Corin opened his mouth to reply, but no words came out. It didn't matter. Artek already knew the answer. Corin had recognized the gameboard and the playing pieces. Like every noble child, he had learned to play the game.

"You have to help us, Corin," Artek said gravely. He gripped the young man's shoulders. "You have to help us get across the room. You're the only one who can do it."

Corin tried to back away, but Artek's strong hands held him firmly. "But I can't," the nobleman gasped. "Don't you understand? If I make a mistake, you'll all be killed."

"And if you don't try, we'll all die for certain," Artek growled.

Tears sprang into Corin's eyes, along with a look of terror. "You don't understand. I can't do it. I tried . . . I tried to be worth something, but I failed. You said so yourself." He shook his head. "He was right. He was always right. I suppose I deserved it," Corin sobbed.

In sudden dread, Artek gazed at the noble. A coldness crept into his heart, and dark realization into his mind. He gripped the young man's shoulders more tightly, searching his frightened face. "What did he do to you, Corin?" Artek asked. "By all the gods, what did your father do to you?"

Beckla, Guss, and Muragh stared at them in shock. A low moan escaped Corin's lips.

"Tell me!" Artek demanded, baring his white teeth.

This time he did not wait for an answer. With brutal force, he spun Corin around. He gripped the lord's dirty silk shirt in two hands and tore it apart.

"Ur thokkar!" he swore in the language of orcs.

Crisscrossing the skin of Corin's back were countless pale scars. Artek had seen enough thieves flogged in public squares to know what the raised weals were—lash marks. As a child, Artek had often received the cruel abuse of his father's tongue, and once or twice, Arturg had even struck him. But never this. Never had he suffered anything like this.

Stunned, Artek released Corin. The young lord pulled the tattered remains of his shirt back over his shoulders, concealing the scars once again. Hesitantly, he looked up with wounded eyes at Artek. For a moment, all Artek could see was a small, golden-haired boy in a corner, injured and afraid, trying with all his courage not to cry.

"I had to bear it," Corin said finally in a quiet voice, barely a whisper. "I couldn't weep. I couldn't resist. I had to bear it because if I did, then maybe he would love me."

Trembling, Corin continued, as if words long dammed up inside were now rushing from him of their own volition. The others could only listen in growing horror. "I was the youngest of three sons, you see. Corlus, my eldest brother, was to inherit the Silvertor estate. My other brother, Cordair, was the most like my father, being skilled at arms and gambling, and well liked by other men. And then there was me.

"My mother died in childbirth when I was born. I think my father always blamed me for that. At least, I used to tell myself that he did. That way it all made some sort of sense—there was a reason that nothing I could ever say or do pleased him." As he spoke, Corin kept his gaze on the floor. "Most of the time he just ignored me and kept busy with Corlus and Cordair. But once a moon or so, he would come home reeking of wine, and feeling sour-tempered from losing at gambling. He would roar for me at the top of his lungs, and I didn't dare refuse to come. I would find him in his chamber, his riding whip in his hands. That was when . . ."

Corin suddenly looked up at the others. A smile twisted his lips. "Fate is strange, isn't it? Who would have thought that my father would outlive my brothers? But Corlus died of the red fever, and Cordair got a knife in the heart when he was caught cheating at dice in a tavern by the harbor. Then this winter my father finally died. The physicians said it was the drink that did it. I came to him at his deathbed. And do you know what he told me? 'You are the one I should have outlived.' That was all he said. Then he died." Corin's gaze returned to his shoes.

"My father's death left me as the sole heir to the Silvertor legacy. And to his seat on the Circle of Nobles. Our House is one of the oldest in the city, and there has always been a Silvertor on the Circle—the vote is a mere formality. I suppose I should have been happy. But I wasn't." He clenched his hands into fists. "I didn't want his House. I didn't want his blasted seat on the Circle. I could never please my father. How could I possibly please all of the other nobles in Waterdeep?"

Forcibly, he unclenched his hands and let out a weary sigh. "The truth is, when Lord Darien Thal in-

vited me on the hunt into Undermountain, I secretly
hoped something would happen to me—something
bad. I told myself it would all be so much easier that
way." Wiping the tears from his cheeks, he looked at
Artek. "And here I am," he finished softly. "I know
you can never forgive me for getting you into this,
Artek. But I want you to know that I am sorry—terribly sorry."

For a long time, Artek could say nothing. All this
time he had thought of Corin as a mere nuisance, as
an object to be rescued and nothing more. In that, he
had been no better than the young lord's father. Perhaps worse. He of all people should have known better. He knew what it was like to be scorned by one
whose love he craved; he knew what it was like to
learn to loathe himself. If Corin's father were still
alive, Artek would have vowed to kill him. But ven-
geance cannot be gained from the dead, and the living are left to bear the scars inflicted.

At last Artek drew in a deep breath. Maybe it was
too late for him, but Corin was young. Maybe there
was still time for the young man to find a sort of
healing, to be whole. Artek reached out and gripped
Corin's shoulders. He gazed into the young man's
eyes and would not let him look away.

"Listen to me, Corin," he said solemnly. "Listen to
me, because I speak the truth. I was wrong. Your father was wrong. You aren't worthless. You have to
believe that. I know that there are voices inside you,
voices that tell you otherwise, but you have to stop
listening to them because they, too, are wrong. No
one deserves what happened to you, Corin. Do you
hear me? No one."

At last Corin stopped struggling and held still within Artek's grasp. Artek kept talking.

"Don't you see, Corin? We need you. All of us. You're the only one who can get us across that lanceboard. You're the only one who can help us." Black eyes bore into clear blue ones. "Please," he whispered. "Won't you try?"

For a long moment, Corin sat as if frozen, staring with unseeing eyes. Artek despaired, fearing his words had fallen upon deaf ears. Then Corin's pale visage seemed to melt, and he blinked, drawing in a shuddering breath. At last he nodded. "I can't promise anything," he said in a hoarse voice. "But I will try."

Artek could not suppress a toothy grin. He encircled Corin in his strong arms, embracing him tightly. The young man stiffened. Then, tentatively, he lifted his arms to return the embrace.

"Excuse me, Artek," Corin gasped after a time, "but I'd like to breathe now."

"Oh, sorry!" Artek exclaimed, releasing the young man from his grip.

Corin stood, smiling shyly. "Actually, you're all rather in luck, you know. Though my father never placed much stock in it—it wasn't a blood sport, you see—I was something of a champion at lanceboard among my peers." He clapped his hands together. "Now, let's get started. We have a game to play."

A new air of confidence and authority gradually crept into Corin's words and actions. For the first time since Artek had met him, the young man truly seemed like a lord. He surveyed the gameboard critically, forming a strategy.

"This isn't going to be simple," Corin murmured, his expression one of intent concentration. "Our opponent has a full complement of playing pieces, and we are only four."

"Make that five!" Muragh piped up, rolling toward the nobleman's feet.

Corin actually laughed as he picked up the skull. "Ah, then there *is* some hope after all," he said.

With crisp commands, he directed the others to their starting locations on the first row of the gameboard. Artek took the King's position, and Beckla the Queen's, next to him. Corin placed Guss on the end, in the role of an Ogre, and took a Knight position for himself. Muragh, to his delight, was a Sorcerer.

After this, Corin instructed each of them on the manner of their movement.

"Artek, when you first stepped onto the board, it was where Muragh is now, on the starting square of a Sorcerer," Corin explained. "Sorcerers can only move along a diagonal. That's why you encountered the magical barrier when you tried to move forward and side-to-side."

Artek nodded at the nobleman's words. As long as they moved according to the rules of the pieces they were playing, they should be able to walk across the board without encountering the glowing barriers.

Corin continued to instruct them in the rules of their movement. As King, Artek could walk in any direction he chose, but only one square at a time. Beckla, acting as the Queen, could also move in any direction. However, she could go as many spaces as she wished. Upon learning of this advantage, she flashed Artek a smug expression. Guss, the Ogre, was informed that he could move as far as he wished along straight lines, but not along a diagonal, which was Muragh's sole ability as Sorcerer. Corin had taken the most difficult role for himself, for a Knight was forced to move in a curious pattern: two squares in a straight line, then one more square to either side.

Once they knew the rules, they were ready to begin.

"It looks like the starting move is up to us," Corin decided. "We're playing from weakness, but that doesn't mean we can't act boldly. King, move one square forward."

Artek stepped from his white starting square onto the black square before him. No magical barrier appeared to block his passage. He let out a sigh of relief.

The moment Artek finished his move, an ethereal figure on the far side of the chamber abruptly began to move. One of the dimly transparent dwarves in the front row—Soldiers, Corin called those pieces—stepped one square forward, then halted, standing as still as before.

"I was afraid of that," Corin said grimly.

"Afraid of what?" Artek asked in growing dread.

"This really is just like a game of lanceboard," the nobleman replied. "Every time one of us moves, one of our opponent's pieces gets to move as well."

Artek shifted uncomfortably on the black square. "Wait a minute, Corin. Isn't the point of this game to capture your opponent's pieces?"

The young lord nodded silently.

"All right," Artek went on. "Then what happens to

one of us if we're captured by another piece?"

Corin took a deep breath. "All captured pieces are removed from the gameboard," he said evenly.

The others shivered as the implication of these words registered upon them. A chill danced up Artek's spine, and he licked his lips nervously. *Removed from the gameboard.* It sounded very . . . final.

"I guess we'll just have to keep from getting captured, won't we?" Artek said, hoping he sounded more confident than he felt.

It was their turn again.

"Sorcerer!" Corin called out. "Diagonal to your left, two squares. Protect your King."

His mandible working furiously, Muragh hopped and rolled into position. As he came to a halt on his square, one of the ghostly Knights leapt the Soldier in front of it and sallied out onto the gameboard. Corin himself moved next, mirroring the enemy Knight's position. The knight moved again. Corin tracked him. This time another Soldier moved forward.

"Ogre, ahead two and challenge!" Corin commanded.

Guss obeyed, lumbering forward toward the middle of the board. One of the opposing Sorcerers drifted menacingly in his direction but could not have captured him anyway, for Guss and the translucent Sorcerer were on opposite colors.

Corin shook his head. "This is difficult with so few pieces. Do you see, Artek? There's a clear diagonal between you and that Sorcerer—and that's the only way he can move. You're in danger now. However, I can move to protect you."

"Wait a minute!" Artek protested. "Won't the Sorcerer be able to capture you then?"

"If so, then our Queen will be able to take him," Corin replied with only a slight quaver in his voice. "We'll have to hope our opponent is not yet ready to sacrifice one of his pieces." Before Artek could argue further, Corin moved two and then one, ending up standing between Artek and the enemy Sorcerer.

Fortunately, Corin's reasoning proved correct. The Sorcerer did not capture Corin. Instead, it moved diagonally back one square, taking itself out of Guss's path.

"Good, we've got our opponent on the retreat," Corin said. "Now is the time to keep pressing forward."

Following Corin's directions, they executed several more moves, making good progress across the board while avoiding the opposing pieces. Then one of the enemy Knights galloped silently forward, lance aimed menacingly at Artek.

Corin let out a sharp laugh. "It seems our opponent grows impatient. The Knight is in your path, Queen, and Ogre is protecting you. Capture him!"

Beckla swallowed hard, straightening her vest. "Here goes nothing," she said dubiously. The wizard steeled her shoulders, then moved boldly forward, stepping onto the same square as the enemy Knight. The Knight lowered its lance toward her, but its horse reared back, opening its mouth in a silent scream. A gout of green fire sprang up from the floor, consuming the Knight as it rose toward the ceiling. A moment later, the magical fire vanished.

Beckla stared at the faint scorch mark on the floor—all that remained of the Knight. "Something

tells me we definitely do not want to get captured,"
she said.

The others could only nod in agreement. They continued to move across the board, but their progress
was slower now. Corin was deep in concentration,
and sweat beaded on his smooth brow. It was becoming steadily more difficult to avoid capture. Artek
took an opposing Soldier, and Guss a Sorcerer—both
opposing pieces were consumed by pillars of emerald
flame.

"Queen, move two to your left!" Corin called out.
Just as Beckla started to step in that direction, the
nobleman shouted in alarm. "Wait! Stop!"

Beckla halted, no more than an inch from the
edge of her present square.

"I'm sorry," Corin said breathlessly. "You'll be exposed to their Ogre from that position. I didn't see it
until it was almost too late."

Corin studied the board again. Seconds stretched
into long minutes. The others watched him in growing alarm. The nobleman muttered under his breath,
going through move after move in his mind. It
seemed he could find none that would not result in
capture. Finally, he looked back at Artek, his expression grim.

"I'm afraid we're out of choices. There's only one
thing I can think of, and I'm afraid it's a rather risky
gambit. If it fails, we're lost."

Artek gazed at him unflinchingly. "I trust you,
Corin."

For a moment, it almost seemed a faint smile of
gratitude touched the young lord's lips. He nodded.
"Very well, then. It's time to gamble our King. Let's

just hope they take the bait. King! Ahead one!"

Artek did as instructed. In response, an opposing
Soldier moved one square out of the way. In sudden
alarm, Artek saw that he was surrounded on three
sides. An enemy Knight, Queen, and Ogre were all in
position to capture him. It had been his last move.
There would be no escaping.

"We've lost," he said, his hopes dying.

"Not yet!" Corin cried out. "It seems you've
forgotten the same thing our opponent has." He
pointed toward a small yellow object that for some
time now had sat unnoticed near the side of the
gameboard. "Now, Muragh!"

Grinning toothily, the skull rolled forward, moving in an unobstructed diagonal line—straight toward the enemy King. The ghostly King's mouth
opened in a silent cry of surprise and fear, but it
could not move aside. Muragh careened directly into
the ethereal form. The King's arms spread wide as a
blazing column of green fire sprang from the floor
beneath its feet. A second later, many more pillars of
emerald magic shot toward the ceiling, each consuming one of the remaining enemy game pieces. As suddenly as they had appeared, the columns of fire
dissipated—the ghostly figures were no more. Artek
stared in wonder. They had won.

With no opposing pieces, all they had to do now
was avoid the magical force walls by moving cor-
rectly. They made their way swiftly across the gameboard and stepped onto the swath of green marble
bordering the far side.

Artek gripped Corin's shoulder. "You did it," he
said with a fierce grin.

Corin smiled. "I did, didn't I?" he asked in amazement.

Their jubilation fell into silence as their eyes turned toward the golden door in the wall. It was time to see what waited beyond.

Together they approached the nave. Any thought of one of them going alone had been dismissed without discussion. There was no doorknob, so Artek reached out to push on the door. Just as his fingers brushed the smooth, gold surface, the door swung silently inward. A puff of dry air rushed out, and they stepped into the space beyond.

The chamber was small, with no other doors or openings but the one through which they had entered. The walls and floor were of the same gold-flecked marble as the outer hall. The only furnishings were a table and chair hewn of polished onyx. A male figure sat in the chair, slumped forward over the table. His rich velvet robes had long ago decayed to tatters, and his withered skin clung like old parchment to his yellowed bones. Rotted gray hair drooped over his bony shoulders. It was the last apprentice. And by the look of him, he had died in this room long centuries ago.

Artek shook his head sadly. Had it all been for nothing—the entire perilous game of lanceboard? He didn't know why he was surprised. He really should be getting used to disappointment by now.

"Look," Beckla said softly. "There's something in his hands."

She approached the mummified apprentice and carefully removed an object from the grip of his brittle fingers. It was a small, silver disk with thin writing engraved upon one side. They gathered around Beckla to read the words:

The deeper you go, the deeper I get.
If you jump sideways, you may find me yet.
                                        —H.

Without doubt the *H* at the bottom stood for *Halaster*. Evidently, this riddle was a clue that the mad mage had left behind to help his students find him. Only it seemed this apprentice had died trying.

Artek glanced down at the inky tattoo on his arm. The wheel continued to spin slowly, inexorably. The moon had long passed the arrow, and now the sun drew near. By his best guess, it was no more than an hour until daybreak in the city above, no more than an hour until the tattoo sent out a fatal jolt of magic, stopping his heart forever. For all he knew, the last apprentice had spent centuries trying to solve Halaster's riddle, and without success. Artek doubted they could answer it in a mere hour. He shook his head sadly. The others sighed. There was no need for words. They had run out of apprentices, and out of hope.

"Well, now what?" Muragh piped up finally, unable to bear the gloomy silence. "Are we all just going to stand here moping at each other until we turn to dust?"

"No, the rest of you shouldn't give up," Artek said solemnly. "You may yet find a way out of Undermountain. You've still got a chance, but I'm afraid I don't have one much longer."

"Neither do we, really," Beckla replied darkly. She

glanced at Corin, a strange sorrow in her eyes. "I haven't seen much food or water in this part of Undermountain. We won't last for very long without both."

After a moment, Artek nodded gravely. He respected the wizard too much to argue with her. She and Corin might be able to keep searching for a few more days before thirst and exhaustion overcame them. But only if they were lucky.

Artek turned toward Guss and Muragh. The gargoyle gripped the skull tightly in his clawed hands, worry showing in his glowing green eyes.

"Even after the rest of us are . . . gone, you two don't have to quit searching for a way out of here," Artek told them seriously. "You can keep looking for as long as it takes. Eventually, you're bound to find a gate that will take you out of here."

Beckla ran a hand through her close-cropped hair. "I'm afraid that won't do them much good," she said sadly. "Muragh and Guss aren't alive in the conventional sense of the word. Neither of them could pass through a gate without a living being accompanying them."

Artek hung his head in sorrow. So they were all doomed together. He started to sink to the floor in despair.

Then, like a bolt of lightning, it struck him. He stared at the wizard, as if looking for an answer. Something was not right.

"Wait a minute, Beckla," he said in confusion. "If Guss can't go through a gate all by himself, why did you send him to test the one we found in the cave in Wyllowwood?"

The question caught the wizard entirely off guard.

Her mouth opened in surprise, and she stumbled backward. After a moment, she tried to sputter an explanation, but Artek cut her off. All this time, something about the wizard had been bothering him. Something had been nagging at the back of his mind, but he had been too busy to really consider it. At last, he knew what it was.

"That gate would have worked for some of us, wouldn't it? Don't lie to me anymore, Beckla," he hissed, baring his pointed teeth in a feral snarl. "I know now that you already *have*. Your hair gives you away. When we first met, you told me that you had lived in Undermountain for over a year. And your clothes look it. But your hair is short, as if it had been recently cut. Don't try to tell me that you did such a fine job with the edge of your dagger."

Beckla did not deny his words. Instead, she braced her shoulders, gazing at him, deep remorse in her brown eyes.

"Damn it, Beckla!" Artek snarled. "Tell me what in the Abyss is going on here!"

The wizard took a deep breath.

"I've betrayed you," she said.

Horned Ring

Crimson rage surged in Artek's head, and blood pounded in his ears. His orcish side howled in silent fury at the utterance of the cursed word—*betrayed*. He gripped the edge of the onyx table, knuckles white, teeth clenched. He could not let go. He did not dare. There was no telling what violence his hands would commit if he did. He glared at Beckla with smoldering black eyes.

"Tell me," he commanded hoarsely.

They were the only words he could manage. The others stared at Beckla in astonishment, trying to comprehend what was happening. At last, the wizard nodded. Pain burned in her brown eyes, but her shoulders were straight, her too-square jaw resolute.

"I'll explain everything," she said solemnly. "I know now that I can't lie to you anymore. Though once I tell the truth, I imagine that you'll most likely decide to kill me. Not that I could blame you. There's only one thing that I ask. Just let me finish before you . . . deal with me. I think you owe me that much."

"No promises," Artek hissed. His arms trembled. He wished to let go of the stone and crush a living throat instead. "Just talk."

Beckla sighed. "As you wish," she said simply. "Not everything I told you was a lie." She shook her head ruefully. "Some of it was all too true. I am indeed a small-time wizard. I've been kicked out of more mage schools than I can count, usually for lack of money." A sardonic smile twisted her lips. "Though once or twice it was for telling the master mage just where he could stuff his wand. In case you hadn't noticed, I can be a little abrasive at times."

"Oh, I hadn't noticed, really," Guss murmured politely.

Beckla winked at the gargoyle in gratitude. Then her expression grew grim.

"All right, here's the part you don't know," the wizard said, crossing her arms across her grubby shirt as she paced before the table. "It wasn't by chance that I happened upon you in the upper halls of Undermountain, Artek. But it really *was* blind luck that I was there in time to help you with those flying snakes. The truth is, I haven't spent the last year in Undermountain. I came in by a private entrance no more than two hours before you entered the maze yourself. Before that, I had been informed of Corin's whereabouts. You see, it was my job all along to lead you to the lost lord—that's what I was hired to do."

"Hired?" Artek asked. "Hired by whom?"

Beckla paused and then spoke without emotion. "Lord Darien Thal."

An animalistic snarl ripped itself from deep in Artek's throat. Somehow he had known he was going to hear that foul name again. He let go of the table, bearing down on Beckla. Only by great effort did he keep his shaking hands at his sides. The others looked on, mouths agape.

"So what did he offer you?" Artek hissed. "A tower of your own? The finest tutors of magic? Money to purchase all you needed to research your precious spells? Was that it, wizard? Did he offer to buy your dreams for you?"

"Yes," Beckla whispered. She gazed, not at Artek, but into space, as if she could see a vision of all she had ever desired floating before her. "He promised to make me a great wizard, a mage of renown. All I had to do was lead you to Corin. Then you would use the transportation device he gave you, which would take you deeper into Undermountain."

Part of Artek's anger was lost to confusion. "I don't understand. If your job was to get us lost deeper in Undermountain, then why did you come with us? And why did you help us every time we were attacked?"

"Lord Thal didn't want to leave anything to chance," Beckla explained evenly. "At first, he wanted me to lead you both to your deaths, and to bring back proof of your demise. But I refused him on that point."

"How kind of you," Artek spat bitterly.

Beckla winced at his words but went on. "We decided that I would go with you through the gate, to make certain you did not return to the surface before two days had passed. By then, the nobles would have held their vote, and Lord Thal would have been elected to the Circle. And the reason I helped out in all those scrapes is easy enough—I was protecting my own neck."

Corin stepped forward, his boyish face both worried and perplexed. "But I still don't understand, Beckla. Why in the world would you agree to such a task? Once you were lost with us, how were you supposed to escape from Undermountain yourself?"

"With this."

She drew something from a pocket of her vest and held it up. It was a bronze ring inlaid with small rubies. Two small prongs stood up from the center of the ring like curved horns, holding a larger ruby between them.

Artek stared at the ring in shock. "You mean, all this time you've had a way out?"

Beckla nodded gravely. "This ring has the power to gate whoever wears it out of Undermountain. I could have left you at any time. But I didn't. I don't suppose that counts for anything, but I wanted you to know.

"I had always thought that I would give anything for my dream, but I know now that a dream at any price isn't a dream at all—it's a nightmare." She hung her head. "Do what you will now," she whispered softly.

Artek bared his slightly pointed teeth. He raised his big hands before him. He knew now what would be the wizard's punishment for her betrayal. Corin and Guss reached for him, as if to hold him back, but he shook them off. A low growl rumbled in his chest. He sprang forward, catching the wizard in his arms, and with his orcish strength began to squeeze her—in a rough but warm embrace.

Beckla's eyes grew large with astonishment, as did those of the others. Artek laughed, lifted the wizard off the floor, and spun her around. At last, he set her down. She gripped the table dizzily to keep from falling.

"I don't understand," she gasped. "Aren't you angry with me?"

"By all the fires of the Abyss, you'd better believe I'm angry with you, Beckla Shadesar. You should have told us before about that ring of yours. It could have saved us a rather large amount of trouble. But the fact is, you *didn't* betray us. You could have, but you chose not to." He reached out to squeeze her hand. "And that's all that matters."

Color crept slowly into Beckla's cheeks. A smile stole across her lips, and a mischievous spark flashed in her brown eyes. "I think Lord Darien Thal is going to be in for a bit of a surprise." She held up the magical ring. "Let's get out of this dump."

The wizard pressed one of the small rubies on the ring, and it popped out, falling into her hand. Thrice more she did this, then gave a ruby to each of the others, sticking Muragh's in his bony ear hole. Finally, Beckla put the ring on her right hand. They gathered close as she held up the ring and spoke in a commanding voice. "Gate—open!"

The ring flashed. In the air before them appeared a glowing line. The line widened into a doorway filled with billowing gray mist.

"All right, everybody," Beckla cried. "Hold on!"

Together they leapt through the misty portal and fell into the nothingness beyond. Once again, Artek felt the terrible, bodiless cold that gnawed at the very center of his being, but it lasted only a moment. There was another flash, and a crackling hole opened in midair, a gap in the very fabric of the world. The five tumbled through the hole and struck a hard stone floor.

"Can't you program these things for softer landings?" Corin complained as they stood. "I'm really not certain I can take much more . . . oh." His words faltered as they gazed around.

A rough-hewn corridor stretched into shadow in either direction. Pale fungus clung to the walls, and dark water trickled across the floor.

Artek swore vehemently.

"I don't understand," Beckla said in confusion. "The ring was supposed to take us to the surface, but this still looks like—"

"Undermountain," Artek spat, finishing for her. He shook his head and almost laughed. Almost, but his chest was too tight with the bitter irony of it all. What fools they were! "Don't you see, Beckla? Haven't you figured it out yet? He's betrayed you, too."

The wizard's face blanched. Then anger ignited in her eyes. She spoke a single, hateful word, as if it were a curse: "Thal."

Artek nodded grimly. "It makes sense. He couldn't have allowed you to live—you knew that he had arranged Corin's demise. So, he made certain that you would never escape from Undermountain either."

A great heaviness came upon Artek, weighing him down. "Well, it looks as if Darien has beaten us to our little surprise. He has defeated us after all. But I suppose it was well that we tried." He glanced at his tattoo—less than an hour left. At least he would not have long to wait for his end to come. The others would not be so lucky. It was hard to believe now that the legacy of the *Garug-Mal* truly ran in his blood, because the darkness held no comfort. It was cold, and bleak, and utterly empty.

"Wait just a second," Muragh piped up suddenly. "Guss, pick me up. Beckla, hold up your hand. I need to take a look at that ring of yours."

The others regarded Muragh in vague curiosity, but they did as he instructed. The skull peered at the ring with his empty eye sockets.

"Hmm," he muttered through his broken teeth. "I was afraid of that," the skull pronounced finally.

"Afraid of what?" Artek asked, not certain he had the energy to play the skull's guessing games anymore.

"This is a Horned Ring," Muragh replied. "Not a common find in Undermountain, but not so rare either. Halaster made quite a few of them."

"Wait a minute," Artek protested. "You mean Halaster himself made this thing?"

Somehow the fleshless skull managed to look annoyed. "Granted, I don't have lips, so sometimes I tend to mumble, but I'm pretty certain that's what I said."

Beckla studied the ring with new interest. "If it won't take us out of Undermountain, what will it do?"

"Take us down," Muragh replied. "A Horned Ring will gate you anywhere you want to go in Undermountain, as long as it's below where you are at the moment. With every jump, it takes its wearer deeper."

Artek looked at the skull in sudden shock. "What did you say?" he demanded hoarsely.

"Really, Artek," the skull grumbled. "Why don't you clean the orc cheese out of your ears? I'm getting awfully tired of repeating myself."

But Artek was no longer paying attention to the skull. He paced quickly over the damp stone floor, his mind working feverishly.

"Of course!" he exclaimed, smacking his forehead with his hand. "That's the answer!"

"The answer to what?" Beckla asked.

"Halaster's riddle," he replied in growing excitement. "Remember? 'The deeper you go, the deeper I get. If you jump sideways, you may find me yet.' "

"I think maybe you've jumped a little too deep yourself," Muragh noted acerbically.

Artek ignored him. "Don't you see, Beckla? You said it yourself, back when you were explaining to me the difference between teleporting and using a gate. Teleportation is a fast but direct journey between places." He brought his hands together. "But using a gate is like jumping—"

"Sideways," Beckla breathed.

Artek snapped his fingers. "Exactly! That's the key to finding Halaster. If every use of the Horned Ring takes you deeper, eventually you would have to reach the deepest part of Undermountain. And where else would the Mad Wizard be except at the very bottom of his own maze?"

"Do you think we really dare disturb Halaster himself?" Corin asked, a startled expression on his smudged face.

"It's our only chance," Artek replied. "He's the only one who could transport us out of here. What have we got to lose?"

"You can count me in," Guss said with a grin.

"Me too!" Muragh added.

"And me," Beckla said firmly.

Corin smoothed his grimy, tattered silk shirt, then gripped the rapier at his side. "Well, I'm not about to miss all the fun."

Artek surveyed the determined faces of the others. He had entered Undermountain alone. Never had he expected to find such allies, such friends, in its dark depths. His heart swelled. "Let's do it," he said.

They gathered close together, making certain each still had a ruby. Then Beckla raised the ring. "Gate!" she ordered. "Open!"

The misty portal appeared before them.

"Here goes nothing," Artek murmured.

Together they jumped through.

They fell sprawling to the floor of a great cavern. An acrid smell hung in the dank air. Artek heard a strange clinking sound and looked up.

Glittering blue scales armored the vast, sinuous body of a blue dragon. Like sapphire sails, leathery wings spread open in a menacing display. Red eyes flaring hotly, the dragon stretched its serpentine neck, rising off the mountain of gold, silver, and jewels upon which it sprawled.

"Thieves!" it shrieked in a deafening voice.

The dragon opened its toothy maw, preparing to kill them with its deadly breath.

"Beckla, the gate!" Artek cried. "Open it!"

The wizard needed no prompting. She shouted the words. Instantly, the glowing portal appeared in the air before them. They threw themselves toward the billowing mists just as a terrible crackling filled the air. Blazing bolts of blue lightning emanated from the dragon's maw, sizzling toward them. Just before they were engulfed by searing, sapphire death, the magical fog swallowed them. Dragon, cavern, and lightning vanished.

They quickly lost count of the jumps they made using the Horned Ring.

Sometimes they landed in musty stone corridors and dim tombs. Other times they found themselves suddenly facing snarling abominations ready to rip their throats out. Once, they plunged into bone-chilling water, and another time they landed on a small basalt islet lost amid a sea of molten lava. Each time, Beckla quickly resummoned the gate, and they leapt through, passing from one peril to another in dizzying succession.

Then they landed on a stone floor. Thick clouds of dust billowed sluggishly around them. They were in a cobweb-filled antechamber. By the look of it, no one had set foot in this place in centuries. But there was no time to waste—they had to keep jumping.

"Gate, open!" Beckla called out.

The portal appeared, and they lunged through.

They landed on a stone floor. Thick clouds of dust filled the air around them.

Artek blinked in surprise. It was the same antechamber they had landed in a moment ago. The jump had taken them no deeper. Then he realized why.

"We're here," he said.

This was it. The very bottom of Undermountain.

As they stood, their eyes fell upon a small, nondescript wooden door set into one wall. There was no other exit. The five exchanged uncertain looks but there was only one thing to do. They approached the door, and Artek turned the brass knob. The door swung open.

"Blast it—company!" hissed a cracked voice. "I must have forgotten to reset the poison-spiked welcome mat again. Well, don't just stand there like you don't have the brains of a black pudding among you. Shut the door. You're letting in a draft!"

They were so startled by these words that they could only numbly obey. Closing the door, they took a step into the chamber beyond. No, not *chamber*, Artek corrected himself. Make that *laboratory*.

If there was any rhyme or reason to the laboratory, it was beyond Artek's comprehension. Chaos ruled supreme here. Vials and beakers balanced precariously on makeshift tables fashioned from moldering books. Weird objects cluttered crooked shelves: mummified animal parts, jars filled with staring eyeballs, and small stone idols with leering expressions. A bucket carelessly filled with jewels sat next to a glass case that enshrined a collection of toenail clippings. Candles had been stuck with melted wax to every available surface: floor, shelves, books, jars, and the skulls of articulated skeletons. However, they seemed to cast more smoke than light, filling the room with flickering shadows that tricked the eye. In all, it was like the locked attic room of someone's mad uncle—peculiar, musty, and vaguely sinister.

Then Artek saw the old man. It took some concentration to pick him out from among the mess. He was clad in a drab black robe that was belted crookedly around the waist with a frayed bit of rope. Scraggly gray hair hung loosely over his stooped, bony shoulders as he bent over a wooden table, muttering and cackling to himself as he worked on something hidden from view.

Artek guessed that the man was a lackey of Halaster's. However, if he *was* a doorman, he wasn't a very good one. The fellow seemed to have completely forgotten about their presence. After a moment, Artek cleared his throat. "Excuse me," he said hesitantly.

The old man continued to mutter to himself, poring over the table before him.

Gathering his courage, Artek took a step forward. This time he spoke more loudly. "Excuse me, but we're really in a bit of a hurry. We were wondering if you could tell us where we might find Halas—"

The old man looked up, twisting his head to peer back over his shoulder. His ancient face was nearly lost beneath a long gray beard and spiky eyebrows— all Artek could make out was a bladelike nose and two colorless eyes as cold and piercing as ice.

"What?" the old man interrupted. "You're still here?" He blew a snort of disgust through his ratty mustache. "I must have forgotten to oil the trigger on the boulder over the door as well. Well, if you're not going to have the decency to die, at least stop being such a nuisance with all your chatter. Can't you see that I'm working? Now make yourself useful and hand me that."

He thrust a bony finger toward a small jar of

black paint on a nearby shelf. Before Artek even knew what he was doing, he hopped forward to obey the command. Chagrined, he brought the jar of paint to the ancient man. Artek craned his neck, but could not quite glimpse what the other man was working on. It was something very small. After a moment, the old man cackled in glee.

"Done!"

Scooping up several tiny objects into a withered hand, he marched with surprising swiftness toward an opening in the far wall and disappeared beyond. Artek exchanged curious looks with the others. After a moment's hesitation, they followed after. Stepping through the opening, they found themselves not in another chamber, but on the edge of a vast cavern. A red-gold light hung upon the dank air, but it appeared to have no source. Artek blinked in astonishment as the others gasped behind him.

Arranged in haphazard fashion around the cavern were a score of tables, every one a dozen paces long and half again as wide. Sprawling atop each of the tables was what appeared to be an intricate maze. Artek approached one of the tables and shook his head in wonder. This wasn't just any maze, he realized.

It was Undermountain.

"What in the name of all the gods is *that*?" he asked in awe.

From the center of the cavern came a shrill cackle of glee. "It's my masterpiece!" the old man cried. "My most marvelous toy ever. Impressed, aren't you? Well, you should be!"

Rendered in tiny but perfect detail, every single one of the vast labyrinth's many subterranean levels

lay before Artek. He had never seen anything so
wondrous in his life. The model was roofless, so that
he could gaze within, and every wall, every door,
every minuscule stone had been fashioned with exquisite care from wood and clay and paint. Tiny figurines populated the miniature halls and chambers:
skillfully rendered monsters and adventurers, each
no taller than the knuckle of a finger. So flawless
was the model that Artek felt almost like some great
god, peering down upon the diminutive world of mor-
tals below.

"Look!" Beckla whispered in amazement. She and
the others had wandered around, gazing at other
levels resting on other tables. The wizard pointed to
a chamber filled with tiny trees fashioned from bits
of green moss. "I think this is Wyllowwood."

"And this must be the River Sargauth," Corin
added from nearby, pointing to a thin strip of glittering blue fashioned from crushed sapphire.

"And here's the tomb where you found me," Guss
said excitedly, pointing to a small chamber at the
end of another table.

"It's times like these that make me really wish I
still had fingers," Muragh muttered to no one in particular.

Artek shook his head in disbelief. "Everything's
here. Everything. It's absolutely perfect."

The old man approached. "Of course it is," he said.
"I made it, didn't I? And it's taken me quite a few
centuries to get it just right, if I do say so."

Startled, Artek stared at the ancient man. A chilling suspicion began to coalesce in his mind.

Just then the old man glanced down and frowned.

Near the center of the table, a band of adventurer figurines faced a dozen clay goblins. "Humph! I don't like those odds." The old man reached into his pocket and drew out a strange-looking pair of shears. Opening the handles, the shears extended like an accordion, stretching toward the figurines. A cruel light flashed in his eyes as he squeezed the handles together, and the blades of the shears snapped shut, lopping off the heads of three of the adventurer figurines. Only one remained intact. The old man let out a burst of maniacal laughter, retracting the shears. "That's better!"

The others watched with growing discomfort as the old fellow wreaked further havoc upon the miniature Undermountain. He moved from table to table, flooding rooms with water, melting wax monsters with the flame of a candle, and smashing tiny adventurers at random with a silver hammer. All the while, he let out hoots of malevolent glee, as if it were all a capricious game he was inventing as he went along.

A small white mouse suddenly scurried down a tiny corridor in one of the models, squeaking shrilly.

"Ah, Fang, there you are," the strange old man said, clucking his tongue. "You've been hiding again, haven't you? You know I don't like it when you hide. Next time it may be *bang* with my silver hammer."

The old man picked up the mouse and held out a tiny object. It was a miniature sword. "Go give this to the warrior on level four, chamber sixty-two. I don't want her to die just yet. She's been far too much fun." He set the mouse back down on the table. "Now shoo! Shoo! And don't hide the next time I'm looking for you."

Fang let out a decidedly recalcitrant squeak, then took the sword in its mouth before scurrying away through the tabletop maze.

Meanwhile, Corin had been studying the miniature labyrinth on a nearby table. "I've always simply adored models," he murmured. He pointed to a dark circle of polished onyx. "What's that?" he asked in delight.

The old man peered over the young noble's shoulder. "That's Midnight Lake."

"And what about this?" Corin pointed to a tortuous series of chambers and corridors.

The old mage let out a snort. "That's the Gauntlet of my idiotic half-spider apprentice, Muiral. He never could find me. But then, none of them did. Poor students one and all, they were."

Artek and Beckla exchanged shocked looks. However, Corin wasn't really listening. "And how about this?" He pointed to a small square that glowed with an eerie green light.

The old man glowered at him. "You're certainly full of questions, aren't you? That's Wish Gate. It will take you anywhere you wish to go."

Artek's pointed ears pricked up at this. "Even out of Undermountain?" he asked.

"I said anywhere, didn't I?" the old man grumped. "Now, I've had more than enough of your questions. I'm quite busy, you know. So be quiet—or get yourselves killed. Do anything, as long as you just stop pestering me!"

The others drew away, gathering on the far side of the cavern.

"Did you hear him?" Artek asked softly. "He called Muiral his apprentice. It can mean only one thing."

Corin's eyes suddenly went wide. He glanced nervously over his shoulder. "You mean that's . . . I was talking to . . . this old fellow is . . ."

Artek nodded grimly. "Halaster himself."

His gaze moved to the ancient mage. Halaster was chortling over his model. Artek shook his head. *The Mad Wizard* wasn't simply a name, he realized. Halaster truly was mad, an old man playing a child's game, his days of power and glory long forgotten.

Muragh let out a dejected sigh. "If he's Halaster, then we're doomed. I think he's more than a little touched, and not particularly nice. He'll never help us."

"What about that Wish Gate?" Guss suggested. "Couldn't it take us out of Undermountain?"

"Probably," Beckla answered. "But only if we could get to it. Judging by the model, it looks to be miles away from here. And it's much higher than we are now. The Horned Ring won't take us there."

Artek made a decision. "It doesn't seem Halaster much cares for company. I'm going to ask him if he'll transport us to Wish Gate. He just might do it, if for no other reason than to get rid of us."

It seemed they had little choice. Keeping close together, the five approached the ancient mage. Mad as he was, he was still a legendary wizard, and not a figure to be trifled with.

Artek cleared his throat nervously. "I'm sorry to disturb you again," he said as politely as he could manage. "I know you're getting rather weary of us by now."

The old man paused in the midst of pouring acid

over a group of melting dwarf figurines. "What clued
you in?" he snorted.

Artek risked continuing. "Well, there is a way you
can be rid of us for good. All you have to do is transport us to Wish Gate and—"

"Bah!" Halaster spat. "I can come up with something far more interesting than that. But thank you
for reminding me. It's about time I used these." From
the pocket of his robe, he pulled out the small objects
he had been working on earlier. They were figurines,
like the ones scattered throughout the various levels
of the miniature Undermountain. Artek leaned
closer, squinting. He saw now that one of them was a
tiny man: broad-shouldered, with black hair and
black eyes, dressed all in black leather, with a curved
saber at his hip.

Blinking in shock, he realized that the figurine
was *him*. Four more diminutive figurines rested on
Halaster's palm: a short-haired woman in a white
shirt and gray vest; a willowy young man with
golden hair; a bat-winged gargoyle; and a grinning
skull no larger than a pea.

"How do you like my newest playthings?" the mad
wizard cackled. "They're not bad likenesses, if I do
say so myself. I'm going to have great fun with these.
I'm rather sure of it."

Before Artek could wonder what he meant, with
two fingers the old man picked up the gargoyle figurine. He scanned the maze on the table before him,
which depicted one of Undermountain's many levels.
"Ah, this will do!" He placed the gargoyle figurine inside a small chamber next to another figurine carved
in the shape of a flame.

Guss vanished.

The others stared in astonishment. One moment the gargoyle was there, standing beside them, and the next moment he *wasn't*. There was no flash, no thunder, no sparkling magic. Guss had simply and completely disappeared. Humming an eerie tune under his breath, Halaster took the figurine of the golden-haired man and, stretching his arm, set it down in the model, on the edge of a chasm.

This time it was Corin who vanished.

This display before them was not merely a model of Undermountain's levels—it *was* Undermountain. By means of his vast magic, Halaster had bound the miniature and the real mazes inexorably together and what happened in one labyrinth happened in the other. Given his madness, Halaster probably thought this no more than a game. He was like a cruel boy burning his toy soldiers for fun, but each of the figurines he manipulated represented real, living beings: animals, monsters, and men. And now he had created five new figurines to add to his amusing little playhouse.

Artek lunged for the model to snatch up the likenesses of Guss and Corin, hoping that would return them to the laboratory. A thin sheet of crimson magic sprang into being between him and the table, throwing him violently backward. He clambered to his feet in time to see the mad wizard place the tiny skull figurine in a chamber next to a green pool. In the blink of an eye, Muragh was gone.

This time Artek lunged for the wizard himself. Once again crimson magic flashed, tossing him backward like a rag doll. Unperturbed, Halaster set the figurine of the short-haired woman in a chamber lined in shining silver. Beckla shouted in horror, but her cry was cut short as she vanished from sight. Artek watched in dread as Halaster took the remaining figurine—the man in black—and reached toward the model. Though he knew it was futile, once more Artek threw himself at the ancient mage. He was only halfway there when, laughing with wicked glee, Halaster set the figurine atop a miniature stone column.

Everything blurred into gray.

* * * * *

Guss backed against the stone wall as the fire elemental danced closer and closer. The air in the cavern shimmered, and it felt as if he were inside an oven. Guss had tried to take flight, but he had been brutally buffeted against a wall by an updraft spawned by the roaring heat. He could see no other exits. There was no escape.

The elemental was mesmerizing, even beautiful. He almost thought he could see a lithe figure whirling in the center of the white-hot corona. He supposed it was better this way. It was wrong to live on after all his brethren had passed into stone, but now it would not be much longer. Behind him, the stone wall began to sag. Rivulets of liquid rock dripped downward. Searing pain filled Guss's body as the fire elemental danced nearer. Just a few more moments. Then he would return to the stone that had spawned him. Like the wall, he, too, began to melt.

* * * * *

At least it was an adventurous way to go, Corin thought.

With white-knuckled hands he clung to the edge of a precipice. Darkness yawned beneath his feet. Somewhere far, far below he could hear the sound of water, but it was a long way down. His boots scrabbled against the cliff face, but it was no use. The stone was too smooth. He tried to pull himself up, but the darkness seemed to drag him downward. There wasn't enough strength in his arms and what little remained was quickly waning.

At last, his fingers could hold on to the sharp edge no longer. His hands started to slip, then let go. His last thought was of how he wished he'd had a chance to say good-bye to Artek and the others. Then he plunged downward, falling into deep—but not endless—darkness.

* * * * *

Muragh stared at the rising pool of bubbling green liquid.

"Of course you're staring, you ninny," he muttered to himself. "You're a skull. You don't have eyelids. Staring is all you *can* do."

Even before the emerald fluid touched the old bones of a nameless creature—dissolving them in an instant—Muragh had known it was acid. He had hopped and rolled as far as possible to the edge of the small, circular stone room, but he could go no farther. The acid continued to rise.

"I wonder if it can hurt to die when you're already

dead?" he asked himself nervously.

With every second, the edge of the hissing pool drew nearer. It looked as if he was about to find out.

* * * * *

Beckla knew that this was what it was like to go mad.

Countless faces leered at her from the jagged, shardlike mirrors that covered the walls, floor, and ceiling of the chamber—all horribly distorted. Bloated, bloodshot eyes stared at her, and twisted mouths laughed in silent mockery. They were hideous. Yet still more hideous was the knowledge that the faces were her own, each one a broken reflection of her own horrified visage.

Beckla spun dizzily, but in every direction the horrid, shattered faces gazed back at her. Screaming, she sank to the floor, and the sharp-edged mirrors that covered it sliced her knees. She tried shutting her eyes, but that made it even worse, for then she could feel all the loathsome eyes boring into her flesh. She opened her eyes and reeled again. It felt as if at any moment her mind would shatter like the crazed mirrors, breaking into a thousand distorted pieces from which a whole could never again be reconstructed. She had to get out but could see no doorway. Only eyes, mouths, and faces, faces, faces.

Sobbing, she hunched over. As she did, a reflection caught her eye. A thought pierced the growing madness that clutched her brain. Perhaps there was a way after all.

Gargoyle's Gift

Artek stood atop a stone pillar.

He was in a vast, dimly lit hall. A line of free-standing columns stretched in either direction, each perhaps ten paces apart. Like the one Artek stood upon, all ended abruptly, supporting nothing but thin air. If there was a ceiling to this place, it was lost in the gloom above. With his orcish eyes, he could just make out the floor of the hall below. It was writhing. Even without his darkvision he could have guessed the nature of the slithering shadows by the dry hissing that rose on the air—snakes. There were hundreds of them, thousands. And more than a few of them were probably venomous.

Glancing down at the dark tattoo on his forearm, he saw that the sun was nearly touching the arrow now. Dawn was just minutes away. And his death with it.

Artek flinched at a sudden, reverberating *boom!* There was a long moment of silence, followed by a second crash. Then came another, and another. His jaw fell in grim surprise. It looked as if something else were going to kill him first.

The pillars were falling. Even as he watched, one of the columns farther down the line tilted in his direction and struck the column next to it with a thunderous cracking of stone, causing this column to begin to fall as well. It was a chain reaction—one by one, they were all going to topple.

The tenth column from him began to fall. Then the ninth. He turned, took as much of a running start as the constraining surface allowed, then leapt to the top of the next pillar. Letting his momentum carry him forward, he tensed his legs and sprang to the pinnacle of the next pillar in line. Behind him, the columns continued to topple. The seventh farthest from him fell. Then the sixth. He kept jumping.

His lungs burned with effort. The fourth column behind him crashed to the floor, and then the third. He could not jump fast enough—the columns were gaining on him. A few seconds more and he would crash to the snake-strewn floor below with a thousand tons of stone. Then he saw it hovering in midair just ahead: a glowing square filled with billowing gray mist. He blinked in confusion. How could this be?

There was a deafening crash and the stone beneath his feet gave a violent shudder. He fell sprawling to the top of the pillar and nearly went flying over the side. He gripped the edge, hauling himself back up. As he did, the column tilted wildly, then began to trace a smooth, fatal arc toward the floor below. The pillar was falling.

With a desperate cry, Artek sprang up and forward with all of his strength. For a terrified moment, he thought he wasn't going to make it, but then his body broke the surface of the gate, and he fell down into gray emptiness.

As before, his body seemed to dissolve away. He had no substance, no flesh—only a naked, quivering consciousness to be flayed raw by the bitter cold. Thankfully, the horrible sensation lasted only a second. There was a flash. The reek of lightning filled his nostrils, and he fell hard to a stone floor. Groaning, he pulled himself to his feet.

A trio of trolls stood before him.

They reached out with long arms, baring countless filthy, pointy teeth. With a cry of alarm, Artek fumbled for the cursed saber at his hip and drew it with a ring of steel. He did not wait for the trolls to attack first. He swung the saber, striking the arm of one of the creatures. The limb snapped with a brittle sound and fell to the floor. The troll did not so much as blink. Its companions were equally still. Artek stared in puzzlement.

Cautiously, he approached the creatures, tapping one with his saber. It tottered, then fell backward. As it struck the floor, it shattered.

Clay, Artek realized in amazement. The trolls were made of clay. The cursed saber did not compel him to attack the harmless figures. As he stared down at the broken monster, he noticed that the floor looked odd. He scratched the stones with the point of the saber, and a thick line of gray curled up, revealing brown wood below. It was paint. What was going on here?

Before Artek could think of an answer, there was a sizzling sound as a gate appeared in the air above. A form dropped through, landing on the floor with a soft *oof!* It was Beckla. He quickly helped the wizard to her feet as the gate flashed into nonexistence. The wizard's brown eyes were wide and staring, almost mad. At last she shuddered and looked at Artek.

"Where are the others?" she gasped.

Even as she said this, three more gates crackled into existence. Each spat out a single figure before vanishing. Corin and Guss groggily picked themselves up, while Muragh rolled in a dizzy circle.

The young nobleman blinked in bewilderment. "I don't understand. I was plummeting to my death. Then a gray square appeared below me and I fell into it and . . . and here I am."

"I was about to be melted into slag when the same thing happened to me," Guss said with a shudder. Wisps of smoke still wafted from his scaly hide.

"And I was on the verge of being dissolved into skull soup," Muragh said in a quavering voice.

"What is going on?" Artek wondered. "Where are we?"

"We're in Undermountain," Beckla said in awe.

"I can see that," Artek replied dryly.

"No, not the real Undermountain," Beckla countered. Her forehead crinkled in a frown. "Though I suppose we *are* there, too."

"Make up your mind," Artek said.

"Don't you see?" Beckla circled the chamber, studying the clay trolls, the painted walls, the wooden floor. "We're inside the miniature." She waited for the others to absorb this fact and then went on.

"It was the Horned Ring," the wizard explained. "I thought that if each of us still had a ruby from the ring, there was a chance it might be able to gate us all to the same place. So I concentrated on Halaster's cavern as I invoked the ring. And it worked. It brought us all here." She ran a hand through her short hair, gazing around. "Only something went wrong. The magic that binds Halaster's model of Undermountain must permeate the entire cavern. I think there must have been some strange interaction between the Horned Ring and that magic."

In shock, Artek stared at the clay trolls. He had thought them to be statues, but now he knew that wasn't so. They were figurines—the kind with which Halaster populated his model of Undermountain. This entire room was no more than a few inches long.

"By all the bloodiest gods!" he shouted, whirling to look at Beckla. "Do you mean to tell me that each of us is now the size of one of Halaster's figurines?"

The wizard nodded grimly. "In a word, yes. And I imagine that, somewhere in Undermountain, there are now five life-sized clay replicas of us, falling off cliffs and getting dissolved by acid. Somehow the interference between the model and the ring has caused us to switch places with our figurines."

Artek staggered, leaning against a painted paper

column for support—this was too much. "At least it won't be much work to bury me," he said in a slightly manic voice. "No need to dig six feet. Six inches will do fine."

"Wait a minute," Corin said. The nobleman paced quickly back and forth, his face lined in thought. "This might not be as bad as it seems."

"Apparently, you have a better imagination than I do," Beckla noted dubiously.

"Actually, my idea is really rather simple," Corin went on. "Halaster seems to have taken great care in making this miniature an exact working replica of Undermountain. Don't you see?" He paused meaningfully. "It's perfect *in every way*."

"Spit it out, Corin!" Muragh griped. "What are you getting at?"

Artek looked at the young man in astonishment. "I see what Corin means," he said. "Wish Gate!"

"Indubitably!" Corin cried.

"Of course!" Beckla exclaimed. "Halaster has taken almost pathological care in recreating every detail in this model—there's no reason to believe that the miniature Wish Gate won't act just like the real one."

Artek glanced up. Hadn't each of the models been roofless? All he saw above them was a hazy, red-gold glow. He turned to the gargoyle. "Guss, do you think you can fly up and see if you can spot Wish Gate?" Guss nodded enthusiastically. Stubby wings flapping, he rose into the air.

Crimson magic crackled. The gargoyle let out a yelp of pain and dropped back to the floor.

"The magical barrier," Beckla groaned. "It must

work from the inside as well as out. Only Halaster can move something in and out of the model."

Artek was not about to give up so easily. "Well, we'll just have to find our way out of this level the hard way, like mice in a maze. Come on!" Forcing himself not to look at the tattoo on his arm, he kicked open the door and dashed into the painted hallway beyond. The others were right on his heels.

They ran down corridors painted in imitation of damp, moldy stone, passing countless figurines: monsters with glass splinter fangs, wizards gripping toothpick staves, and heroes wielding sewing-needle swords. Artek let his orcish instincts guide him as he tried to home in on their target. Finally, he came to a halt, and the others stopped, panting.

"We've been making steady headway in one direction this whole time," he said between breaths. "We've got to be near the edge of the maze by now."

Guss walked up to the wall before them, eyed it critically, then lashed out with a clawed fist. His hand punched through paint and wood. Ruddy light poured through the opening. "Looks like you're right, Artek," the gargoyle said with a grin.

Artek peered through the opening. Guss had punched through an outer wall and they were indeed on one edge of the maze. Just beneath was the edge of the table upon which this level sat. Beyond that, the drop to the floor below seemed hundreds of feet, not the three or four he knew it to be.

"Help me widen this," he said, tearing away a chunk of wood.

The others lent their hands to the task, and in moments the opening was wide enough for them to crawl through. Once on the other side, they balanced precariously on the edge of the table.

"Hey, how come we haven't turned big again now that we're outside the model?" Muragh asked in annoyance.

Beckla answered his question. "I don't think we'll return to our normal size until we're finally out of Undermountain—that should break the connection between us and our figurines."

"There!" Corin said, pointing across what seemed a vast gap to the next nearest table. "I think that's the table that holds the model of the Wish Gate level."

Artek shook his head doubtfully. "I suppose it's no more than three feet to that table, but it might as well be a mile. How are we ever going to get across?"

"Guss the gargoyle, at your service," Guss announced cheerfully. He hovered over them, leathery wings flapping. "I hope you don't mind, but I'll have to take you one at a time."

Their laughter fell short as a gigantic shadow loomed over them, blotting out the light. A great craggy moon rose over the model, two smaller pale spheres embedded in its surface. Only after a second did Artek realize that it was not a moon at all but Halaster's wrinkled face. The wizard was bending over his model. A gigantic, wrinkled hand stretched in their direction. They cowered against the wall of the maze as the hand loomed nearer. One careless swipe, and they would be flattened like bugs. Artek clenched his jaw, trying not to scream.

The hand hovered directly above them, then continued on, reaching to manipulate some objects elsewhere in the maze. Artek forced himself to breathe again. Halaster had not seen them. But they might not be so lucky next time—they had to hurry.

Artek tried not to think about the seconds slipping away as Guss valiantly ferried each of the others across the gap to the other table. Finally, it was Artek's turn. Though Guss was clearly growing tired, he did not complain, and at last set Artek down gently on the table's edge. They shrank into the corner between wall and tabletop for a moment, but no shadow loomed above. Apparently, Halaster had not noticed their little adventure.

The magical barrier had prevented Guss from setting them down within the maze, so Beckla blasted a hole in the wall of the model with a spell. They crawled through the smoking gap, into the labyrinth beyond.

"You got the closest look at the model, Corin," Artek said. "You lead the way."

For a moment, a look of uncertainty crossed Corin's face. Then—with visible effort—he squared his shoulders and nodded. "All right, follow me."

Artek grinned. Two days ago, Corin would never have accepted such a responsibility—the young lord had grown on this journey.

Ignoring their weariness, they ran down painted hallways and punched through doors of stiff paper. Nothing stood in their way now. They were almost to Wish Gate.

They turned the corner and found themselves facing a gigantic white beast with blood-red eyes. It gnashed its long, yellow teeth and saliva trickled from the corner of its mouth. The five stared in horror. This was no clay figurine.

Emitting a high-pitched squeak, the creature lumbered toward them, dragging a pink, ropelike tail behind. Understanding broke through Artek's terrified stupor—this was no monstrous abomination of the underworld. It was Fang, Halaster's pet mouse. But the creature was now thrice their size, making it a monster indeed. It seemed angry at their intrusion upon its territory. Its claws scrabbled against the floor, gouging the gray paint. Baring its razor-sharp teeth, it lunged for them.

With a roar, Guss lashed out an arm, swiping Fang's pink nose with his talons. The mouse squealed in pain, raising its bloodied snout into the air. The five dashed into a side chamber. They shut the stiff paste-and-paper door, hoping it was enough to keep the mouse at bay. A moment later, they heard a scratching outside.

"We have to keep going down this corridor," Corin whispered urgently. "It's the only way to Wish Gate."

Beckla shook her head. "We'll never get past Halaster's little pet."

Artek clenched his hand into a fist, punching the wooden wall. He could not believe that they had survived so many perils only to be defeated by a mouse.

"There is a way," said a gruff voice.

The others looked up in surprise. It was Guss. "I could go out into the hallway first and run in the opposite direction. That way, the mouse would follow me and the rest of you could get to the gate."

"But that thing will kill you!" Beckla cried.

Guss's serious expression did not waver. For a moment he was silent, and then he spoke in quiet words.

"During all those centuries I dwelled in the tomb

of Talastria and Orannon, I always thought there was something wrong with me. I couldn't bring myself to slay the tomb's defilers as my brethren did. I thought . . . I thought it was because I was a coward." The gargoyle gazed at the others, his green eyes glowing brightly. "But that's not true. I simply had never met anyone whom I wanted to protect. Until now."

The gargoyle reached out to grip Beckla's hand gently in his own.

"Please," he said softly but insistently. "Let me do this thing. It is what I was created for."

Beckla snatched her hand away. Corin and Muragh gazed at the gargoyle with shock. Sorrow weighed heavily on Artek's heart, but a smile touched his lips. Guss knew who he was now—truly, deeply, with all his stony heart, Artek thought. Would that *he* could say so much. He would not deny Guss's chance to be whole.

Artek laid a hand fondly on the gargoyle's spiky shoulder. "Maybe you were created from evil, but you're a good creature to us. Never forget that."

Gratitude filled the gargoyle's eyes, but there was worry as well. "You would do well to heed your own words, Artek Ar'talen."

The others made their farewells then, though time forced them to be quick. Beckla's good-bye was the most tearful, and she was reluctant to release the gargoyle from her embrace.

"I'm going to miss you so much, Guss," she said quietly.

"And I you, Beckla," the gargoyle replied, squeezing her tight in his stony arms. "You, more than anyone, have taught me that I can be what I choose to be. Thank you, Beckla Shadesar. Remember me."

She shook her head fiercely. "How could I ever forget you?" But she could manage no more words beyond that.

The gargoyle flashed a toothy grin and extended his onyx talons, truly looking like the fearsome creature he had been created to be. But the same kindness glowed in his eyes.

"Here I come, Fang!" Guss bellowed. "Your doom is upon you. And its name is Terrathiguss!"

The gargoyle shredded the paper door with his claws and leapt through the tatters. The mouse squealed, its bloody whiskers twitching. Guss ran down the corridor. The mouse scrabbled after him while the others dashed into the hallway, watching in horror.

Guss was fast, but the mouse was faster still. It pounced, landing on the gargoyle. The two caught each other in a terrible embrace. Guss's talons raked across the mouse's belly, staining its snowy fur with crimson. It shrieked, then dug its teeth into the gargoyle's shoulder, and green ichor flowed. Wrestling with each other, the two creatures crashed into a wall. Thin wood splintered. As one, mouse and gargoyle tumbled through the hole and were gone.

Artek was first to the gap in the wall. Beckla and Corin—who held Muragh—were a half-second behind. Together, they peered through the hole.

Beyond the edge of the tabletop, on the floor far below, lay the mouse, its fur drenched with blood. It twitched once, then lay still. Scattered around the mouse were a dozen jagged shards of gray stone, stone that looked just like the remnants of a broken statue—the statue of a gargoyle.

Clutching a hand to her mouth, Beckla turned away. Corin cradled Muragh in his arms. By force of will, Artek swallowed the lump of sorrow in his throat. There would be time for mourning later. He gripped Beckla's hand.

"Let's go," he said.

The others nodded, and they started back down the hallway. Moments later, they burst through a paper door and into a small room. Wish Gate hung on the far wall like a shimmering emerald mirror. Artek looked down at his tattoo. The sun had brushed the arrow. How long did he have now? Three minutes? Two? There was no time to waste.

He gripped hands with Beckla and Corin; the nobleman held Muragh in his other hand. They approached the shimmering gate.

"Where are you going to wish us to?" Beckla asked.

Artek bared his pointed teeth; the expression was not a smile. "If it works, then you'll see."

Fixing his wish in his mind, he tightened his grip on the others. Then, as one, they leapt into the gate.

This time the nothingness was green. Then blue. Then black as ice at midnight. The cold was worse than before, and far, far longer—crueler than anything they had felt. Artek thought it would freeze his very soul to splinters, and his consciousness dwindled, like a dying spark lost in a winter night. Then, just as the spark wavered on the edge of being extinguished, cold dark became blazing light, and the universe exploded.

Falling through a sizzling aperture, they landed

on a cushioned surface. Artek blinked and looked down. It was a thick, luxurious rug—an expensive one, by the look of it. His feral grin broadened. He recognized this room. The wish had worked.

With a snarl, he leapt to his feet. Corin and Beckla pulled themselves up behind him. They were in a gaudily decorated room filled with gilded wood, rich tapestries, and ostentatious displays of gold and silver. Before them stood two men. One was clearly a wizard: bald-headed, hook-nosed, and clad in a brown robe. The other was tall and elegant, with dark hair and gleaming green eyes, fashionably clad in purple velvet and silvery silk. He had frozen in the act of putting on a thick, black walking cloak.

"Going somewhere, Lord Thal?" Artek asked.

Only for a second did shock register upon the lord's handsome face. Then his visage grew smooth once more, his hooded green eyes glittering like a serpent's. A cruel smile coiled around the corners of his lips.

"Artek Ar'talen," he said with an almost imperceptible nod. "Exaggerated as the stories concerning your prowess seemed, it appears now they underestimated you."

Artek took a menacing step forward. Beckla and Corin flanked him on either side. "Save the compliments, Thal," Artek spat. "They're wasted on me. There's only one thing I want from you."

Thal affected an expression of mock regret. "Oh, do forgive me. But I really am in a bit of hurry. I have an important appointment to keep." Wicked laughter rose in his chest. "It seems that a foolish little titmouse of a lord has turned up missing—

hardly a great loss, I know—and in his stead I am to be elected to the seventh seat on the city's Circle of Nobles."

Corin hung his head at Darien's cutting insult. Worried, Beckla glanced over at the young man.

Artek laughed bitterly. "What was it you told me when you first offered me this task, Darien?" He snapped his fingers. "Ah, yes. I remember. 'Among Silvertor's rivals are those with dark ambitions. They see the Circle as a means to rule over all the city's nobility, and as a position from which to launch an all-out assault against the hidden Lords of Waterdeep.' "

"Well, then," Darien said with dark mirth. "I did not lie about everything."

Darien's wizard gripped his staff. "Shall I dispose of this refuse for you, my lord?"

"Hush, Melthis," Darien crooned. "Be polite. These are our guests, after all. Besides, in just a few more seconds, the worst of them will be disposed of for us."

Artek glanced at his dark tattoo. The sun was nearly centered upon the arrow. The windows of Darien's mansion glowed deep red—it was almost dawn.

Artek walked up to the dark-haired lord and thrust out his arm. "Have your vulture take it off, Darien," he hissed between clenched teeth. "Now. If you don't, I swear, you won't outlive me."

Darien sighed deeply. At last he nodded. "Very well, if you put it that way." He turned toward the bald-headed wizard. "Melthis?"

"Yes, my lord?"

"Die," Darien said flatly. The lord pulled his right arm from beneath his heavy cloak, and three whirling prongs sprang from the end of the burnished steel Device where his hand should have been. Before Artek could react, Darien plunged the spinning prongs into the wizard's chest. Melthis jerked spasmodically, his eyes going wide in disbelief, his mouth opening silently.

Darien pulled the bloody Device back. Melthis slumped to the floor, blood pouring from the ragged hole in his chest. The wizard twitched once, and that was all.

"Damn you, Thal!" Artek shouted in fury. "Why?"

Darien's smiled with an almost mad glee. "Melthis was weak and stupid. Had you threatened my life, he might have capitulated and given you what you wanted, removing the tattoo. But now there is no chance of that." His voice rose exultantly. "The seconds are slipping by, Ar'talen. Can't you feel them draining away, one by one? You've lost. If you were wise, you would use these last moments to make peace with whatever uncouth gods you orcish rats worship in your rancid little holes in the ground."

Beckla raised her hands to cast a spell. "No!" Artek roared. "He's mine!" Orcish rage cast its blood-red veil before his eyes. Drawing the saber at his hip, he lunged forward. He swung the blade in a whistling arc, precisely aimed to sever the lord's neck.

But before it connected, the saber jerked in Artek's hand, wrenching his arm painfully. The blade changed direction of its own volition, and Artek twisted his body, barely managing to keep from severing his own leg.

"You are a fool, Ar'talen," Darien laughed. "You should have known you could not harm me with that blade. I was the one who gave it to you, after all."

Artek tried to cast down the sword. He would squeeze the life out of Darien with his bare hands if he could just release the cursed blade. But it was all he could do to keep the saber from turning on him again.

Darien tossed his cloak back, holding the bloody Device before him. He started moving for the door. "Out of my way—all of you! Waterdeep is going to be mine. And no one can stop me."

There was a sharp ringing of steel.

"I can," someone said.

All turned in surprise. It was Corin. He stood before Darien, rapier drawn. Gone from the young man's face was all the pale uncertainty of before. Authority blazed in his brilliant blue eyes, and despite his ragged, grimy clothes and smudged cheeks, his nobility seemed to shine forth. For all of Darien's rich velvet and silver silk, he looked like a lowly beggar next to Corin.

Mocking laughter escaped Darien's throat. "You can't kill me, *boy*. And even if you could, you wouldn't. You haven't the guts. Now scurry back to your little House of Silvertor, and perhaps, when I rule the city, I might let you live. After all, you're really not even worth killing."

Corin said nothing. He gripped his rapier tightly, his jaw set in firm resolution. The Device buzzed on the end of Darien's arm. For a protracted moment the two stared at each other, deciding who would make the first move.

Without warning, Darien let out a cry of pain. He hopped on one foot, clutching the other with his hand.

A pale, round form gnawed with yellow teeth at the flesh of his ankle: Muragh. With his left hand, Darien grabbed the skull and hurled it across the room. Muragh struck a wall with a sickening *thud*, then fell to the floor. After that, the skull did not move.

Muragh's teeth had done little damage, but Darien had been thrown off balance and Corin did not waste the chance. His rapier flashed in a bright arc, severing Darien's right arm above the wrist. The Device bounced to the carpet, its steel prongs still whirling violently. Darien stared in horror at the gory stump of his arm. He clutched it to his body and stumbled back against a polished mahogany wall. The cruel arrogance in his eyes was replaced by terror as Corin advanced, leveling his rapier at Darien's chest.

Darien shook his head slowly, tears streaming from his eyes. "Please," he whined piteously. "Please, Lord Silvertor. I beg of you. Have mercy!"

Corin hesitated only a moment. "No, Darien," he said quietly. "Mercy is for innocents."

Darien opened his mouth to scream, but was cut short by the whiplike sounds of Corin's rapier. Corin withdrew the blade. For a moment it seemed his blows had done nothing—Darien stared forward with an almost peaceful expression. Then blood began to flow from a dozen wounds on his arms and torso. A line of crimson appeared around his neck. Cleanly severed, Darien's head rolled to one side while his body slumped to the other, and both fell to the floor in a rapidly growing pool of blood.

"Do forgive me," Corin whispered. The rapier slipped from his numb fingers as he stared at the grisly scene he had wrought.

Artek lifted the cursed saber. He willed his hand to release the hilt. To his amazement, the blade fell to the floor. Then he felt it: the first pinpricks of pain in his arm. His eyes locked on the tattoo. The sun was centered squarely on the arrow now. Sparks of crimson magic sizzled around the lines of dark ink, and he shuddered as blazing agony traveled swiftly up his arm, reaching toward his heart.

Now that he had finally come to the end, he found that he was not afraid anymore. Perhaps it was because he finally knew who he was. And it was Guss who had shown him, with his noble sacrifice. If a gargoyle could be good, then so could Artek. It didn't matter what one was created to be. What mattered was how one lived one's life. He knew now that he didn't have to choose between being good and being part orc. He could be both.

Artek threw his head back, calling out to the heavens. "Arturg! Arthaug! My fathers before me! I come to you!"

"No!" a voice screamed.

It was Beckla.

The wizard rushed toward him as he fell to his knees. She raised her hand. Something gold and crimson shone on her finger. "Gate!" she cried. "Open!"

As she spoke the words, a glowing square filled with billowing gray mist appeared before them. Deadly crimson magic crackled around Artek's tattoo. He arched his spine in agony. His heart jerked in his chest.

Filled as he was with pain, he almost didn't notice as Beckla grabbed his arm and thrust it into the shimmering gate. The wizard held his arm fast, keeping the magical portal from pulling Artek fully into its cold mists. Instantly, Artek's pain vanished. The fire in his arm turned to ice as his flesh melted away in the nothingness beyond. His heart gradually slowed to a steady pace. Finally, the wizard pulled his arm out of the swirling mists. The gate sizzled and vanished.

Artek stared at his arm in wonder. The tattoo still marked his flesh, but the crimson magic was gone, and the image no longer moved. Golden daylight spilled through the glass windows into the room. Dawn had come and he was still alive.

"What happened?" he asked in amazement.

Relief flashed in Beckla's brown eyes. "Our bodies become incorporeal when we pass beyond a gate," she explained. "I figured that the tattoo's death magic couldn't work if there was no arm for it to travel up."

"Good reasoning," he murmured, flexing his arm.

"Lucky guess," she replied with a smirk. "The spell was set to work at a specific time. That time has passed. I think the magic has been negated. It's just a mundane tattoo now."

Artek grinned at her. "You're really not a bad wizard at all, you know."

"And I'm going to get even better," she said. From the pocket of her vest she pulled out a score of folded parchment sheets. "I picked these up in the lair of the silversanns, in Trobriand's Graveyard. The spellbooks there were all torn up, but some of their pages were still whole. Every one of these is a new spell, Artek, enough for years of study." She carefully tucked the papers back into her vest. "Maybe I won't ever be the greatest wizard in the city. But I'm well on my way to becoming a good one."

Artek could only laugh in agreement. They stood up, looking to Corin. The nobleman, tears streaming freely down his dirty cheeks, turned away from Darien's corpse.

Artek's mirth was replaced by concern. "Are you all right, Corin?" he asked quietly.

The young lord nodded, roughly wiping the tears from his cheeks. "I am now—thanks to you, Artek. I won't ever let anyone tell me I'm worthless again."

Artek said nothing. He reached out to grip Corin's shoulder. After a moment, he tousled the lord's hair. "Don't you have a vote to be getting to?" he asked.

"As a matter of fact, I do," Corin replied, suddenly beaming. He glanced down at his ragged clothes. "I'm not exactly dressed appropriately, but it will have to suffice. I've decided that I really don't care if I please the other nobles or not."

Beckla cast a sideways glance at Artek, then stepped toward the lord. "Do you mind if I go with you, Corin?" she asked, her eyes shining.

Corin grinned shyly, then nodded. "I would like that very much," he replied gently, taking her hand in his.

Artek gaped at the two in shock. "But I thought women always fell for the roguish type!" he sputtered.

Beckla winked slyly at him. "Not in this story, Ar'talen. I need a dose of goodness in my life."

Artek could only shake his head, his expression both chagrined and bemused.

"Oh, before I go," Corin said, "you should know that my first action in the Circle will be to recommend that a certain Artek the Knife receive a full pardon for all past crimes. The fellow will have a completely clean start."

Artek looked up at the young man in surprise. "He won't waste it," he said.

Corin nodded solemnly. "I know."

Without further words, Corin and Beckla dashed from the room and out into the dawning streets. For a moment Artek stared after them, feeling terribly alone. He wondered how it was possible to feel so glad and so sorrowful at the same time. At last, with a sigh, he turned to leave.

"Hey!" a reedy voice piped up. "Don't forget about me!"

Artek swore. How could it have possibly slipped his mind? He hurriedly knelt and picked up the skull. "Muragh, are you all right?"

"I'm going to have a nasty headache," the skull groaned. "And believe me, when all you *are* is a head, headaches are no fun. But I'll be all right."

Artek grinned, his spirits rising. It looked as if he wasn't so alone after all. Picking up the skull, he headed outside. The city was just beginning to stir, getting ready for the day. He couldn't remember the last time he had seen so bright a morning.

"So," Muragh said, his jaw working, "did I ever tell you about the time the mermen in Waterdeep Harbor used me to play an impromptu game of finball?"

"No," Artek laughed. "But I'm sure you will."

"Well," the skull chattered happily, "it all began when I had the misfortune of getting eaten by a swordshark . . ."